The
Secret
Language
of Sisters

The Secret Language of Sisters

LUANNE RICE

Point

All rights reserved. Published by Point, an imprint of Scholastic Inc., *Publishers since 1920.*
SCHOLASTIC, POINT, and associated logos are trademarks and/or registered
trademarks of Scholastic Inc.

The publisher does not have any control over and does not assume any responsibility for
author or third-party websites or their content.

Library of Congress Cataloging-in-Publication Data

Rice, Luanne, author.
    The secret language of sisters / Luanne Rice.
        pages cm
    Summary: Mathilda (Tilly), fourteen, and Ruth Anne (Roo), sixteen, are sisters and best
friends in Connecticut, but when Roo crashes her car while texting she is confined to a hospital bed with "locked-in syndrome," aware of her surroundings, but apparently comatose—
and Tilly must find a way to communicate with her sister, while dealing with her own sense
of guilt.
    ISBN 978-0-545-83955-6 (jacketed hardcover) 1. Sisters—Juvenile fiction. 2. Traffic
accident victims—Juvenile fiction. 3. Coma—Patients—Juvenile fiction. 4. Text messaging
(Cell phone systems)—Juvenile fiction. 5. Guilt—Juvenile fiction. 6. Connecticut—Juvenile
fiction. [1. Sisters—Fiction. 2. Traffic accidents—Fiction. 3. Coma—Fiction. 4. Text messaging
(Cell phone systems)—Fiction. 5. Guilt—Fiction. 6. Connecticut—Fiction.] I. Title.
    PZ7.1.R53Se 2016
    813.54—dc23
    [Fic]

2015016008

10 9 8 7 6 5 4 3 2 1   16 17 18 19 20

Printed in the U.S.A.   23
First edition, March 2016

Book design by Abby Dening

For Audrey O'Brien Loggia

Prologue

Roo

I'm late.

And I'm hardly ever late, that's the thing. I tend to be so on time it drives some people—namely my sister, Tilly—crazy. She says I make her look bad. Right now she's waiting for me to pick her up at the river museum, and I should have been there five minutes ago.

It is four o'clock on Saturday afternoon, bright, clear, and cold. Driving through the marshes, I see ice on the banks, sparkling on the golden grasses and the splintery old dock. The Connecticut River is nearly frozen over, but it turns dark blue in the wide-open sections where it meets the salt water of Long Island Sound, and the late-afternoon February light is perfect. I slow down to take another shot.

I am unfashionably into landscapes; I apologize to no one. I park my dad's old Volvo in the sandy lot behind the bait shop, shuttered for winter. Grabbing my camera, I cross the street to snap a few shots of cold winter sunlight on the broken ice.

The phone in my pocket buzzes. I ignore it and keep taking photographs. I had set today aside to do this, but driving Tilly around has cut into my plans. I can't help that I'm a little compulsive about getting things done, and if one thing has to slide today, it's going to be punctuality. My portfolio for the Serena Kader Barrois Foundation Photography Contest needs more work. Although it's not due until June, I want it to be as perfect as I can make it, and capture these winter days. I'm a junior and want to apply to Yale early decision. The award would boost my chances of being accepted at my dad's old university, but it also includes a thousand-dollar scholarship, and that would help my mom a lot, no matter where I go.

Just as important as the scholarship: If I win, I'll dedicate the prize to Dad. I think that's partly what's got Tilly acting so mad at me. He died last summer, and to say we both miss him is a slight understatement, like saying the sun is bright. Taking pictures of nature is my way of staying connected to him, making him feel alive to me. Tilly and Dad used to go owling, searching for the owls that live in the woods at the far end of the beach. She hasn't returned to the owls since he died, hasn't found a way to keep him close.

I miss him so much, glancing over at the car actually hurts. It was his before he died. There's a shadow in the front seat, cast by the bait shack, and for one sharp instant I pretend it's his ghost or, even better, *him*. I'll get in the car, and he'll be there, and we'll go pick up Tilly, and none of the last year will have happened.

Another buzz. My fingers are stiff from the cold, but I pull the phone from my jacket pocket and check. Four texts: Two are from Tilly. *Where are you?* And then, *I mean it, WHERE ARE YOU?* My heartbeat picks up—her anxiety is contagious, and I write her back: *On my way, O impatient one!!!*

And she *is* impatient, my little sister. Two years and a lifetime younger than I am. The world revolves around Mathilda Mae. Well, it always has for me, anyway. I'm sure I had some normal sibling jealousy, being the first child, then having her come along. Mostly, I adore her and try to protect her. Sometimes I feel like her mother. Still, she can be incredibly annoying.

The third text is from Isabel Cruz, my best friend. She's also entering the photo contest, and she has shot me a picture of the shrine to the Virgin of Guadalupe in her mother's bedroom. The photo shows the most recent addition: Her mother is constantly making offerings, and now the brightly colored doll has four dead roses, no doubt taken from one of the tables her mom had cleared that day, wedged into her veil.

I write back, *Brava, preciosa!* Then I take a photo of the bait shack's faded sign with my phone and send it to her.

The fourth text is from my boyfriend, Newton. How can I explain what one question from him can do to me? We have been together for so long, through the best of times and the worst of times. He sat in the row behind me at my father's funeral, and I reached back to hold his hand through most of it. So why have I been pulling away? It's not that I don't love him. I want to say, if anything, I love him too much.

He's written: *How can you say being apart is better?*

Oh, Newton. That's too hard to answer by text, and I'm late for Tilly. Or at least that's my excuse. It's Saturday, and he and I haven't seen each other once since getting out of school yesterday, and to tell you the truth, I plan to avoid him until Monday.

I get back into the car; my father's ghost is gone. I throw my phone and camera on the passenger seat, and head north on Shore Road. Now I really need to hurry to Tilly.

My sister's not that strong, academically. She's having senior slump, and she's only a freshman. So the fact she spent hours at the museum doing research for a school project deserves praise and encouragement. Our mom is grading papers, so I am Tilly's designated chauffeur. I'll make up for being late by taking her out for hot chocolate.

Long shadows fall across the road, dappling the two-hundred-year-old stone walls with black and silver. Everything is a photograph. I want to stop here, see if I can capture the spare and haunting beauty, but my phone buzzes again. It's on the seat beside me, right against my camera. The metal on metal sounds loud and jarring. It's Tilly, of course.

If she could just wait, I'd be there soon, and we could take the long way home, listen to the radio, and when we stop for cocoa, I'll make sure she gets extra marshmallows. But my phone is exploding with texts, little Tilly-isms: *Whatcha doin that's more important than your ONLY SISTER?* Followed shortly by *Um, I'm still here.* Then, *Just here killing time while the MUSEUM is trying to CLOSE! You are keeping people from their DINNERS.* Maybe I'll take the passive-aggressive route and ignore her. SO TEMPTING. Instead, I speed up.

And here she is again: *At least tell me how long you'll be.*

My hand hovers over my phone; I'm a bit torn about whether to just keep going, or to waste time pulling over to respond.

She sends another, all caps, as if she's screaming at me, so obviously agitated she misspells: *ANSERE ME!*

That makes me laugh, which she would hate.

I'm heading down the long straightaway toward the bridge. The two white church steeples that mark the town of Black Hall rise above bare trees scoring the low hills. It's a sleepy little town in wintertime—summer people come from New York and Hartford, with fancy cars and lots of money—but in February it's just us locals, and the roads are empty. So I grab my phone.

Everyone knows: Don't text and drive. And I don't! I swear. Well, I do. But only when I am sure it's safe, when there are no other cars, no bends in the road, only in daylight, and only when it's a quick reply.

I see our town's single traffic light half a mile ahead. The bridge is on my left; it arches over the Connecticut River, a simple span with the most beautiful views in the world. Fields and wetlands, winter brown and crisscrossed with frozen tidal creeks, glisten on the right. I am going forty-three miles an hour, just slightly over the speed limit. I pump the brakes as I approach the light. Forty miles an hour.

Phone in my right hand, thumb hitting the keys as my eyes dart from the road to the keyboard. There's a pickup truck coming toward me, but still far off, on the other side of the traffic light, and even from this distance, I recognize it: the Johnson family's farm wagon, bright red with wooden slats around the truck bed.

Plenty of time, slowing more, thirty miles an hour, and I press the numeral 5, and I look down directly at my phone to quickly type the next part: *mins away.* And I hit SEND just in time to look up and see that I have veered off the road onto the shoulder, where an old woman is walking her dog in the shadows, and I am going to hit them.

I see it all: She is wearing a black coat, and she has gray hair and glasses, and I don't know her name, but I have seen her in the grocery store, and her dog is a Labrador retriever with a red collar and has darted after a blur that might be a squirrel, and the woman's eyes are wide open and so is her mouth. I can read her lips: *Oh, NO!* And I have dropped the phone and I am yanking the wheel left as hard and fast as I can. The car turns, the bumper misses the lady by an inch, no more, and I feel a thud and my heart sickens because I know I have hit the dog.

I scream out, and I would do anything if I could turn back time just eleven seconds, just thirteen seconds, to save the poor dog, and the car spins around so fast, one circle, then another, and I remember my father saying steer into the skid, which makes no sense, especially because now the car is somersaulting down the bank, the windows are smashing and glass is flying, and just trying to breathe I gulp a piece of it down and have time to wonder if it will cut my insides, shred my throat and stomach, when the car lands in a place no car should ever land, nose down, on its roof, in the frozen creek.

I am hanging by my seat belt. I look around, and everything is quiet except the sound of rushing water. Only, the stream is solid ice; it isn't moving at all. The only liquid is the hot river of my blood, and then the world goes away.

Tilly

Roo is taking forever. She sent me a text, *5 mins away*, and that was over an hour ago. Forever, right? She is usually so on time it makes you want to jump out a window. But in this case, what's up?

With sisters, everyone always says, "She's the pretty one, she's the smart one," and yes, Roo is both. I, according to my teachers, parents, and even Roo, am impatient to a *fault*.

It's why I'm here in the first place, at the Hawthorne River Museum, amassing material for my American history project, due next week. Nona and Emily, my two best friends, have already finished theirs, and I'm feeling the pressure. I feel like plagiarizing, I swear. But my dad was a Yale professor, my mother teaches earth science in middle school, Roo is a genius, and I Know Better Than to Copy. But it's tempting.

Roo suggested I do my report on the *Turtle*, the world's first submarine used during a war, built right here in Connecticut and used to spy on the British in the Revolutionary War.

I've spent the afternoon sketching and learning about the museum's scale model. Mostly, I've been getting crushes on the sub's inventors, David Bushnell and Phineas Pratt. Hot guys of history.

Still: *5 mins away.* Now it's been an hour and a half, and it's dark out. I look at my phone again, a little worried. Being so late is most un-Roo-like.

She doesn't know it, but I had wanted her to drive us to the pine trees where the owls live in the graveyard. The same graveyard where our father's buried. There would be a chance the owls would fly out for their nightly hunt, and I could see them for the first time since our dad died. Also, I know the ice dripping off the needles would look cool and mystical in the sunset, and Roo could take photos that would be good for her portfolio. We could say hi to Dad while we were at it.

I was doing her a *favor*, trying to get her to rush. But now the sun is down, and it's too late.

So I'm mad. I'm about to blow, standing by the museum door, with the staff shooting me looks because they obviously want to go home, when I see my sister's boyfriend's car drive in. Was she hanging out with Newton when she should have been getting me? Were they laughing at me, making fun of all my texts begging her to hurry up?

That makes me even angrier. So instead of running out the door, I pick up a museum brochure and pretend to read. I'll make them come inside for me.

But out of the corner of my eye, I see that Newton is alone in the car. No Roo. My sister is not in the car. I drop the brochure. I can't explain the feeling that goes through me. I've never felt it before, but it's a panic that I can taste, as if I've bitten down on tinfoil. I leave the museum, step into the cold.

Newton gets out of the car. He is tall and so gangly and awkward the kids at school call him Gawk behind his back, and sometimes I do, too, but right then we walk toward each other and he puts his hands on my shoulders and the tinfoil taste gets worse.

"Where's Roo?" I ask.

"She was in an accident," he says. "Come on."

"What do you mean, an accident?"

"Tilly, just hurry up."

So we rush. Driving out of town, he tells me the basics: Roo flipped her car, my mother called him to ask him to pick me up, we are heading for the hospital in New London.

Flipped her car?

That's a sentence that belongs on the news, in the paper, on the lips of kids talking about their juvie drinking-and-drag-racing friends—not Roo, not my perfect, made-for-the-Ivy-League sister. In fact, it can't be possible—Newton has made a mistake. Or he's pulling a cruel joke on me. That in and of itself would be funny, because Newton is such a dork, jokes are not his thing. He's a tad on the humorless side for me.

I glance over at him: He has both hands on the wheel in the suggested ten-and-two position. His brown hair is long, but not cool long—he just needs a haircut—and his black-rimmed glasses are slipping down his nose. Without thinking, I reach over to push them up for him.

He doesn't say thank you. He is a laser aiming down the highway, Route 95. His phone beeps. I glance around, but it's not in sight. What if it's Roo? What if she's texting to ask how the joke on me is going?

"Someone is trying to get in touch with you," I say.

"I hear that."

"Aren't you going to check?"

"I'm driving, Tilly," he says. And I think: *Duh*. He would never check a text while at the wheel. That gives me a weird shiver, but I don't follow it to a specific thought.

"Where's your phone?" I ask.

"In my pocket."

"Okay, excuse me," I say, and reach into the right-hand pocket of his dark-blue fleece with the words WOODS HOLE YOUNGER SCIENTISTS BIODIVERSITY CAMP embroidered in gold on the chest. I pull out his phone and see the message. It is from my mother's number: *Come directly to the 3rd floor—she's in the ICU.*

I gasp. My heart stops, then starts faster than ever. It is smashing into my ribs. I am only fourteen, but I feel I'm having a heart attack. The taste of aluminum floods my whole mouth, nose, and head. It's like an extrasensory signal that Roo is in major danger.

"It's not a joke?" I ask.

"A what?" he asks. The concept, that someone would kid around at such a time, is so alien to him, he can't even grasp my question.

"Oh my God, oh my God!" I say. "I can't breathe."

"You're hyperventilating. Put your head between your knees."

It's weird that my sister's boyfriend knows how to deal with my freak-outs, but I tend to have them even when my sister is not in the ICU. Roo is the calm, logical one. I am the emotional, reactive one. *Breathe, Tilly,* my father used to say. *Just breathe.* He always knew how to calm me down, and just then my thoughts jump to him, and how he should be here for this, to help Roo, and I start to cry.

Newton actually takes one hand off the wheel and pats my head. Strangely, it helps a little. So by the time we turn off Ocean Avenue into the hospital parking lot, my eyes are dry. We hurry in, take the elevator to the third floor, tell the nurse at the desk who we are visiting, and my mother sees us and ushers us into a little room off to the side.

My mother is wearing a black sweater and beige wool pants; she must have come straight from school. She looks at me with a slight smile in her blue-gray eyes, and in them I see that it's going to be okay. After what we went through with my father, I know how to read my mother. She hugs me.

"Where is she?" I ask.

"Now listen," she says. "They have to do a lot more tests. But everything looks good so far, and they'll move her to a regular floor as soon as her vital signs stabilize. She's alert, wide-awake. She's very upset, though. She hit a dog, and she's worried about how he's doing."

"A dog?" I ask, and for the first time, hearing that Roo is awake, I start wondering about the actual accident, where she was, how it happened. "Can I see her?"

"Yes, she's been asking for you nonstop. You too, Newton. Typical Roo, worried about everyone else. The doctor is limiting her visitors right now, so you first, Tilly. Five minutes, no more. She's right over there, the third cubicle down."

So I go.

The ICU has beds arranged around the nurses' station, each partitioned from the next by curtains, and filled with machines that are humming and beeping. I tiptoe, not wanting to disturb anyone, but then I can't help it and I run the last few steps and stand breathless at my sister's bed.

"Oh, Tilly!" she says the second she sees me. She is pale, bruised, bandaged, forehead stitched. She is stuck all over with needles and tubes. I crack in half and spill all over the floor and into her arms.

"Ouch," she says weakly. I realize I have jostled a needle in her forearm. It is attached to a tube that runs up to a bottle of clear liquid hanging on a bracket over the bed.

"I'm sorry." I jump back and stare at her. How is it possible she looks even more beautiful than usual? Milky white skin, almost translucent, that spill of dark hair, the bandage on her head making her appear more vulnerable and delicate, a princess who has fallen from the tower. She is tall, willowy, and black Irish with long mahogany hair and blue eyes, and I am anything but: three inches shorter, ten pounds heavier, with garden-variety reddish-brown hair and "hazel" eyes. Roo used to tell me they were green, but she was just trying to make me feel more special—trust me, they're mud brown.

"Is this my fault?" I ask. I blurt it out, straight out of nowhere. And suddenly I know why I am nervous and my stomach is turning: It's not just that my sister is in the hospital, it's that I'm worried *I'm* the reason she's here. If she hadn't been driving to get me, it wouldn't have happened.

"What are you talking about? The dog ran out. Is he okay?" she asks, her sapphire-blue eyes brimming with tears.

"I don't know. Roo, what happened?"

"He ran out of nowhere," she said. "That's all I remember."

"You were coming to get me."

"Tilly, my head hurts."

My stomach does cartwheels. I glance around the room, because seeing the blood seep through her head bandage is making me sick. I notice her stuff is missing: Where is her camera, her backpack, her phone?

"Tilly. Can you find out about the dog?"

"I will."

She's trembling as if she's cold. I glance around for an extra blanket but don't see one. So I take her hand, which is freezing, to warm her up. She's wearing a plastic hospital bracelet, her full name looking so official: RUTH ANN MCCABE.

"Tilly, I don't feel so good . . . my neck aches. I want Dad." Her voice breaks. "I want him now."

"I know," I say. "Me too."

Just then she throws up on herself. I give a feeble, hysterical chuckle—I am so inappropriate sometimes, I hate myself. I start to dab her with a washcloth I find on the tray table, and I gag from the smell of her barf. A nurse comes in to clean her up.

"My head," Roo says to the nurse. "And I have a stiff neck."

A doctor walks in, shines a light in Roo's eyes and says to the nurse, "Corneal reflexes." Then he tells Roo to touch the tip of her nose with her right index finger. "Good, now the left. Good."

So she's fine, I'm thinking. She's passing the dumb tests. She threw up, but that's probably normal, right? Meanwhile the cartwheels in my stomach have turned into backflips, as if my insides know something my mind can't deal with.

I realize my time is up. I should let Newton come see her, but I can't leave; I want Roo to reassure me she's okay. I want her to ask about my project—it's so Roo to talk about homework. That would be how I'd know she's going to be fine.

The doctor and nurses walk out, and Roo and I are alone again.

"Feel better?" I ask.

She doesn't reply. And I notice that her lips look parched. Roo, whose mouth always looks like it belongs in a lipstick ad, perfect and cherry red and just-licked shiny, whose blue eyes are huge and whose lashes are thick and long and dark, unlike my eyelashes, so pale and reddish you can barely see them, my gorgeous sister, Roo, seems to be fading before my eyes.

"What's the matter?" I ask.

"I feel strange," she says.

"Your head's really hurting?"

"It's buzzing," she said.

"What do you mean?"

Roo lets out a low moan. It sounds like a whisper, then a rumbling laugh, and then an earthquake, and she starts shaking in her bed, like a demonically possessed girl in the movies, my angelic sister, her arms and legs thrashing around, her eyes rolling back into her head so only the whites are visible.

"Mom!" I yell, and I'm still clutching her hand as I throw myself on my sister's body to hold her down. Her wild movements have yanked the needle and tube from her arm, and a thin stream of bright-red blood writes a soaring, exuberant, and illegible note on her white pillowcase.

My mother and Newton run in, and a bunch of nurses, and that same doctor who made her touch her nose, and Roo is tossing around like a cat on a trampoline, and I finally let go of her hand as the nurses push me away, and we don't know it yet, but our world has just changed forever.

Tilly

TEEN IN COMA AFTER SHORE ROAD CRASH

BLACK HALL, CONNECTICUT—*A Black Hall High School junior, 16, remains in critical condition at Shore Hospital after a single-car accident Saturday afternoon on Shore Road. Conditions were icy, and it appears she swerved to avoid hitting a dog and lost control of the vehicle, said Black Hall Police Department spokesman Sgt. Paul Simpson.*

"It was a very serious accident," Sgt. Simpson said. "Our emergency crews had to use the Jaws of Life to extricate the victim. She was conscious and alert when pulled from the vehicle."

Hospital officials say the star student is paralyzed from the neck down and has lapsed into a coma after suffering a seizure. They refused to speculate on whether she is expected to remain in a vegetative state. The cause of the crash is unknown.

"She must have hit ice, because I saw the car coming straight at us," said Martha Muirhead, who had been walking the dog. "I ran to her right after the crash, and she knew she'd hit Lucan. Her only concern was for him."

School officials contacted Monday said the victim is an honors student and active member of the junior class. On Sunday, friends and family of the 16-year-old were keeping vigil at the hospital. "She's in there fighting for her life," her sister, 14, said, hurrying past reporters. There was no additional comment from the family.

The victim had been driving to pick up her sister at a local museum. After she drove north on Shore Road, she lost control just before Haley Creek, and according to Ms. Muirhead, the car flipped end over end, landing upside down in the marsh.

"Lucan has a broken leg, but he'll be fine," Ms. Muirhead said. "I just hope she knows that somehow. She was so caring. I pray she pulls through."

Investigators will continue examining the scene to determine the cause of the accident, and will conduct tests to determine whether drugs or alcohol were a factor. The victim's name is not being released because she is a minor.

I sat by Roo's bed with Mom and Isabel, the article on the bedside table next to us as we listened to the sounds of Roo's machines. Her breath sounded like dragon fire, whooshing in and out as the respirator pumped air into her body; her chest rose and fell in a way that looked artificial and violent, not the sweet, soft breaths of my big sister.

Isabel leaned over Roo, her thick brown hair falling into her red-rimmed eyes. She wore a white sweater and a bunch of necklaces, a gold one with a cross, and chains with little tin charms on them: a winged heart, another cross, a dolphin, a skull, a praying girl, and also a pendant Roo had given her, with two pressed violets encased in a glass circle.

"Roo," Isabel said, kissing her forehead. "We love you."

"She knows that!" I said.

"Don't snap at Isabel," my mother said.

"Just stop talking to her," I said. "Or tell her that the dog is okay instead. *That's* what she'd want to know! Not lame stuff she already knows. You're acting like people in a movie talking to someone in a coma."

"Honey," my mother said gently, as if I were a time bomb. "She *is* in a coma." She paused. "And paralyzed." Her voice sounded hollow.

"That's just because she's asleep!" I protested. "She'll move when she wakes up."

My mother stared at me but didn't reply. Her silent pity toward me was deafening.

The doctors weren't sure of the precise cause of Roo's paralysis—MRIs and every other test known to medical science revealed her spine was unbroken—but still my sister couldn't move or respond to stimuli. It might have been due to the stroke.

Yes, sixteen-year-olds can have strokes, and Roo had one right after the seizure—that's what it was, those wild, uncontrolled movements the last time I talked to her. As the doctors had rushed her out of the room, she apparently suffered a brain stem stroke affecting the basilar artery system. They called it a pediatric stroke, which bothered me, as if it was in any way less devastating than the kind adults get.

And Roo has been lying in her hospital bed, eyes wide open, on a ventilator, ever since.

"We do love you," Isabel said, stroking Roo's cheek, purple and yellow with bruises, caked with dry spittle. It made me insane seeing her do that, partly because I couldn't bear to touch my sister, to even go close enough to smell her.

I stared at Roo. Her eyes were open and protruding, practically popping out of her skull, but she wasn't in there. Roo's doctor, Dr. Danforth, told us open eyes were normal in coma patients—as if *anything* was normal. Roo didn't blink, there was no consciousness, no intelligence. And her expression was shockingly, terribly startled. Dr. Danforth said that Roo was incapable of emotion, that her face had just been frozen that way, left behind by the stroke.

It made me think of an essay by Roo that our father had loved. She had written about Hubbard's Point, our beautiful rocky coast, and how a glacier from the last ice age had carved out Connecticut's craggy and immovable rocks and ledges in its wake. That's basically what Dr. Danforth was saying: My sister's expression had been sculpted by not a glacier but a stroke. Her face had turned to stone.

The injured parts of her head, bruised and bloody, were shaved for stitches—there were bald patches beneath the big wads of gauze bandage, and the rest of her hair, once thick and glossy, with the color and shine of ebony piano keys, was flat and dirty. Her skin, formerly as fresh as a peach, was pale and grainy, almost gray, as if there was no blood left inside her.

Her long, dark lashes were encrusted with yellow goo. Her lips behind the breathing tube looked cracked; nurses drifted in and out constantly to dab them with Vaseline.

Why? I wondered. *She can't feel it. She's not even breathing on her own.*

A plastic tube snaked into her nostrils and down her throat, held in place by clear tape and attached to a ventilator that looked almost like a kitchen appliance, with dials and a screen, right next to the bed.

That machine is keeping her alive until they can figure out what to do with her organs, I thought.

"My sister is going to die," I whispered.

Or maybe I didn't speak. No sound came out, and neither my mother nor Isabel reacted.

I looked back down at the newspaper on the bed stand, skimming over the words again.

"This article is disgusting," I said, slapping the paper. "Drugs and alcohol? Roo?" I once saw a show on E! about a Disney actress who sued a magazine that had claimed she'd been drunk on a yacht. She'd said those lies could wreck her career. She'd called it slander, or maybe libel. Or defamation? "It's slander, Mom," I went on. "Defamation! I'm going to write a letter to the editor."

"Tilly, they're not saying she took any—it's normal to test after an accident. That's all they're saying," Mom said calmly.

"Still, it gives the wrong idea about her," I said.

Yesterday, the reporter from the newspaper had been waiting in the hospital lobby, and I remembered talking to her. She'd seemed nice, but now I realized it was phony sympathy. She was just a defaming wolf in sheep's clothing.

"We know Roo," Isabel said. She glanced over at me, attempting solidarity. "The tests will come back negative. She was taking photos, not partying. We texted about it."

"Oh, God. Don't tell me she was texting," my mother said.

"No, not while she was driving," Isabel said, sounding a little outraged. One thing about Isabel, she was always clear about the difference between right and wrong. She had a little bit of moral outrage going on at all times.

"Could we stop talking?" I asked. My stomach flipped, thinking about how Roo and I had been texting. But she must have pulled over to answer me. Roo was not the text-and-drive type. I shivered the thought away.

"Sweetheart," my mother said, leaning close to Roo. "We have some good news. Lucan, the dog, is fine. He's going to recover. Tilly said you would want to know, and . . ."

I stopped listening. I remembered how Roo had teased me in the fall for talking to Dad's grave. He wasn't there, he couldn't hear me, she had said. She was being all scientific and rational, and I was acting like an emo baby. So I had stopped.

My mind prickled with the fact that I had promised Roo to be rational. Would she consider it "rational" for us to be talking to her now?

I got up and left the room. Hearing my mother talk to comatose Roo was a nightmare I had to wake up from. The hallway felt chilly. I had this morbid thought: They want this neurological floor cold because the patients can't feel anything, and if the temperature is down, it will keep those lifeless bodies on machines from rotting.

Help. I'm thinking horror-movie thoughts about my sister.

"Hey."

I looked over, and there was Newton unfolding his lanky self like an origami crane from a vinyl sofa. He swallowed a few times, his Adam's apple bobbing in his long throat. His glasses looked crooked and smudged, as if he'd slept in them three days straight. Then I realized he probably had; none of us had left the hospital for very long.

The four of us—me, Mom, Isabel, and Newton—took turns sitting by Roo's bed while the others went in search of food and coffee. I'd always thought I'd be happy for any excuse to miss school, but ha: I was so wrong. I hadn't been back since Roo's seizure, and I'd give anything to be stuck in algebra till the end of time, if only Roo could be okay.

"Hey," I said.

"How is she?" Newton asked.

"The same."

"That's a scientific impossibility," he said. "Nothing remains static."

"Why do you have to talk like that with me? It sounds so stupid. 'Nothing remains static.' "

"I'm trying to reassure you," he said. "You idiot."

"Thank you for that."

"No problem."

But coming from Newton, with his goofy smile, the word *idiot* had a ring of affection.

"So tell me why I should be reassured," I said.

"Well, her vital signs have been stable. Her blood pressure has stopped falling, so they're not worried about internal bleeding anymore."

"But they said she's paralyzed."

"True, but the reason is unclear, so that could mean movement will return. Her C3, 4, and 5 are intact."

"Huh?"

"Oh," he said, as if suddenly remembering it was nonscientific me and not Roo he was talking to. "Cervical discs. Quadriplegia can be caused by injury to the spinal cord above those three. And as we know, her spine is intact. So it must be related to the stroke, and . . ."

"You're a doctor now?"

"I know how to do research, Tilly. What do you think I've been reading about since it happened? Anyway, her doctors are continuing to do tests."

He was right about that. The doctors huddled around Roo throughout the day, maintaining intravenous lines and saline locks, administering blood tests and brain tests, pushing her eyelids up with their thumbs and shining tiny flashlights into her eyes to see if her pupils dilated, throwing around phrases that belong in science fiction—or at least someone else's sister's life: *anticoagulants*, *diffuse axonal brain injury*, and *cerebral thromboembolism*.

"Nothing is conclusive yet," Newton added. "It's an evolving diagnosis."

"Have you *seen* her?" I asked. I wanted to shove him for saying "evolving diagnosis." I realized that being brainy was his default mode, but it really got under my skin and made what was happening to Roo sound so distant. "The way she stares without seeing."

"I know," he said.

"Machines are keeping her alive. True or false?"

"True." He cleared his throat, looked straight up at the ceiling. We both stood there staring at a tiny dot that might have been a fly. No, it was just a dot. It hypnotized us for a couple of minutes. Then the horrid thoughts returned.

My sister is gone—or she might as well be. Not only is she comatose, she is a Q—quadriplegic. However she got that way, whether her C-whatevers are intact or not, she is in a vegetative state.

If anyone at school uses the word vegetable, *I will kill them.*

I took my phone out of my pocket. There was a long thread of a group text from Emily and Nona, sent from school earlier.

How is she, everyone wants to know???? Emily had texted.

Did she wake up yet? Does she recognize you? Nona had asked.

Give her a HUUUUGGGGEEE hug from me! Emily had written.

Me 2, Nona had added.

Miss u luv u, Emily had written.

I wasn't exactly in the mood to tell anyone anything. But Emily and Nona were the people closest to me besides Mom and Roo. Standing beside Newton in the hall, I wrote back: *She hasn't woken up, we're here with her now, thank u luv u.*

So yes: Everyone was talking; Roo was the topic of the year.

"Uh," Newton said.

"What?" I asked, looking up from my phone.

"Did Roo say anything to you?"

"No! She can't talk, you know that."

"Not today," he said. "Before. The accident."

"About what?"

"I don't know. Did she mention me? Mention us?"

"You and Roo?" I asked, confused. What was there to say? The two of them were pretty much inseparable.

"Yeah," he said.

"Not really," I said. But thinking back, I did remember a couple of weird moments Saturday morning—the day of the accident. Our landline had rung, and I'd seen Newton's name on caller ID. Just as I reached for it, Roo had said to let it go, she'd call him from her cell phone. But then her cell had buzzed. Newton again, and she'd ignored that, too. What had that been about?

"Why?" I asked.

"Never mind," he said, looking away. I felt a little unsettled. What could the problem have been? With the entire world falling apart, I didn't want another dreadful thing to worry about.

"Tell me," I pushed.

"It's nothing," he said. "Seriously."

I heard the loud and ever-present sound of Roo's respirator coming from her room. I wanted to go in there and ask her what Newton was talking about, and why she hadn't taken his call that day. I wanted to snuggle up next to her while she braided my hair, the way she'd always done, clipping the braids with tortoiseshell barrettes that had been our mother's in college. I wanted everything to go back to the way it was.

My breath caught in my chest, and it came out in a sob.

"Listen to her," I said.

"It's bad," he said.

"My mother and Isabel are in there talking to her as if she can hear. Do you think she can?"

"I don't think so," he said, very quietly, and I appreciated him for not pretending things were more okay than they were—or at all.

"So what's going to happen?" I asked.

My sister's boyfriend stared into my eyes. He was at least a foot taller than I was and, aside from Roo, the smartest kid at school. His eyes filled behind his glasses, and his lower lip began to wobble. With one finger, I touched his bare, gangly wrist, jutting out from the sleeve of the same sweater he'd been wearing since Roo's accident.

Then, with his right index finger, he touched the top of my head. We stood there, in the hall of Shore Hospital, the two people who love Roo most, not counting my mother and Isabel, locked in a dorky circuit of pain and index fingers and the unspoken answer we both feared most: that Roo was going to die.

I backed away. Everywhere I moved in this hospital was destined to rip my heart out. In the hall with Newton, in the room with Roo: Either way, I couldn't take it. Every time I breathed, I thought of Roo, of how she couldn't do something as simple as breathe. If she wasn't going to live, I had to spend every last second with her. So I walked back to her room.

Roo

I was totally immobile, wrapped in sheets and blankets and bandages; that's what it felt like.

I was in a tomb, in ancient Egypt, surrounded by funerary objects, scarabs and baskets and amulets.

Okay, I am dreaming about a history project. What are those dreams where you know you're asleep, you're fully cognizant of that fact, but you're swept along in a strange world?

Lucid dreams, that's what they're called. I was having one of those.

And it had been going on forever, days at least. Ever since I first figured out that I'm in a hospital.

Time to wake up now, come on! Wiggle your fingers, kick your legs!

I commanded my limbs to move, but they didn't. How bizarre. I was trapped, mummified. That word was so weird, *mummified;* just try to say it in a regular sentence, not home-work, with a straight face. Especially when talking about yourself.

My head itched, and there was a cold breeze blowing. *Where's my hair?* I had a sharp memory of someone shaving part of my head, stitching up cuts. I'd hit my forehead on the steering wheel, and there was a gash behind my ear. I felt the stiches pulling now and wanted to raise my hand to touch the scar, but I couldn't move my arm.

Here is my mother leaning over me. Here is Isabel holding my hand, whispering in Spanish.

I recognized the phrases, a prayer, similar to one she said for my father when he died.

Don't pray for me, you're scaring me, I said, but the words didn't come out. Isabel kept praying, her lips moving. She looked so pretty, a little blush on her angular cheeks, the tiny gold cross necklace her grandmother gave her mingled with the tin *milagros,* the Mexican charms she wears on long chains. All that metal catching the light.

Light came in through the windows. I was on heavy medication, I knew that much, because I felt so confused and thick, and my stomach was upset. *Am I dreaming or am I awake?*

My dream of an Egyptian tomb wouldn't contain light, it would be pitch-dark in there, and it wouldn't have my mother and Isabel, and a sense of Tilly and Newton nearby. I thought I could hear their voices out in the hall.

And through the drugs I also thought: *crash.*

One little word, and a whole lot of sound, the loudest noises I'd ever heard smashed into my memory.

Glass breaking, metal crunching, a dog yelping, water splashing. No, wait, that's blood rushing. My blood running down my face, upside down, from a cut in my head into my nose and mouth. I'm choking, I can't breathe, I'm drowning in my own blood.

It terrified me, and I thrashed around, but my limbs didn't move, and that made me panic even more.

Did a crash really occur? . . . Was I in a car wreck? Or was that a different dream?

The old lady and the dog. I remembered them, and the horror I felt at hitting him, the dog. It happened. It was real. I was in an accident.

"Sweetheart," Mom said now. "We have some good news. Lucan, the dog, is fine. He's going to recover. Tilly said you would want to know, and it was in the paper, he's really okay."

Oh, that sweet dog, black Lab, red collar, and I hit him, my car went off the road. I drove it straight at him. I remembered the sound of the car's bumper striking his hip, the thud, and the old lady's scream, and then my own screams.

I tried to flinch, but I couldn't do that, either.

Mom? I said. *Please help me. I have a million questions; why won't you listen?*

Mom just kept murmuring in a flat, zombie tone about the dog. She seemed not to notice that I was frantic. She couldn't hear me. I was stuck, a leaf in just-poured concrete. Pull me out before it hardens.

Isabel, can't you help me?

She and Mom, the two of them sat there doing nothing, just talking, soft voices, prayers and stories. I was here, but they weren't paying attention.

GET TILLY! I screamed. *NEWTON! They will understand! Tilly and Newton will know what's going on immediately and get me out of here.*

Where is here?

Here is the hospital, I realized.

Tubes and needles dosed me with pain medication. How many days had it been since the accident? How many hours? Did it matter?

I remembered my seizure, Tilly standing there—the worst feeling I've ever had, thrashing around with no control, hearing her scream just before I passed out. I woke up being restrained—or at least that's what I thought. I thought they had tied me down. Then I realized, *No, there are no straps. It's me—I can't move. I can't speak. I can't get anyone to hear me.*

I must have looked like a lifeless lump, but inside my mind I was wild, alive, in agony, going crazy.

The worst part, beyond any pain, was not having my family realize that I was awake and completely conscious, hearing everything. How could they not know?

Mom? You're right here, and you can't hear me. Tilly! Get in here, come into my room. I need my sister! She's the one.

Of everyone here, all these people I loved, Tilly spoke my language. She got me. One look and she'd know.

Hurry, Tilly, I need you.

The nurse entered, saying hi to my mother and Isabel, blocking my view of everyone.

Nurse, I see you holding that needle, tapping the IV. I can't make you hear, but will you look into my eyes? Please, no more

*medication, not now. I need to stay alert, to make my family know
I am here.*

I could see out the hospital window. The sky was blue, and
there were big fluffy white clouds moving past, just outside. I
could see their shadows on the brick wall opposite the window.

Help me help me help me.

The nurse bustled around me.

*No, stop filling the syringe from that little bottle of clear liquid.
Please, no, don't inject it into my IV. You know it's going to make
me go to sleep, don't you? That's what keeps happening, that is
why I have to begin again, to remember all over again, to get
through the grogginess of the medication. I need to stay awake, to
get you to notice me.*

And this was my favorite nurse, an older, African American woman. I saw her before, today and yesterday and the day
before, but it was like encountering her for the first time again
and again, remembering and forgetting, a horrible cycle.

Right now I decided to call her Pearl because she wore a
necklace with three pearls on a chain, and I heard her telling
Mom, "Each one represents one of my daughters."

"My baby, my Roo," my mother said, starting to sob. She
clutched Pearl's hand. "What am I going to do?"

"You stay strong for her," Pearl said. "Her doctor is the best
there is, you can count on that. Dr. Danforth is taking good
care of her."

"Will she wake up? Will she come out of the coma?"

"It's early days yet," Pearl said. "We live with a different
clock on this floor. We don't keep time the same way. You just

be with her when you can. And we'll be here with her when you can't."

"My baby," my mother said again. "I can't stand to see her this way."

But I'm okay, I wanted to scream. *I am here! Please see me, talk to ME.*

The tall, thin neurology intern who always brooded and studied me and took notes and looked into my eyes came into the room. I always hoped he would see, but he never did. He'd done test after test, but he didn't know I was there. And he said very little. I named him Dr. Quiet.

"Mrs. McCabe has questions," Pearl said to Dr. Quiet.

So do I—talk to me. I am freaking awake!

But they didn't.

"The stroke caused damage," Dr. Quiet said. "And as long as she's in the coma, we have to watch and wait."

Watch and wait? That's what they teach you in med school? It's not a coma—I am awake and shrieking; can't you hear me?

"How long will the coma last?" my mother asked.

"You'll have to discuss that with Dr. Danforth," Dr. Quiet said.

Right. My main doctor was Dr. Sarah Danforth. She was a specialist in pediatric neurovascular disease. I remembered that she introduced herself by name, looking me in the eyes, and even though she thought I couldn't hear, I appreciated her treating me as if I were real. She was brilliant but kind; she made rounds with a little teddy bear pinned to the lapel of her white lab coat. She had a Boston accent. Would a coma patient you have to watch and wait for know that? But I hadn't seen her today.

Or had I? It felt so blurry. I was used to having my mind sharp and clear.

Isabel wiped something sticky from my eyes. I tried to blink, to capture her attention, but I couldn't get my eyelids to move. She seemed focused on her task, cleaning gunk from my eyes, then my mouth. This was awful, gross, having my best friend attend to me this way.

Isabel came from Mexico when we were in fourth grade, and it was best friends at first sight. Back then she spoke very little English—her family hung out mainly with other Mexicans who had immigrated here, her cousins and a group of family friends who had come from the same Mexican town to the Connecticut shoreline to find restaurant work.

Isabel credited me with how quickly she learned English, because I was a pedantic little thing with a tiny blackboard and a bunch of storybooks, and I'd go through them with her, word by word, nearly every day after school, and teach her the names of things as we walked the tide line and picked up smooth beach stones. She called them *piedras de amistad*: friendship stones.

"Well, you're a sweetheart," Pearl said to Isabel now.

And she was and I loved her, but right now I was yelling at her—*Why can't you help me, why won't you see me?*

My throat was raw from strain, and my heart was tired. I wanted to stay awake, but I couldn't. The medicine was rushing through me now; I felt it in my tissue, in my bones. I heard Isabel's milagros rattling—she had a nervous habit of grasping the charms she wore around her neck. Among them was the glass locket containing two white violets I gave her for her thirteenth birthday, the flowers symbolizing two best friends.

"Hail Mary," she whispered, starting to pray again. She was Catholic, very devout.

Isabel—look at me. Don't pray, talk to me.

"Full of grace," she continued, the milagros clanking against my bed rail.

When she kissed my cheek, I smelled her lemon shampoo, and I just wanted to cry. I heard the rest of the prayer, and then she stopped speaking.

I love the smell of lemons, I wanted to say. *I want to go outside with you and run on the beach. I want to go home. I am so scared*, I wanted to tell her. And I also wanted to push her away, as hard as I could. *Get Tilly*, I wanted to say. *You don't see me, you don't love me like Tilly. Get me my sister. She's the only one. The only one who can help me. Oh, Tilly.*

And it worked, because Tilly finally came through the door. She barreled right past my mother and Isabel and Pearl. And Newton was behind her, and my heart felt liquid with love for him.

Tilly, I said, but of course she didn't hear me.

No one heard me. The medication filled my system yet again, and I fell asleep.

Chapter Two

Tilly

*M*y first day back at school, walking up the stone steps, knowing Roo wasn't going to be there, I felt the heat of everyone's mad curiosity.

Eyes on me as I walked down the hall, stopped at my locker. All through morning classes, I kept thinking, *Who cares about equations, about Ralph Waldo Emerson, about minerals in the soil of Chile, about the first submarine, when Roo could die any minute? I need to be back at the hospital.*

At lunch I met TEN in the cafeteria. Emily and Nona know I call them my quasi-besties, and they get it, because of course my real best friend is my sister. But put the first initials of Tilly, Emily, and Nona together and there you have it—the child hood name of our club, TEN. We've known one another our whole lives, even before we were born because our mothers had sat together on the beach back when they were pregnant with us.

"How is she?" Nona asked.

"The same," I said, scrunched down in my seat, wearing Roo's Nantucket hoodie with my jeans and boots.

"Holding her own," Emily said, always so loving and positive. She and I were about the same height, i.e., short. She had silky, light-brown hair and unusual amber-colored eyes, and she wore glasses: Today's pair were cat eyed with blue frames. Her dress—probably made by her mother, who was a seamstress—had tiny red and blue flowers all over it. On anyone else it would have been reminiscent of a tablecloth, but Em pulled it off with a chunky silver-link belt and made it look country chic.

I smiled at her and tried to eat my sandwich, but it tasted like sawdust.

"What *happened*?" Nona asked. "You hardly told us anything."

"I was slightly busy," I said.

"Too busy to tell us what's really going on? All you had to do was text."

I was ticked, but this was quintessential Nona. She always pushed, and sometimes leaned close to the edge of being slightly offensive. She occasionally made me feel she wasn't completely on my side—the opposite of Em, who was always caring, and often the peacemaker.

Today, Nona was wearing a black leather jacket in her ongoing attempt to look older and tougher than she was. She had turquoise eyes and white-blond hair that had started turning a little darker—still blond, but more yellow than white—once she turned fourteen. This year, she gave herself an asymmetrical haircut: buzzed the left side of her head, and tragically the hair underneath was almost brown. The overall effect, as Em and I had discussed on the phone a few days before the accident, wasn't quite working.

"Uh, her car flipped," I said, as if I hadn't already told her, and as if the news hadn't reported it a hundred times.

"It just seems so random," Nona said. "That's, like, the straightest part of the road."

"Yeah, it was icy."

"I know, but it's crazy she lost control."

"She didn't want to hit the dog."

"I was just thinking, it had to be the brakes, or the steering. Maybe there was a malfunction with the car. Your mother could sue."

"That's gross. You sound like a lawyer on TV," I said, even though I had similar lawsuit thoughts when reading that awful article.

"I try," Nona said.

But the weird thing was, she'd gotten me thinking, and NOT about lawsuits. Roo's accident *did* happen on a straightaway. And if the dog was all the way off the road, on the shoulder, why would Roo have had to maneuver at all?

The toxicology report had come back negative—of course Roo hadn't been drinking or taking drugs. But did the newspaper print the update? No. The cops had returned her camera and backpack to us. They checked the digital photographs, which provided a map of the last half hour before the crash: gorgeous shots of the saltwater marshes and tidal flats, ones she obviously planned to submit to the contest. Her phone was missing, which was weird. They figured she must have lost it at one of her last stops.

It had probably slipped out of her jacket pocket; she wouldn't even notice, the way she got so involved in her photography. The rest of the world disappeared when she had her eye on the viewfinder. If I'd been there, I'd have teased her the way I always did.

"Hey, Roo, photograph this!" I'd said to her a week ago, walking on my hands along the high tide line.

She had been crouched down in the sand, photographing the way the February wind blew the soft, creamy white tops off the waves. She had wanted to capture the delicate saltwater lace foam against the powerful, almost solid-looking steely-gray waves.

"Over here!" I called. I was upside down, skittering through the nasty dry seaweed on my hands, and gravity had pulled my jacket and shirt down over my face. My bare midriff was all goose bumps.

"Hang on a minute, Tilly," she called back. "I want to get this set."

"No, check this out!" I clamored as annoyingly as possible, but she stayed focused on those waves. I wished I had a talent like hers, but I took the worst pictures, when I even bothered trying. I couldn't seem to stay still long enough, and my photos always looked like blurs of movement, caused by me whirling around or getting too excited and jumping up and down.

I wound up doing somersaults down the beach, getting my hair all sandy. Finally, when Roo had gotten the shots she wanted, she turned and I did one last triumphant handstand. She chuckled—I could always make Roo laugh—and clicked a photo of me.

The next morning, at breakfast, I found she'd printed out the photo and propped it up in the fruit bowl. She thought it was hilarious. Our mother was not amused. I sat there eating my cereal, staring at the picture. Roo had caught me at the exact perfect moment—my hands in the sand, my feet straight up in the air, my bare belly winter white, my pink striped bra the only bright spot in the frigid beach landscape. But my shirt hadn't quite covered my face, and you could see me smiling with total love at my sister.

Sitting in the caf with TEN, I shook my head hard, dispelling this terrifying thought—Was it possible Roo and I would never run down the beach together again?

"Are you going to go see her after school today?" Em asked gently, looking at me over the rims of her pale-blue glasses.

"Of course," I said.

Emily nodded; she could see right under my skin and knew just how I felt, that there was nowhere else I wanted to be.

Nona, though, was looking down at her right shoulder, holding the remaining blond thatch in her fist, probably contemplating a bleach job.

My emotions started getting the better of me. As much as I fought them, and I did, they tended to do that. I thought of Roo, how unfair it was for her to be in the hospital while people at school, even my best friends, talked about her at the same time they were worrying about dumb real-life things like hair color.

Roo was so smart, so good; I didn't even care that I had always been in her shadow. Well, maybe I cared. A little. Before the accident, that is. Nobody would ever mistake me for either a beauty or a genius. My sister was—is—both.

"My mother can drive us," Nona said.

"Us?" I asked.

"We want to go with you," Emily said. "To visit Roo."

"But you can't," I said, swallowing down the lie. "No visitors except family."

"But it would be good for her," Nona said, still frowning at her hair. Then she looked up, and I loved her again. "We could talk to her about Hubbard's Point, the beach and stars, stuff she loved. *Loves*, I mean. It will bring her back."

There was no rule about Roo having visitors. And Nona and Em loved Roo, too; they'd grown up with her. They wouldn't judge her. But somehow, in a coma, Roo had become my responsibility. She needed protection, and I didn't want anyone outside the little circle of my mother, Newton, Isabel, and me visiting her.

Across the cafeteria, I heard Marlene Nossiter laughing with a bunch of the popular kids, her snobby friends. She was in Roo's grade, the kind of girl who was in the bathroom curling her eyelashes whenever possible. I looked over, and she smirked at me before turning toward her boyfriend, Andy Newell, and her pals Deb Bonner and Allison Meyrier. I heard Roo's name whispered. I stood up, started over.

"Don't do it. Don't give her the satisfaction," Nona said, grabbing my wrist. I saw genuine concern in her eyes, but I pulled away and kept going.

"What's so funny?" I asked, stopping at Marlene's table.

"Oh, nothing," Marlene said. "We were just talking about the good news, saw it on TV. That dog your sister hit will be totally fine. Broken leg—no biggie."

"Yeah, I saw him and his owner at the Big Y," Andy said. "He has a blue cast. Limping through the dairy aisle."

"Ha-ha, you're hilarious," I said, and felt like jabbing Andy in the throat. But I did feel relieved to know the dog was well enough to go to the grocery store.

"His owner is so weird," Marlene said. "She's, like, a witch. She's probably putting spells on your family after what your sister did. I would be careful."

"Maybe YOU should be careful," I said. I could barely speak or breathe.

"The dog's owner is Miss Muirhead. My mom took care of her sister," Nona said as she and Em came up behind me. Nona's mother, a nurse's aide, worked for half the elderly people in town. Then, glancing at Em and me, Nona added, "She *is* a little bizarre."

"What kind of name is Lucan for a dog?" Andy asked. "It's not Luke and it's not Lucas."

"It sounds Wiccan, actually," Deb said.

"Told you she was a witch!" Marlene said, giggling and dancing a little in her seat.

"You think it's funny?" I asked, moving closer.

"Um, no," she said, jerking back as if I'd invaded her super-precious personal space, which I totally had. I had this horrible desire to grab her hair in both my fists and pull it as hard as I could.

People began to gather. Isabel walked over with her cousin Melanie Torres, a sophomore. Two freshman boys—Teddy Messina, who'd been in our class since first grade, and Slater Jones, the quiet new African American kid from New York City—stood there looking vaguely uncomfortable.

"Mathilda," Marlene said to me. "I am not saying this to be cruel. But it is possible Roo is a vegetable because that crazy old lady did some evil magic on her."

I felt a surge of anger. "Shut up, Marlene. I mean it. Shut your ugly face," I hissed.

"Nice, Tilly. Classy as ever. I'm just basically saying what they said in the paper. Vegetative state. It is what it is." She shrugged, got up, and started to walk away. That wasn't happening. Rage overflowed, and I lunged at her.

And then I felt the thud of someone bumping into me from behind, a pair of arms clamping around my waist. It was Slater Jones.

"Don't get into a fight," he said into my ear. "Don't give her the satisfaction—just forget it, walk away."

"Are you serious?" I asked, wrenching free to look straight into his dark-brown eyes. "*Forget* it? Did you hear what she said? About my sister?"

"Yeah. But walk away from her."

"You don't even know us!" I said, boiling over with frustration at everyone and everything. Slater just happened to be in my way. Marlene sat back down, a smug look on her face as she watched the drama.

"No, but I know fights," Slater replied. "I'm a New Yorker. Fights get you nowhere. Rise up, don't sink down."

"Wow, you're so tough," I said loudly, sarcastically. I saw him flinch just slightly.

"Well, maybe I have to be. I know how it is to have a disabled family member," he said.

That gave me a moment's pause, and I studied Slater's face. "I'm sorry for you," I said. "But my sister's going to get better."

"Woo-woo," Allison said. "Not if she's got a spell on her."

Marlene, Allison, Deb, and the others started laughing. I knew my checks were bright red; Slater just stood there with this weird, quiet dignity on his face. I felt humiliated, and worse, I knew I had hurt him.

"Miss Muirhead wouldn't do anything to Roo," Slater said, standing between me and Marlene and her friends.

"How do you know?" I asked.

"I work for her. I do odd jobs after school, and she's really nice. She feels bad about what happened."

Mr. Gordon, the principal, came into the cafeteria, and I used that opportunity to leave as fast as I could. Emily called my name, but I kept going. I was too wrapped up in what a jerk I'd been to Slater and the truth of what Marlene had said.

Roo *was* a vegetable.

My sister had two separate brain injuries—the traumatic one caused by the car crash, and the acquired one caused by the stroke. And she would never be the same again.

I went to the library, to lay out the pages of my report on the *Turtle*, the one I'd started the day of Roo's accident. I was still seething about Marlene. She had always been mean. I remembered seeing her make Roo cry, when they were eight and I was six. Roo had found a robin's nest in the hedge behind school, and she would sit a short distance away, watching the parents fly in and out.

Roo loved all birds the way I loved owls. She'd let me sit with her, and she'd show me her notebook where she'd sketched pictures and written poems about the birds of Black Hall. Robins were Connecticut's state bird, their eggs a perfect deep turquoise blue. Seeing us there, Marlene cackled, "Nature lovers, nature lovers!" as if it were the worst insult.

The next day, the nest was on the ground. The eggs were broken, the woven twigs and leaves pulled apart, strewn under the hedge. I had a lump in my throat watching Roo crouch down, gathering the bits of blue shell together while the heartbroken adult robins twittered overhead.

"Maybe they'll build another one," Roo said, tears running down her cheeks. She never mentioned Marlene's name, but I knew that she had done it, and looking back, I even knew why: She had envy for Roo's curiosity and goodness, for the way her interests would lead her to drawing pictures and writing poems and taking photographs that got her recognized. I knew because I sometimes felt that way, too.

Right before the end of the day, I got a text from my mother:

> *They took the breathing tube out. She's*
> *breathing on her own! No more ventilator.*
> *Dr. D says this is very good news. Meet me*
> *outside school. We'll head straight to see her.*

I couldn't believe it—but what did it mean? It didn't matter—I could hardly wait.

Although my mother taught at the middle school right next to Black Hall High, she'd been taking time off to be with Roo and deal with insurance problems. So she drove from home and picked me up; I was so anxious to get going, I met her halfway down the school's long driveway.

We headed toward the bridge along Shore Road, past all the scenic spots Roo photographed just before her crash. My mother and I passed the accident site; it looked innocent in the afternoon light: the marsh, a winding coastal stream, a great blue heron fishing in the shallows.

"If she's breathing on her own, does that mean she's waking up?" I asked.

"Honey, I don't know yet. Dr. Danforth said we have to manage expectations," my mother said.

"But she said '*very* good news,' right?"

"Yes."

My pulse galloped, making me feel I could run alongside the car and beat my mother to the hospital.

"And being off the ventilator is huge," I said.

"It is."

"It means she's going to get better, right?" I asked.

"We have to believe that."

"She's strong! She's amazing. Now that she's breathing on her own, she can really start to improve. It means her body is starting to work again. She's going to know us, Mom. She is!"

"Let's wait and see."

"'Very good news,'" I repeated. "Those were the doctor's exact words?"

"Yes, exact words."

I pictured Roo awake. I would probably have to break some of the terrible news to her. She would want to know why she couldn't move. She would be so devastated to learn the extent of her injuries. But I was planning the words I would say to her: *I'm here for you, I will take care of you, you can count on me for everything.*

I pictured us at school, Roo and me. She'd be in a wheelchair, and I'd push her to all her classes. Yale might be out, because I would never get in; she would have to go to a college I could eventually be admitted to. But I would stay by her side.

Mom and I found a parking spot on the street, a small victory because the parking garage was costing a fortune. Although I might not have been a genius like Roo, I was no dummy, and I knew those papers spread across the dining room table meant Mom was cashing in our savings bonds and taking out a loan to cover medical expenses not covered by insurance.

Just as we were getting into the elevator, my mother gave me a small smile and hug. And I beamed back. That elevator ride was the happiest I had been since before the crash.

We ran down the hall, past the nurses' station, into Roo's room.

I don't know what I expected, but it wasn't this. Oh my God, oh, Roo.

The breathing tube had been taken out: That much was true, but it was the only difference I could see. Dr. Danforth was making notes on her chart. I threw myself at the bed, eye to eye with my sister. But she still wasn't there. She stared straight ahead exactly as before: no smile, no recognition. Her lips were drawn back in a horrible expression—previously hidden by the tape holding the ventilator tube in place. Her head was still partially shaved, only they'd changed the bandages, so more of the baldness showed. Her incisions were more visible, dark and jagged on her scalp, stitched up, the tied-off black thread looking like tiny angry insects. I felt sick.

"Roo, can you hear me?" I asked, and then, just in case I was missing something, "Are you awake now?"

She didn't answer; she still didn't know I was there. I felt a sob in my throat and turned to the doctor.

"That look on her face, what is she feeling?" I asked.

"She still doesn't feel emotion, Tilly," Dr. Danforth said in a very quiet voice, just as she'd explained before. "That's part of her condition. The expression on her face is purely physical."

I grabbed Roo's hands, held them to my lips while I cried, kissed them, and burbled spit all over: "Roo, it's me, please talk to me, please, Roo!"

My mother tried to pull me away. "Stop it, Tilly!" she said.

"Why did you say it was very good news?" I wailed, turning back to the doctor.

"Because it really is. The fact she can breathe without the respirator is a tremendous step," Dr. Danforth said. She was wearing her white lab coat with the little teddy bear pinned to the lapel; I am not proud of the fact that I felt like ripping that bear right off her collar and throwing it out the window.

"But I thought she'd know us!"

"Tilly, we can't jump ahead of ourselves. Roo's brain injuries are severe. We just don't know when, or even if, the next development will occur. We have to be grateful for every step, even when it seems small."

"Oh, Roo," I said, turning back to my sister, sitting beside her on the bed, crushing her hand in mine.

"And this one *wasn't* small. It might not seem like much to you," Dr. Danforth said, "but breathing on her own is clinically significant."

Clinically? The word was so cold, so unconnected to the love I felt for my sister. Rage boiled through me. My mother murmured something, and she and the doctor left the room. And here I was with Roo.

She lay in bed, on her left side because she'd started getting sores on her right hip. Her open eyes disturbed me exactly as they had ever since the seizure, staring with what seemed to be anguish, straight into nothing. Her lips, pulled back from her teeth in a horror-movie rictus, were forming the expression she might have had at the time of the crash: terror and dread.

A nurse came in, checked the plastic bag attached to Roo's bed: It was full of dark-brown urine. I had gotten used to the idea of Roo having a catheter, having the smell of pee around all the time, but I hated being in the room when the nurse emptied the bag.

"You want to step out for a minute?" the nurse asked, picking up on my discomfort.

"That's okay," I said, steeling myself. If Roo had to go through it, the least I could do was stick by her side during the procedures that made me feel the worst.

I was the least science-oriented member of my family. Roo would probably have scientific curiosity even about what was happening to her now. The closest I came to that was checking out owl pellets—gross, slimy things gagged up by owls after eating, filled with the indigestible remains of whatever they'd just devoured: fur, blood, bones, claws, little mice skulls, sparrow beaks. I had a collection of them, picked up by me and my dad on our owling walks. Thinking of Dad right now, wishing he were here to help us through this, brought tears to my eyes.

The nurse reached up under Roo's hospital gown, adjusted the thick tube; I tried not to think about how that felt to my sister. This was one of the few moments it helped to tell myself Roo was gone, that she couldn't feel pain, but I felt it for her, cramps and twinges like the worst possible UTI.

When the nurse walked out, I noticed she'd left Roo's legs uncovered. I knew Roo couldn't feel the cool air, but didn't the nurse realize she was at risk for pneumonia? Dr. Danforth had said Roo's whole system was compromised. My mother had taken that and run with it, told me in a grim way that if Roo CAUGHT EVEN A COLD, it could turn into an infection, and she could develop pneumonia that she might not survive. I had become paranoid and felt like chasing the nurse down and yelling at her to keep my sister covered up, to safeguard against colds. I was furious at everyone.

Instead of berating the hospital staff, I took a deep breath. I stepped closer to my sister. I pulled the blanket over her legs, then took off the hoodie I'd worn to school; it happened to be one of Roo's, from a vacation we'd all taken to Nantucket. I tucked the sweatshirt around her, to keep her warm.

It hurt to swallow. This was the closest I'd been to Roo since her seizure—the smells, the sight of her empty eyes, had been too much. But now I buried my face in her neck and held her in my arms till my heart slowed a little.

Then I eased my arms from around her, crouching down so my face was about an inch away from hers. Stroking her cheek, I brushed a strand of hair behind her ear, being careful not to jostle her stitches. In spite of what the doctor said about Roo not feeling, I didn't want to hurt my sister.

Everyone had been telling me to talk to her, that it would be good for me, therapeutic. And my mom said maybe somewhere, deep inside, Roo could hear. I had resisted all this time; that had been my way of holding out for Roo to really wake up, to talk to us, to not be a coma girl but to be my old Roo.

"Hello," I said. My voice croaked as if I had never spoken before.

Of course Roo didn't answer.

"I'm supposed to talk to you," I said. "I feel stupid."

If only Roo would laugh, or stick her tongue out, do something to prove she was there. Talking to her now felt oddly right, and so did being this close and looking into her eyes. They were surprisingly unclouded.

"Are you in there?" I asked.

No answer.

"Blink if you can hear me," I said, and even though there wasn't a hope in the world, I realized I was holding my breath. What if Roo DID blink? But she didn't. She just kept breathing. I moved closer, so I felt her breath. It was warm and steady. It was normal, so everyday, because what could be more everyday than breathing? It nearly tore me in half.

"Roo," I said.

She didn't answer.

"I want to ask you something," I said, but my throat ached so much it was barely a whisper. "Are you here because of me? Was the accident my fault, for making you come pick me up that day? Do you hate me?"

"She doesn't hate you."

At the sound of Newton's voice, I jumped about a mile. It was one thing to talk to Roo, but it was another to have someone hear me. I looked out the window so Newton wouldn't see, and wiped my eyes with the back of my hand. He and Isabel must have driven to the hospital together. I could hear Isabel talking to my mother in the hall.

"Don't ask that again," Newton said.

"What?"

"If she thinks it's your fault."

"It was."

"Shut up, Tilly."

"If I hadn't needed a ride, she wouldn't have been on that road when it was so icy."

Newton sighed. "She'd have been out taking photos no matter what. It was an accident. That dog ran out. If it was anyone's fault, it was hers. She shouldn't have swerved like that."

Suddenly the fury I'd been holding inside, from Dr. Danforth and the nurse, exploded. I hurled myself straight at

Newton, both fists pumping, socking him right in the nose so blood sprayed out of his face. I heard my knuckles crack against his jawbone or a tooth, I didn't know which, I didn't care, and the crazy thing was I really loved Newton, I appreciated him staying in Roo's life through it all, but I was yelling at the top of my lungs, "SHUT UP, IT'S NOT HER FAULT! TAKE IT BACK, NEWTON! NOTHING IS HER FAULT, NOTHING!"

And then the arms of the nursing staff or hospital security encircled my waist from behind and hauled me out of Roo's room, kicking and screaming, and then I went limp as a dead jellyfish.

*O*h, Tilly. She came so close to knowing. She even asked the blink question, but I can't blink. If she had just looked at me longer, maybe she would have seen me fix my gaze on her.

Since they've started cutting back on my medication, I feel a lot more conscious. I saw and heard exactly how hard Tilly smacked Newton. I knew she'd pay the price for attacking him. No one can ever punish Tilly the way she does herself. She was a girl of passion and regrets. She always had been, but it had gotten worse over the last year, since our dad died.

Mom and Tilly came back into the room, followed by Isabel and Dr. Danforth. Mom and Tilly were crying so hard, they had to support each other. My arms ached to hug them, and my voice wanted to scream, *I am in here, I love you, help me!* Newton walked in, too, an ice pack pressed to his lip.

My mother kissed me good-bye and hustled Tilly home for some combination of love and punishment. Isabel wanted to stay, but Newton told her to go. Pearl and Taylor Swift, the twentysomething blond nurse who always wore red lipstick and did little dance moves while she sang to herself, rolled me onto my back and splinted my hands around foam grips, to keep my fingers from becoming rigid—this had become normal treatment, but it felt so strange to have them doing it in the midst of my family drama.

When the nurses left, Newton sat close to my bed. My skin tingled. I felt like exploding, I wanted to touch him so badly.

I felt as if I was behind a screen, watching everything close-up but unable to be seen or heard. I was a prisoner in a tiny cell. Tilly's rage was as ferocious as my own. Her scream echoed in my chest as if it had come from my own throat. I felt it in my ears, shattering my eardrums, and I could almost feel the impact of her fist hitting Newton.

It killed me that she hurt him, the boy I had loved so long, but finally I *got* Tilly in a way I never had before: the heat of her emotion, the way she reacts. I was always the calm one, but just then I wanted to punch the walls, tear down the curtains and the ceilings and all these tubes and wires connecting me to the IV and heart monitor. I wanted to run out of here faster than I'd ever run before. I wanted to act wild, like Tilly, instead of calm and logical, like me.

My mind raced instead of my body, but it continued in the same circles. I wondered if I was going crazy. What if I was? Who would know? My mind chased itself, told me to move my fingers, inch my arm across the bed, and curl my toes: But my body wouldn't obey the commands. My mind repeated itself, went through the same thought processes, the same impossible challenges, and each time my hand refused to lift, my toes failed to move, I felt more helpless and insane. My heart was going to jump out of my chest.

I tried to control my mind. To test myself, to see if I could still think. My father used to tell me I had a good mind. He meant that I used reason and logic, like a scientist or a mathematician.

So I tried to map the stars. It was the very end of February, I knew, but I chose a spring date: April 1. Because this really did feel like a bad April Fool's joke.

Although it was broad daylight, and I was stuck in a hospital, I tried to enlarge my mind, zoom out. I imagined the night sky over Hubbard's Point.

There was Gemma in the small constellation Corona Borealis, hiding behind Boötes, with Arcturus blazing bright. Ursa Major would be almost straight overhead; if I were standing in my yard, the Big Dipper would be just above our tallest oak tree, peeking out of the crown of branches as it rose in the sky. And because it was imaginary April, it was almost time for the Lyrids, with twenty fast meteors an hour at its peak, the meteor showers radiant somewhere between Lyra and Hercules.

Okay, I could still map the star chart, I could still remember the night sky. Did that mean I wasn't crazy? Did I still have a good mind or was my brain slowly turning to mush, like the rest of me?

I stared at Newton. His lip was bleeding, but he wasn't paying attention to that. He was watching me.

What did I look like to him? I hadn't seen a mirror, but I knew from the feeling of air on my scalp that they'd shaved part of my head. And from the feeling of stitches pulling my forehead and the skin behind my ear, I knew I had stitches. I knew I looked terrible, but when he gazed at me, he had the same old look in his eyes.

He just turned seventeen, yet he spent so much time here with me. He was that rare tall boy who doesn't play basketball, or any sport. He still hadn't grown into his arms and legs, and it used to kill me, the way kids nicknamed him Gawk, when they weren't calling him Fig, à la Fig Newton.

We met when we were ten, the year his family moved to Hubbard's Point from Chicago. His father was a biochemist, and he had come to work at Drysdale, the big pharmaceutical company in Easterly. His mother, as if to counteract the chemicals her husband put into the world, had an incredible organic garden.

Our dads were both scientists, and that's what made me and Newton become friends at first. My dad not only taught at Yale, he worked at the Peabody Museum and sometimes took groups of people, including me and Newton, on deep-sea trips called pelagics, on oceanographic vessels out to the Atlantic canyons beyond Montauk, to Stellwagen and Georges Banks, to see humpbacks, minke whales, and even critically endangered North Atlantic right whales.

Newton's dad worked in a lab, developing drugs, but he taught us how to use chemistry sets and let us use his Bunsen burners. We made homemade sparklers when we were twelve, gave them to our families for Fourth of July, and got in tons of trouble for working with dangerous chemicals without his dad there.

Both Newton and I grew up paying attention to nature and the way things worked. When we were eleven, a nor'easter blew wildly off the Atlantic and drove a few lobster pots onto the beach. He and I salvaged one and took it apart, figured out how it was made, where the bait went and how the lobsters were lured in, how the metal mesh doors were tied to the trap with fine twine, designed to decompose so if the buoy line was cut, the trap wouldn't stay on the bottom of the ocean, catching lobsters until the end of time.

Newton, I miss you. I wish you could hear me.

And oh my God! It was as if I had willed him to come closer to me. He scraped his chair across the floor, leaned his elbow on the bed. I could smell his soap, and my throat ached with the beautiful familiarity.

Newton picked up my right hand and looked at the spot where the splint had chafed my wrist. There was a raw patch of skin, red and oozing. I stared at him. He had long, dark-brown hair and, behind his black-rimmed glasses, green eyes the color of Four Mile River at dawn. Those eyes were fixed on my wrist. And he let go of my hand, and I wanted to cry. *Don't leave,* I wanted to say. *Don't let go.*

But he walked to the tray where there was a stack of gauze pads, and he ripped open the sterile package.

He turned on the water at the sink in the corner of the room and let it run until I saw steam. Then he soaked the pad and tested it on the back of his own hand, and when it was cool enough, he came to me. He loosened the splint's Velcro strap and removed it, and then he washed the pus off my raw wrist.

"There," he said. "Does it feel better?"

Yes! I wanted to say. *So much better. Don't let go, Newton. Just stay with me.*

And he did.

I let my mind drift to another night sky. Back in November, one school night when my mother had parent-teacher conferences and Tilly was sleeping over at Emily's, Newton and I bundled up, grabbed beach blankets and my camera, and headed out. My house sits on a low granite cliff overlooking a crescent bay, and steep steps lead down to a footbridge that crosses a saltwater creek. It was dark, but that didn't matter. Newton and I knew every inch; if we were blindfolded, our feet could find the way.

We ran down the beach, wide-open sand with the Long Island Sound lapping at our boots, the wave crests white and rippling in starlight. The tide was coming in. I stopped to photograph the waves' lacy froth, and then I snapped Newton silhouetted by blazing stars.

At the end of the beach, we climbed up a rocky hill, onto a secret path; it led into the woods, but just for a short way. At night the darkness was total—scrub oaks surrounded us, and pure instinct drove us along. Within five minutes we emerged onto Little Beach—the most beautiful and romantic place on earth.

Newton spread one of the blankets while I set up my camera to take time-lapse shots of star trails. We lay down, pushed the sand around beneath us, carving out a nest, and tugged the second blanket over us. The November air was cold, but we slid our hands up under each other's sweaters.

We kissed, his glasses bumping my cheeks. I reached up and gently took them off.

"Now I can't see you," he said.

"But I'm right here."

He kissed me again, slow and tender, and I saw stars—literally, little white sparkles inside my eyelids. My body was firing on cylinders I didn't even know I had. There was a scientific explanation, but for once I didn't stop to consider it.

Overhead, the Leonids cast a skein of glitter in the sky. Meteor showers were our thing, Newton's and mine. We had seen the Perseids on Nantucket last summer, and now we were kissing beneath November's Leonids. Sparks showered overhead, falling to earth. My father was buried a mile away. Since summer I had been held captive with thudding grief.

"Where are we going to go to college?" Newton asked, holding me.

"That's what you're thinking about?" I asked, laughing.

"Yeah," he said. "Because I want this to last forever, and college is coming up fast, and we have to apply to the same places next year."

"Well, I already know," I said.

"Yale," he said. It wasn't a question.

I nodded, my face pressed into his shoulder.

The idea of going to Yale had started out being for my dad—he had gone there and later taught there, and he'd been so proud of my test scores, all the academic stuff, and we'd planned on driving into New Haven together, if I got accepted, if I got in.

He died of a heart attack, my dad. It happened last summer, August 4, a perfect summer day. He had driven home from his office in New Haven, dropped his briefcase by the kitchen door, where he always did. He kissed my mother, my sister, and me hello. He had brought me a bunch of pamphlets, brochures, and forms from the admissions office.

"Thanks, Dad," I said.

"No problem, Yale girl."

"Not yet," I said, and laughed. "Don't jinx it."

"As if I could." He stretched, gave me another hug. "We'll go through them later, okay? I'm going to lie down for a minute before dinner."

"Okay," I said.

"See you later," he said.

Then he went upstairs for a nap and didn't wake up.

That last minute in the kitchen was his last minute with us. *See you later* were the last words he said to me.

He was only fifty. He had a heart attack in his sleep. And he'd been healthy—he ate well, he ran on the beach with my mom, we hadn't known anything was wrong. It would have been unbearable, no matter what. But losing him so suddenly was a nightmare. I still can't believe it.

Now, going to Yale meant even more to me. It meant everything. I had read through every single paper he'd brought me the day he died. I had already started filling out forms that weren't due for a year. I was all set to make appointments to see admissions advisors, and his friend in the dean's office, and I was working harder than I ever had at school to get straight As in AP classes, to complete my portfolio and win the Serena Kader Barrois Foundation Photography Contest, and to get into Yale early decision my senior year.

Getting in, attending my dad's school, knowing that he had spent the last day of his life gathering information for me to apply, became the most important thing. It was a way to stay close to him, to be inspired by him, and to follow in his footsteps. Nothing in life, even loving Newton, compared to this. If only we'd had longer than that last minute in the kitchen, maybe I could have adjusted my goals. But life doesn't let us plan that way. So for me it was Yale or nothing.

"You're number one in our class," Newton said that night on the beach. "Your test scores are off the charts, and your dad taught there. You'll get in, no problem. But I won't."

"Stop it, boy genius," I said.

But I knew what he meant. Anything to do with math or science, Newton got top grades. But he was so absorbed by those subjects, he tended to neglect English, history, and art, and his grades reflected it. His advisor had told him he could get into a great college but that the Ivies in general and Yale in particular would be long shots.

"Could we try for somewhere else?" he asked.

I felt this awful swooning, as if I were going to fall off the world, into space, and leave him behind.

"Newton, even if we go to different colleges, we'll still stay together."

"But we won't *be* together."

"We will as often as we can."

"It will be too different," he said. "I don't want to be apart from you."

"I don't want that either," I said, feeling sad and troubled, because I knew that no matter what, I was applying to Yale, and if I got in, I was going to go.

"Hold me, okay?" I asked.

"Always," he whispered, wrapping his arms around me even tighter. "No matter what, forever and ever." Then he paused, and added, "I love you."

"I love you, too," I whispered. And even though we had known each other forever, even though we had loved each other since we were twelve, it was the first time we had said those words.

And then he kissed me.

I felt split in half that night. My feelings filled the sky. I wanted life to stop, go backward, I wanted my father to still be alive. Science is about how things are, not how we wish they could be. Newton and I were meant to be together in the long run—to me, that was a scientific truth as clear as gravity. My heart ached because I knew we'd have to be apart for a while— for college. But that night, I tried to forget that messy reality and just live the laws of heaven—the beach, the ocean, a kiss, and the fact we said we loved each other.

Newton was my tall boy with the geeky glasses and sweaters whose sleeves never quite reached his wrists, my friend who loved meteors and astronomy as much as I, who shared my dream of outfitting a boat and turning it into an oceanographic research vessel and sailing every one of the world's oceans. How could I ever find anyone more perfect?

It was funny. That night my camera was pointed at the sky, but it might as well have recorded our words, our feelings. The series of time-lapse photos I hoped would anchor my portfolio for the photography contest came out really well. They showed star trails written on the sky, and for me, it was a digital record of that night, that moment when Newton and I said *I love you.*

But the photos also showed that everything passes.

Stars pass through the sky. Minutes pass through the night. Flowers bloom and die. You can try to hold fast to the people you love, but everything changes. Newton and I were changing. He told me how he felt about applying to the same colleges, and I realized I couldn't wait to be at Yale.

Now, in the hospital, he finished dabbing water on my wrist, he cleaned off the nasty leaking fluid, and he stood by my bed, holding the wet gauze in one hand and my wrist in the other. I watched him look down, his fingers encircling my wrist bone, possibly measuring how much smaller it was becoming. It was atrophy. My flesh was shrinking away, and with it went the girl I had been, the girl Newton had loved.

Then he did something that killed me. He lowered his head, pressed his lips to the inside of my wrist. I felt his breath on my skin. I felt his tears. His lip was bleeding from where Tilly had hit him. It must have hurt. I wished I could make it better.

He gently replaced the splint, doing a much more careful job than the nurse. He made sure the Velcro wasn't too tight, and that the edge of the fabric didn't chafe the sore.

Then he picked up his backpack and, without looking at me again, left my room.

Always, he had said to me that night on the beach. *No matter what, forever and ever.*

I would call to him if I could. Or maybe I wouldn't.

Maybe I would just let him go.

Maybe that would be the most loving thing I could do.

Chapter Three

Tilly

On the way home from the hospital, Mom and I went to the Big Y. I pushed the cart. My knuckles hurt from punching Newton, and my hand was so stiff I could barely grip the cart handle. As we'd left the hospital, the nursing supervisor had spoken to us sternly, telling my mother I couldn't be in Roo's room without adult supervision again. That meant my mother or a doctor. And she thought it best I not return for a few days.

My mother walked along looking numb. Her back seemed extra straight, as if having one daughter comatose and the other a juvenile delinquent had given her exceptional posture. She was ashamed of me. I felt it.

Being at the grocery store made my stomach hurt. I grabbed some of the usual stuff our family liked, but every time I reached for one of Roo's favorites, I felt like crumbling inside. Would we never have corn toasties in the house again? With organic peanut butter? Would we never again argue about whether to get McIntosh apples (my choice) or organic Gala (hers)?

"What should we have for dinner?" Mom asked, standing in the meat department.

"Uh, I don't care," I said.

The glass counter was filled with packages of red meat, and it all looked so disgusting I wanted to throw up. Maybe it did to my mother, too, because she seemed to forget about getting anything and just drifted along, down the frozen food aisle. She would have kept walking, around and around the store in a daze, without remembering we needed a meal, so I pulled two cheese enchilada dinners from the freezer.

My fingertips stung from the cold and because they had grabbed only two packages. There should be a third, for Roo. We went down the tea and coffee aisle, and my mother reached for a box of Lemon Zinger, Roo's favorite, then just stopped dead, hand in midair, as if she were a statue.

"Mom?" I asked.

"Roo can't drink tea," she said.

"Maybe not today," I said. "But she will again."

"She won't." She just stood there, her arm straight out. She seemed as immobile as Roo, except for her face. It was a mask of anguish. People walked past us, and I cringed with embarrassment. I wanted to help my mother move along, get out of the public eye of our small town, away from all these staring people.

"Mom?" I asked again.

"I'm her mother," she said. "I can feel it. If she were going to get better, I would know. She's not going to come home, she's never leaving the hospital. I've lost her, I've lost Roo. I'm afraid she's going to die."

"No, Mom. Don't say that!"

I gently took her arm, lowered it to her side. I put my arm around her, tried to lead her down the aisle, toward the front of the store. She wore a navy wool sweater and plaid skirt; her graying brown hair curled softly over her shoulders. She looked just like my mom, but she felt like a stranger. I felt panic racing through me. What was it like for her, saying these words, saying she'd lost Roo? What was it like for her to feel that way?

To feel that Roo might die?

But I felt it, too. Leaving that Lemon Zinger on the shelf was like admitting Roo would be in a coma forever. And one step worse than a coma: that she would die. I had thought it before, even during her seizure. And of course my mother had been fearing deadly colds turning into pneumonia. But this felt different, as if Mom thought it could happen at any time. I wanted to cry, but I had to stay strong for my mother.

I swore then and there that I would never lose my temper again. I would never hit anyone, I would never be banished from being alone with Roo at the hospital. I vowed it.

I would be the perfect daughter, and my sister would come home.

We wheeled our cart to the checkout. My mom paid while I bagged. Walking out the glass door, I saw an African American woman in a motorized wheelchair heading from the parking lot toward the entrance. She wore a red jacket and big dark glasses, and there was a Metropolitan Museum of Art sticker on the back of the chair.

"Hey, Tilly," Slater called out, running to catch up with the woman.

I waved. I watched him push the door open and hold it for her. He'd said he had a disabled family member. *His mother*, I thought.

Following my mom to our car, I paused to glance over my shoulder at him. I saw that Slater had done the same. We stood there looking through the grocery store's glass windows at each other while our mothers went on ahead.

I wondered what had happened, why his mother couldn't walk.

Then I opened the car door and got in and my mother and I headed home. I was already worried the phone would ring when we got there. I was so afraid it would be the hospital saying my sister had died.

This was one of those times I wished I had a talent like Roo's, a way to take pictures or write a brilliant paper, to let the world know what I was feeling.

"Poetry of expression," my dad had said, sitting at the kitchen table last July, of the photos Roo had taken of a family sail across Long Island Sound.

"Poetry of life," my mother had said, looking through the images. "She captured the day so we can keep it with us forever."

I had sat in my usual spot, looking anywhere but at Roo's laptop screen. *We get it*, I'd wanted to say. *Roo is the best at everything.* Finally, I couldn't resist, and glanced over at the photos. These were not for her portfolio, but they were just as good: all of us on the boat, taking turns at the tiller, putting up the sails, with sunlight dancing on the water and all around us the expressions on our faces, eating the picnic lunch Mom had made, our parents in an unguarded moment with our dad's freckled arm over our mom's shoulders.

When I looked up, I saw Roo watching for my reaction.

"Nice," I said, barely able to get the word out.

"Can't you say more about your sister's photos than that?" my dad asked.

"Very nice," I said.

"Tilly," my mom said. "Why don't you have Roo show you how to use her camera? We'd like to see pictures by you, too."

"I've tried," I said. "I'm just not talented. I'm going upstairs. Thanks for a fun sail, though!"

And I went up to my room. I sat on the edge of my bed, wishing I could fly out the window and find a family that wasn't so smart, so good at everything. I instinctively reached for my owl pellets and held them in my hands. There were five, and each was about two inches long, an inch wide, and to the untrained eye they might look like small bundles of sticks and leaves, or spools of horror-movie thread—there were brown feathers sticking out of one, and a tiny shrew skull poking out of another, little white femurs and backbones and bits of sinew.

I tried to remember every owl I had ever seen. I had seen great horned owls every month of the year. And a barred owl three Octobers in a row. Eastern screech owls sounded like the whinny of a horse played backward, and my dad and I had followed their calls through the swamp and woods, to the black gum trees behind the salt pond. My dream was to see a snowy owl one winter day, preferably with my dad, who had told me they look like soccer balls, plump and round, on icy beaches in years when food is scarce on the tundra and they fly down here in search of mice and voles.

I heard a knock at my door and looked up. Roo walked in, leaned on my desk and didn't say anything. We stared at each other for a long time, and my eyes felt hot with tears.

"I know," she said.

I couldn't speak; my voice was too tight, my throat too sore.

"I know how you feel," she continued.

How could she possibly, my beautiful, brilliant, talented sister? All she had to do was point a camera and bingo, everyone fell at her feet. I stared at her, so tall and thin, her eyes so blue and her dark hair so long and shiny, and I felt like an owl pellet in comparison: small, undistinguished, with mud-colored hair and eyes.

"Or maybe I don't," she said, coming to sit next to me on the bed, starting to play with my hair. It felt good, her fingers separating the strands into three, giving me braids. I leaned against her, and the bad feelings started going away.

"I'm not good at anything," I whispered.

"Oh, that is so not true," she said, finishing one braid and starting another.

"Compared to you, I'm not," I said.

"Well. Because I have poetry of expression," she said. "Poetry of life!"

We both broke up laughing but kept it quiet so our parents wouldn't hear. She began another braid. I hoped she would cover my whole head with them. I didn't want her to stop.

"But you have something better," she said.

"What?" I asked, totally not believing her.

"Poetry of owls," she said.

I laughed again, but she didn't.

"Owls, Tilly. You're good at owls. No one is better at them than you."

"But who cares?" I whispered. "Loving something doesn't mean you're good at it. I'm not going to be an owl scientist or anything."

"How do you know?"

"I'm not good at science."

"You're only thirteen," she said. I turned fourteen in September. "You're so smart, but in a different way. The reason you don't like taking photos is that you don't like to stand still. That's how your mind is, too. It moves around, flying over everything."

"Like an owl?" I asked, a little sarcastically.

"I was going to say, like a dragon," she said. "Something imaginary, not of this world. You go everywhere in your imagination. I am stuck with facts. But you're different, Tilly. Just look at your shelves."

We both did. All my toys, my collections, were jammed together: owls, dragons, unicorns, white horses. But mostly owls and dragons.

"See, if it were me," she said, "I'd keep them apart. In taxonomic order, probably, owls on one shelf, horses on another. I'd even apply Linnaean taxonomy to dragons."

Growing up with a dad who worked at the Peabody Museum and in one of the biology departments at Yale, it was hard not to have heard about Linnaeus and his scientific classification, but I honestly didn't know and didn't care about the difference between orders, families, genera, species, and whatever.

"But not you," she said. "You put owls and dragons together because they're part of a story that only you know. And someday I want you to tell me."

"Really?"

"Yeah."

And I leaned into her even harder, and knew she meant it. We sat there for a long time that day, after she had done so many braids I couldn't even count them, until the sun began to go down over the beach, shining through my window straight into our eyes. I don't remember what we talked about after that, or even if we did. Sitting together was enough. And laughing about the poetry of everything.

We understood each other like no one else. She didn't mind that I got jealous sometimes, and I mostly didn't mind that she made our parents so proud.

She made me proud, too.

But driving home from the Big Y with Mom, worrying that the call could come at any time, that Roo had taken a turn for the worse, I couldn't get it out of my mind: I wished I had some way to create something that would express the way I felt about Roo.

And what she was going through.

Roo

I woke up abruptly, wondering again, for the hundredth time, where I was. But the harsh yellow overhead light and the sight of a nurse moving around my bed, checking my heart monitor, quickly reminded me. I was in the hospital. The clock on the wall read 3:20. In the morning.

As soon as I became aware, the dread began again, my mind resumed the endless cycle. How could I get people to hear me, to realize I wasn't in a coma at all? If Tilly hadn't flown off the handle, beaten up Newton, she might have figured it out. I was so mad at her for it, but at the same time I wanted to comfort her. Tilly was scared.

I pictured our house as if I were there right now. The idea of it comforted me, took me out of this sterile, antiseptic-smelling neurology unit. I imagined myself tiptoeing up the creaky wooden stairs of our salty old beach house, into her room. Most kids wanted their own rooms, but I loved having a sister, always wanted to share with her. I had once asked my dad if we could knock down the wall between our rooms, and he had laughed and hugged me.

"Roo, look, it's snowing!" Tilly whispered one night, waking me up, when I was eleven and she was nine.

We stood at the window, watching snow blow sideways off Long Island Sound. It swirled and drifted against our house and the big granite boulders in our yard. The wind howled, and Tilly shivered, pressing close to me.

"What's it saying?" she asked. It was funny, her asking what the wind said. Our dad being a marine biologist, specializing in humpback whales but with a huge soft spot for owls, we were urged to use our imaginations, though never to give human qualities to forces of nature. So it seemed extra fun to play along with her.

"It's saying, 'Tilly and Roo, I want yooooooo,'" I said.

"Don't make it scary," she said.

"Okay, I won't. It's saying it came all the way from the Arctic, across Canada, to bring us snow to play in. To build forts and to make snow angels."

"Not snow angels."

"You love making them."

"Not anymore."

"Why not?"

"They come to life at night and fly past the window; their wings are white, and they brush against the house, trying to get inside. They're ghosts of little girls who died."

"Who told you that?"

"I dreamed it," she said. And she was trembling, so I hugged her harder.

"No, Tilly. They're not scary. They're not even real. We make them ourselves, lying in the snow, moving our arms and legs; that's all they are."

"They're not dead girls?"

"Not at all."

I never wanted Tilly to be scared. I never wanted her to lie awake on a winter's night, hearing the wind blow and imagining ghost girls flying past our house on the hill.

Lying in the hospital bed, I tried to calm my pounding heart. I tried to picture Tilly in her room, the cozy blue quilt on her bed, posters of owls on her wall, her collection of creatures on the bookshelf beside her bed, the owl pellets she and my dad had collected from under the pine trees, a postcard of a snowy owl my parents had picked up in British Columbia before we were born, tacked to the wall by her bedpost.

Tilly and her owls. Were they bringing her peace now? I knew she must miss me the way I missed her. I wished I could sit on her bed now, braid her hair and look out at the beach and let her know everything would be okay.

I tried to imagine Tilly sleeping peacefully, not worried about anything, and I tried to keep myself alive, here on this earth, in a hospital bed, so I wouldn't die, so I wouldn't become a snow angel and scare Tilly.

Chapter Four

Tilly

$\mathcal{F}$ ive days after I'd socked Newton, I took my books outside during morning study period and sat on a bench in the school garden. February had turned to March and the piles of snow had melted, with the brown grass just starting to turn green.

I had gotten a D on my history report. Mrs. Addams had said I could get extra credit by writing another paper; it was due soon, but I was getting nowhere. I just couldn't seem to care about the Revolutionary War in Connecticut when my sister's life hung by a thread.

Staring at my own handwriting, it blurred, and I tried to remember what I'd been trying to say. The first report had been about the *Turtle*, the first submarine, made of wood, built in Connecticut to bomb British ships. I had started researching it the day of Roo's accident. Good scholarship had fallen by the wayside. This one was my chance for a redo. But who cared? I closed my eyes, let the sun warm my face. A shadow fell across my eyelids, making me glance up. Slater stood there smiling cautiously.

"I wanted to apologize," he said.

"You?" I asked. "No. It was me. You're not that tough." I gave him a smile.

"Yeah, but I am, compared to this place," he said. "I shouldn't have grabbed you. I'm sorry. I just didn't want to see you take Marlene's bait."

"Rise up, don't sink down, right?"

"Yeah."

"Did you make that up, or hear it somewhere?"

"Heard it from my basketball coach in New York. What's Marlene got against you?"

"Nothing in particular," I said. "She's just mean. Roo says we should feel bad for her. That she obviously has problems."

"Your sister is wise."

"Yes," I said. "You have no idea."

"How's she doing?"

"Not good. I look at her, and she doesn't seem like my sister." I was horrified to hear my voice coming out in a croak; equally, I was surprised because I hadn't said this to anyone.

"Wait for the miracle," Slater said.

"What do you mean?" I felt my brow wrinkling.

"It might seem really bad right now, but people's conditions can change really fast and really deeply, in a minute. You've got to watch for it, and be there, ready for it, for her."

"I saw you with your mother," I said.

"Yeah," he said, giving me a soft smile. A bunch of kids walked out the gym door and started jogging toward the track. I waited for them all to pass.

"Why is she in a wheelchair?" I asked after they were gone, followed by Mr. Trombly, the gym teacher.

"Multiple sclerosis," he said.

"I'm sorry," I said.

"Thanks. She's had it a long time. It goes through different phases. Right now it's affecting her eyesight." He sounded calm, but his face looked sad.

"That must be awful," I said.

"It is. She says she's gotten used to not being able to walk by herself, but she can't stand the thought of going blind. The world is so beautiful. She wants to be able to see it."

"I hope . . ." I began. But how to finish that sentence? Even with Roo I didn't know what to hope for. Should I say I hope his mother gets better, I hope her condition doesn't get worse, I hope she has a complete recovery?

"I know," he said, flashing a smile that I couldn't help noticing was really cute. "I hope the same for your sister."

"Thanks," I said. Then I spotted Newton walking toward us. My stomach flipped—I had avoided him since I'd belted him. He and Slater nodded at each other, and Slater walked away.

"Mind if I join you?" Newton didn't wait for a reply; he just put his backpack on the bench and sat down.

"I'm surprised you want to."

"Would you prefer I hold a grudge?" he asked.

"I would if I were you," I said. I peered at his mouth. It was five days since I'd punched him, and I felt relieved to see that his lower lip was no longer swollen, and the bruise was turning yellow.

"It's given me a little credibility, to tell you the truth," he said.

"Newton, you're such a nerd. It's called cred, and this isn't the kind you want, trust me," I said. "What, are you telling people you got in a street fight?"

"I let them use their imaginations."

"Huh," I said. I knew he was just trying to make me feel better, but the strange thing was, it was working. He'd actually made a semi-joke.

"You going to the hospital today?" he asked.

I shrugged. "Maybe."

"What do you mean?"

"I mean no. I'm on hospital probation for hitting you. I really am sorry."

"Don't worry about it, I already told you. You were upset."

"Uh, yeah. A little. But I shouldn't have taken it out on you. I have all this sideways anger, apparently. I'm mad at the universe, so I go after whoever's handy." I glanced around, looking for Slater, but he'd walked around the corner of the school, out of sight.

"Does she seem better to you?" Newton asked.

Better. An interesting word. What did better mean, when it came to Roo? Did it mean that she had lost only two pounds this week instead of five? Did it mean that the new foam hand splints had stopped her fingers from crabbing, permanently clawing at the air, quite so badly?

"Yes, much," I said.

"Now you're being sarcastic."

"No, I swear."

Newton smiled, a wicked look in his eyes. He was so lanky, his narrow shoulders hunched over as he sat, his long wrists sticking out of the cuffs of his shirt. For a second it was like the old days, when the three of us would hang out. Except now there was no Roo. I used to feel like a third wheel sometimes, but I'd give anything to have her here and feel that way again.

He wiped his lip, breaking the scab from where I'd hit him, and a drop of blood fell onto my extra-credit history report. I smudged it into a diagram of the *Turtle* with my thumb.

"Oh, Newton," I said. "You're Scarface because of me."

He wiped his lip. "It'll heal."

"If it makes you feel better, I had bruised knuckles the next day," I said, flexing my hands.

"It doesn't, Tilly. But maybe you should talk to people instead of being aggressive. Your friends might actually help. What were you and Slater talking about?"

"Nothing," I said, not sure why I didn't want to say how close I'd felt, for just a second, to Slater.

"*Hola*," Isabel said, walking over. She sat down, put her arm around Newton, closing her eyes so her long, dark lashes rested on her cheeks. He leaned his head on her shoulder for two seconds, and I wanted to pull her away. She might have been Roo's best friend, but she shouldn't be taking liberties with him. She should keep her arm off his shoulder.

"Do you have class next period?" she asked.

"English," Newton said. "In fact, I'd better go now. I'm supposed to be memorizing some poem. Not my strong suit."

"Hard to concentrate on poetry, *cariño*," Isabel said, giving him a sorrowful look.

"Hard to concentrate on anything," he said.

"What about you?" she asked me.

"I'm working on my report."

"Take a walk with me," she said. "You can get back to it, okay?"

"More than okay," I said, relieved to take a break.

Officially we weren't supposed to leave school during the day, but no one really got in trouble for driving off campus during lunch. A lot of kids went to Paradise Ice Cream or Black Hall Pizza and ate there or brought food back. But it wasn't lunch period yet, and Isabel didn't have a car, so I had no idea what she had in mind.

We walked single file through a worn deer path in the marsh, toward Shore Road. I gazed at the back of her head. Both she and Roo had dark-brown hair, but Isabel's was shoulder length, wiry and tightly curled, and Roo's was long and silky-straight. Isabel wore hers pulled back with a turquoise papier-mâché barrette, and I stared at the yellow butterflies and pink flowers painted on the shiny surface and wished so hard I was walking behind my sister instead of Isabel.

When we broke through the reeds onto Shore Road, I could barely move. This was the exact spot where Roo had flipped her car. Isabel walked along the road, to the edge of the gully. As often as I'd driven past, with my mother or on the bus, I'd never actually stopped here since the accident.

"This is where it happened," Isabel said.

"Let's go," I said. "I don't want to be here."

But she ignored me and started to climb down the steeply sloping bank into the marsh. I stepped off the pavement and went closer to the brink to see what she was doing.

Morning sun sparkled on the tidal creek, four feet down from where I was standing. The light split into a million pieces, riding on the shallow water. Willows curved over the banks, new spring leaves just starting to emerge, throwing shadows. A great blue heron stalked away from us, then spread its enormous wings and rose like a pterodactyl, legs trailing out behind, then landed twenty yards away.

The tide was low, and the creek smelled of sea creatures and rotting vegetation. With much of the bank exposed, Isabel crouched down and began to examine what was there. She collected a handful of broken glass, a twisted metal shard, and a piece of clear red plastic.

"From her taillight," she said.

"It's still here?" I asked, shocked and feeling sick to see bits of Roo's car left over from the crash.

"It's been buried," she said, "but last night was the new moon."

"The ebbiest ebb tide," I said.

"*¿Qué es eso?*" Isabel asked.

"The apogee, the lowest tide of the year," I said. "Roo always called it that."

"Yes. You're right. I've come here a lot, since the accident, to talk to her. It's weird, but I feel as if she can hear me when I'm here. Yesterday, when the tide was so low, I walked a little farther into the marsh."

"Okay," I said, my pulse thumping. Why was she acting this way? She was talking strange. The marsh grass was brown with mud, or could that be some of my sister's blood? It made me feel dizzy, and I wanted to leave.

"I don't feel good," I said. "Let's go."

"I have to show you something," she said, staring up the small hill at me.

"You can show me on the way back."

"No, it had to be here, where she nearly died," Isabel said. I knew she was religious and superstitious, and I really didn't want to get a whole bunch of that right now.

"I'm not going to pray by the river," I said. "Or anything like that."

"No problem. Just get down here, Tilly."

My shoulders tightened up. It really upset me, Isabel acting this way, high and mighty, closer to Roo than I was. That happened sometimes, Isabel acting as if their friendship was as important as Roo and me being sisters. One thing about me: Push me too hard one way, and I'll go the other. This was making me feel stubborn.

"I can see everything from up here," I said.

"Not this," she said, pulling a shiny object out of her jacket pocket. It glinted in the sunlight, and I recognized the red polka-dot plastic case and Roo's cell phone in it.

I scrambled down the bank, tumbling four feet straight into the marsh, barely thinking. I sloshed toward Isabel; my sneakers squished, sinking into the mud, silvery with bits of clamshells, mussel shells, and broken glass. I reached out to grab the phone, but she held it away from my grasp.

"You shouldn't have done it, Tilly," Isabel said, her eyes hard and glittering with angry tears.

"What are you talking about?"

"It was dead when I found it," she said.

"Let me see," I said, my heart pounding, as if deep down I knew something horrible was about to happen.

"I took it home, plugged it in, charged it," Isabel went on, pushing against my shoulder and holding the phone just out of my reach.

"What's on there?" I asked.

"I have to admit, I was *muy inquieto*," she said. "*Preocupado*."

"Isabel," I said, needing her to get to the point. She often lapsed into Spanish when she was excited or upset.

"Okay," she said. "I was very worried. Terrified, if you want to know the truth, because I'd been feeling so guilty, texting her the day of the accident. She'd sent me a photo of the bait shop right around the time the police say she crashed. So I looked at the texts, and did the math."

"You caused her accident?" I asked, practically screeching.

"No, Tilly. You did."

Now she gave me the phone, and I saw all the texts I had sent Roo that day, and the very last one she'd written in response: *5 mins away*. And I remembered getting the text. It was on my phone, too—I had looked at it a few times, to remind me of Roo—until it got too painful, realizing she might never text me again. But I had assumed Roo had sent it while the car was stopped. She was too smart to text and drive; she had pulled over, texted me while taking pictures.

"No, you're wrong," I said, looking into Isabel's brown eyes. "Why are you doing this?"

"She loves you, and so do I," Isabel said, her voice breaking. "But this horrible thing happened. I couldn't keep it to myself, you see? I had to tell you. You needed to know. She went off the road right here, texting to you."

"You don't know that," I said, staring at the text. "It could have been from earlier, when she was stopped!"

"Tilly," Isabel said, her eyes starting to flash. "Look at the time. It's stamped 4:05 p.m. Her last photo was taken at 3:59."

"Six minutes before?" I whispered.

Isabel nodded. "That's how long it took her to drive from the bait shop, where she took her last picture, to this spot."

"NO," I said.

But Isabel was right.

I scrambled blindly up the hill, wanting to get away from her, from the phone, from the truth that was staring straight at me. I was on my hands and knees, on the side of the road, wishing I could die, wishing Roo could live, wishing Isabel had never shown me the phone.

The horrible thing was, I'd known I was somehow responsible. I had felt guilty and thought it was just because I'd made Roo come to pick me up.

I had tried telling myself I wanted her to get a shot of the sun going down behind the pine trees by our dad's grave, but that wasn't true. Deep down I had wanted to see the owls fly out for the night. That had been selfish, but *this* was a million times worse. I might as well have grabbed the wheel and yanked the car off the road.

"What do you think we should do?" Isabel asked, climbing up the bank, sitting beside me on the road.

"About what?" I asked.

"The texts," Isabel said.

I felt even more jarred, as if she had shaken me. "What are we supposed to do about them?" I asked.

"We have to tell someone," she said.

"WHY?" I asked, shocked.

"Because it's the right thing," Isabel said stubbornly. I knew she was obsessed with being good and doing right, but in this case, how could telling help?

"It's not going to do any good, or make Roo better," I said, fighting back tears. "It'll just upset people."

"That's the easy way out," Isabel said, her brown eyes flashing.

"But . . ." I began, but she interrupted me

"*Tu madre, claro. Y yo no quiero ser . . .*" She started in Spanish, but switched quickly to English. "Your mother at least. And I really don't want to be the one to tell her. You have to come clean. Tilly, this is for your own sake as much as anything. It's too big a burden to carry, for both of us. I almost wish I hadn't found her phone."

"Why did you even go looking for it?" I asked bleakly.

"I'll give you some time, but if you don't tell your mother, I will," she said, not answering me. "End of the week, okay?"

I couldn't respond. Inside, I was shaking so hard I felt I might come apart at the seams. I wrapped my arms around myself, trying to hold my skin and bones together. It was impossible to think about what Isabel had just said, that I had to tell

my mother. I was still trying to face the fact th
driven Roo off this road.

The skid marks were fading, but were still visible.

"You can see where she hit the brakes," a voice said. "She tried so hard to avoid us."

I looked up, over my shoulder. A tall, stooped woman in a long blue dress and straw hat had walked along the road, and as soon as I saw the black Lab with his leg in a blue cast, I knew: This was the dog Roo had hit.

"You saw it happen?" Isabel asked.

"Yes," the woman said. "This is the same route we walked that day. We come here every day. Do you know Ruth Ann?"

"She's my friend, and Tilly's sister," Isabel said.

I barely heard the voices. I stared at the dog, put my hand out, let him come close and investigate. He was a beautiful, stock Labrador retriever with a gray muzzle, a red collar. He had a cast and walked with a hitch in his gait. He licked the back of my hand.

Petting him, I buried my face in his ruff. I felt destroyed. My text had nearly killed my sister, and this dog, too. Then, glancing up and shading my eyes against the sun, I looked at the woman. She was old, the age of a grandmother, with long white hair and, behind gold wire-rimmed glasses, lines around her eyes. She had a gentle smile.

"How is he?" I made myself ask.

"Lucan is doing well," she said. "I'm Martha Muirhead. I was the first one to see your sister after the crash. How is she now?"

"I don't think she's going to get better," I said.

Miss Muirhead didn't speak; she just tilted her head and stared at me.

"What happened that day?" Isabel asked.

Miss Muirhead seemed not to hear her. She gazed straight at me, as if I were the only one there. I was still sitting on the road, and after a few moments, she bent down next to me, to meet my eyes. She reached out a quavering hand, and so did I. Our index fingers met.

"I talked to her," she said. "Until the police came. She was in and out of consciousness. She was badly injured, but she wanted to know how Lucan was. Whether she had hurt him. Her eyes were very bright, almost glittering. Such blue eyes. Even though yours are hazel, I can see the resemblance between you. You look so alike."

"No one says that," I said.

"Oh, but they're wrong. You're just like her, so caring. You asked for Lucan, first thing. And he's fine. He broke his leg, but it's healed cleanly. Will you tell your sister that?"

"She can't hear us. She's in a coma, and she won't understand," I said, my voice ragged. "And it wouldn't be rational to try."

"Oh, I think it would be. Very rational," Miss Muirhead said. "And I very much think she will understand."

"She's in bad shape—" I stopped myself. For one thing, my voice wouldn't work. For another, I didn't feel like discussing Roo's vegetative state with a stranger, especially after what I'd just learned from Isabel.

"That may be true," Miss Muirhead said calmly, her gaze so

warm and direct it made my heart thump. "But I believe she will understand very well. Please tell her, okay?"

I couldn't answer. I turned away, let out a ragged sob. I heard Isabel assuring Miss Muirhead that she would pass on the message. She explained about Roo's condition, how the doctors said she had no awareness, but that Isabel believed in God and knew that He was taking care of Roo, and that her spirit was exactly the same as before. Through it all, I could think only of Roo's cell phone and how I'd ruined her life.

"I want Tilly to be the one to tell her about Lucan," Miss Muirhead said. "It will mean more coming from her."

Now I did turn around. The old lady was staring at me with such intensity, I felt weird. It was as if she could see right through me, read my mind. Did she know? Marlene had said she knew spells—had she magically realized we'd been texting?

The morning had been relatively warm for March, and still, but just then the breeze began to blow. It swept in from the south, and although we were a few miles inland, it brought scents of Long Island Sound: salt, seaweed, a storm far at sea. I shivered. Miss Muirhead straightened up, tapped her thigh so Lucan limped to her side. The two of them stood there for a few seconds, then walked away.

Isabel was saying how we needed to get back to school; morning study period had ended and we were missing class; we'd get in trouble if we didn't hurry, but I barely heard her. I watched Miss Muirhead and Lucan go. I swear it had nothing to do with what Marlene and her friends had said, but I had the feeling I had just met a witch.

*T*he days went on and on, and no one knew I was there.

Mom, Newton, and Isabel visited nearly every afternoon, but Tilly hadn't been here in days. Pearl was off today, and so was Taylor Swift. The indifferent nurse was on. She touched me as if I were an inanimate object; she never said hello or how are you, the way the others did, even when they obviously thought I couldn't hear them.

Indifferent was giving me a sponge bath. I could smell myself, and it wasn't good: pee and sweat. Pearl always used a special soap she brought from home; it was light and sweet, and made me think of the honeysuckle growing at Hubbard's Point. She left it on the sink, and Taylor Swift now used it to wash me, too. But Indifferent didn't bother. She used liquid soap straight from the dispenser, and it was harsh and institutional-smelling. She wasn't rough, but she wasn't kind.

It hurt my feelings to have her act this way, as if I didn't matter, as if I weren't there. To her, I was just a lump; she was doing her job, nothing more. My eyes filled with tears and spilled over. They ran down my face, but the nurse didn't even wipe them. She just assumed they were simply more leakage from my useless body. To get away from her, I went inside my mind.

I thought of Tilly. The day she punched Newton she was wearing jeans and my Nantucket hoodie. Pretty daring of her to wear it straight up in public without my permission—we've always been a little possessive of our clothes—and I know she was wearing it for a reason. Wrapped in my hoodie, she was keeping me close. I got that completely. She left it behind, wrapped around me, to keep me warm.

She and I could speak in silence with a look, a birdcall, a hoodie. When it did involve words, they could be oblique. Like that time in the fall when I was driving her and Mom to school. I was so full of grief from losing Dad, I missed him so much, I had faked a sore throat so I could stay home and read the Yale papers he'd brought home the day he died. *See you later*, he'd said, but we hadn't.

Mom had made a doctor's appointment for me, and I was supposed to go straight to Dr. Whitcomb's office after I dropped off her and Roo.

I was driving Dad's car, the old Volvo, with his sunglasses over the visor and his faded Red Sox cap stuck in the door pocket, and I pulled into the parking lot our two schools shared. Tilly had just joined me at the high school, and Mom taught at the middle school next door. The teachers were heading in, students were milling around waiting for the 8:10 bell, and Tilly called from the backseat, "See you later."

It was the way she looked at me, the spark of our eyes meeting in the rearview mirror. Even the words: *See you later.* He'd said them to me, but Tilly had heard, too, and she was giving me a message. The back of my neck tingled, and I knew. After I dropped Mom off, I sped around the block, and when I returned to the school lot, the bell had just rung, kids were streaming in through the open doors, and Tilly ran the opposite way, straight to the car.

"What took you so long?" she asked.

"I hit traffic coming over the Matterhorn," I said, something completely nonsensical because in those first months after losing our dad, the world had seemed surreal. Why shouldn't my route back to school and Tilly have included a detour to Europe and over the Alps? It made as much sense as our father dying.

"Next time I advise you take a hot-air balloon," she said, catching on right away.

"Let's go test-drive one now," I said.

And because Tilly and I instinctively share everything and I'd taught her how to drive as soon as I got my license, I shoved over and she sidled under, and my fourteen-year-old sister took the wheel and we went straight across the bridge to the nearest Dunkin' Donuts drive-through. She couldn't get her permit for another year; I just considered that I was giving her a head start.

We picked up a half-dozen crullers and chocolate-frosted donuts along with two black coffees—we had both developed a taste for black coffee, and it was handy because supposedly it was healthier than drinking it with milk and sugar. You're saying, *But what about the baked goods?* and I know, but our dad had barely been dead three months, and we were a little on the despairing side, and donuts helped.

Tilly drove us carefully through town, past the old white church so many famous artists had come to paint. Our town is the prettiest stretch of land on Long Island Sound.

Rich people come in summer, but our family was working- and middle-class. Our grandfathers had been a firefighter and a telephone lineman, and they'd just had the brilliant sense to buy shoreline property before it got expensive. They sent their kids, my parents, to good colleges. Education meant a lot to them; they saw it as our family's way to a better life.

We have silver sands and golden salt marshes, deep blue bays, and that secret path to the hidden beach where Newton and I escaped to kiss and watch the stars, where we said we loved each other. Our parents met at Hubbard's Point, too, and we grew up barefoot and in the water whenever possible. Our father taught us binomial nomenclature—the Latin names of every bird, tree, fish, and mammal at Hubbard's Point. Now he is buried there. That day, Tilly and I went to visit him in the cemetery.

Dad's grave was on the hill, shaded by oak and pine trees, near the tree where great horned owls roost. In the five miles between the drive-through and the train trestle that marked the entrance to Hubbard's Point, we had already inhaled the donuts and crullers, but we still had our coffees. We carried them up the small hill, sat down next to him.

The headstone was made of Connecticut granite, smooth and plain. It was engraved with his name, Thomas McCabe,

and the dates he was born and died. Underneath was the phrase
WAIT FOR THE EARLY OWL.

Tilly and I had the idea for the T. S. Eliot inscription. In fact, our mother let us pick out the stone and choose the lines. She wasn't up to handling much; the shock of having him die so suddenly had shut her down. Our parents loved each other the way other kids wished their parents would. We were the best family.

"Hey, early owl," Tilly said, glancing at the stone. Then she began to quote from the poem, "East Coker" in Eliot's *Four Quartets*. "*Wait for the early owl . . .*"

And I continued, "*In that open field if you do not come too close, if you do not come too close, on a summer midnight, you can hear the music.*"

Owling had been Dad and Tilly's special thing. The truth is, I'd rather have used a phrase from Rainer Maria Rilke's "Falling Stars," but I had let Tilly choose the lines about an owl because I sometimes worried about her, felt sorry for her. But just then I felt jealous.

"We brought coffee," Tilly said, spilling a few drops.

"He can't feel that."

"No kidding. We're a science family; we don't believe in the afterlife. But still," she said. "I want to do it anyway."

"Okay," I said, softening my tone. "But do you think you're being a little irrational?"

"Who cares?" she asked, slashing tears from her eyes. We both cried, but we didn't reach for each other. It was one of those rare moments when we were trapped in our own private grief.

She told Dad the owl fledglings, hatched in June, were probably getting ready to fly from the cavity in the hollow tree. And she said she wished he were there to see them with her.

"We're skipping school," I said when she stopped.

"Do you have to say that?" she asked.

"Well, he can either see everything and already knows," I said, "or he's just plain old dead in the ground and doesn't care. Like you said, we're a scientific family."

"So why say it? Either way?"

"I don't know."

"Isabel's the superstitious one," she said. "You're acting like you believe in ghosts and spirits or something."

I hid a smile. I wasn't the only one feeling jealous; it bothered Tilly that I had such a close friend, that I shared some things with Isabel that I didn't with her.

"Tell him the Red Sox are in the play-offs," she said. "Tell him all the ospreys have left on their migration. Tell him we miss him too much to go out for Halloween."

"You tell him," I said. "If you honestly think he can hear you."

"Dad, one more game and the Red Sox will clinch and be in the World Series again," she said.

"If they make it," I said.

"Don't be so mean," she said.

"I'm just being a realist, like him."

"Yeah, but you had to say that, Roo," Tilly said. "About us skipping school."

I couldn't argue with her there, and it was a sign of how unhinged we were by his death, by missing him, that we were talking to his gravestone. That we had skipped school at all, that I was letting a whole day go by without working for the grades I would need to get into Yale.

The sun was bright and lowering in that October way, the air cool and smelling of fallen leaves, the sky golden blue. Picture autumn light so beautiful it can make you cry for no reason. You're not even thinking that soon the branches will be bare, and the ground frozen, and the weather more often gray than not. It's just that the sky is so blue, so saturated with sunlight, and you want it to stay that way forever.

Tilly spilled more coffee. Our father had loved a good mug of joe. I could see him at his desk, writing about whales and deep dives or reading T. S. Eliot—head bowed, chin in one hand, a steaming cup of coffee by his elbow; sometimes, when he was reading student papers during baseball season, he'd have the radio on low, listening to the Red Sox game.

"I should get back to school," Tilly said, standing up. "I have algebra next period and I'm already getting a C. I really am a loser."

"You are not, Tilly."

"You're just being nice," she said. "You're smarter, that's just how it is. You did so much better as a freshman than I'm doing, and I don't even care."

"Yes, you do."

She shrugged. "One thing for sure. I'll never talk to a grave again. Or anyone who can't hear me. I'll be *rational*. I promise, Roo, just for you."

I smiled at her, but she wouldn't smile back.

"Come on. Let's go," she said.

But neither of us moved. We stood staring at the headstone. It was beautiful in a cold, hard way. He taught us a lot of things, and one of them was to read poems and memorize them; he had taught us his favorites, said they were part of him.

Eventually we got back into the car, only this time I drove. I knew the teachers of Black Hall were tight and loyal to Mom, and they were used to cutting Tilly slack.

I thought they felt sorry for her. There was no point in having false modesty, especially now—*just look at me*—but the truth was, Tilly had to deal with me, the fact that I scored high on tests and she didn't, that I loved to study and my grades reflected it. Tilly told me Principal Gordon had actually said to her face, the day she started freshman year, "It's a hard act, trying to keep up with a sister like Roo. Those are big educational boots to fill." Educational boots. Yes, he said that.

Tilly got Bs and Cs. She was used to hearing the phrase, from both teachers and my parents, *"You're not working up to potential."* Sometimes I think she was actually distinguishing herself, setting herself apart from me, by not trying.

"You're a brain," she said one time. "And so is Newton. You're perfect together."

And for so long we were.

I still loved him, even though so much had changed. Before the accident I'd been thinking of taking a break, putting space between us. But that was in the past. Right now I just needed to survive.

The harder I tried to remember the accident itself, the more I pushed it away. The dog, I pictured running into the street. Did I crash trying to avoid the dog?

No. I was distracted even before I saw him. My mind wasn't on driving. Was it on Newton? No. It was on Tilly. I was late to get her, but more than that: I had taken my eyes off the road. I wasn't concentrating. Oh, God, I was texting. That's what I was doing.

I did this, I brought this on myself!

The awareness pricked my brain, jabbing me like a pin. Everything was shockingly clear, the memory of what I was doing just before I drove off the road, my eyes on my phone, my thumb on the keys.

Stephen Hawking was one of my favorite writers, weaving webs of possibility, quantum physics and cosmology, with his words. I used to think maybe we were all living on a parallel path to the alternative, the scary things that lurk. But that for today we were fine.

Now I was on that other path. And today I was not fine.

I won't get better, I'll never leave this bed, and it's my fault. I am scared and screaming, but no one can hear.

Tilly won't even try, because she thinks I'm just a comatose body. She's keeping her promise.

Do you know how it feels, knowing I did this to myself? It's the worst feeling in the world.

Chapter Five

Tilly

*T*he bus drove along Shore Road, and when we got to the spot where Roo crashed, every single person on the bus turned to look, as they did every day. And there just above the creek bank, as if waiting for the bus to go by, was Miss Muirhead. She watched us pass, and my face burned. I could almost feel her watching me.

"Why does she keep going back there?" I asked, more to myself than to TEN. "You'd think it would be a bad memory, after what happened to Lucan."

"Maybe she likes the scenery along the marsh. It's so pretty," Em said.

"This whole town is pretty. She's going there for a reason," I said. "She seemed weird to me."

"You met her?" Nona asked.

"Yeah." I hadn't told them about my visit to the creek with Isabel, for obvious reasons. The truth about the phone needed to stay a secret. It was eating me up. I could barely sleep, going over and over the memory in my mind, the texts I had sent, so impatient and awful.

I wanted to convince myself I'd thought Roo had stopped the car. But deep down I knew she'd been behind the wheel. Even if she had pulled over to take photos, she would have to start driving eventually, and some of my texts would have landed while she was speeding along Shore Road.

It's all my fault.

"Martha Muirhead's eccentric, that's for sure," Nona said now. "My mom used to talk about her when she worked there. Martha and her sister lived together almost their whole lives. I guess they never got married or had kids or anything. It just about killed Martha when Althea got sick."

"Feeling bad about her sister getting sick makes her eccentric?" Em asked. She glanced at me, and I nodded. It was so Em; I knew she was thinking of me and Roo.

"More than that," Nona said. "She has a big herb garden, and the whole time her sister had cancer, she was cooking up potions. She'd make these silk pouches and fill them with dried goldenrod and thyme and stuff, for her sister to wear around her neck."

"They didn't help, though," I said. It was a statement, not a question. Daughter of a scientist and all.

"Not really. Althea got better for a while, and even my mother started to wonder. But then she went downhill really fast."

"That's sad," Em said, and I agreed but didn't say anything. Miss Muirhead obviously knew how it felt to see a sister suffer. But I still felt strange about the way she'd been so vehement that I be the one to tell Roo that Lucan was better. I hadn't. Not yet. I hadn't been back to see Roo. I was afraid to look at her now, knowing what I'd done, that I'd put her there.

Last night, I'd lain awake. I had surrounded myself with stuffed animals, both mine and Roo's. One of my arms was around an old teddy bear of hers, and my other embraced my stuffed snowy owl and purple dragon. Most of the fuzz had been worn off all three animals.

Roo's bear smelled like her. I buried my nose in him, thinking of how often she had held him. My owl and dragon felt so familiar, snuggling into my side. I loved fierce creatures and had always hoped they would make me brave. Because dragons fought battles, and owls were the most efficient hunters in the forest. I clutched my owl and remembered holding my dad's hand. He had taught me to walk silently through the woods on owling nights.

I'd always tried to be brave, but things scared me: the dark, a snapping twig, the mystery of what was hiding just around the next rock. Trees loomed over us, gigantic monsters. My father would whisper to me that he had my hand, nothing would happen. One night when I was ten, we crouched by the big curved boulder, as quiet as could be. He pointed toward the tall pine, and as my eyes got accustomed to the dark, I looked for the shape that shouldn't have been there.

That's how I'd learned to spot owls—my father had told me to look up, scan trees for anything out of place. You don't expect to see a huge pumpkin-shaped blob in an oak, or a tall black oval in a pine, but if you do, pay close attention, because it might be an owl.

Sure enough, as the dark deepened, the rods and cones in my eyes allowed me to see the owl. It was waking up after its long sleep throughout the day, and it moved and stretched first one wing, then the other, just like a person stretching before jumping out of bed. Starlight caught its yellow eyes; they seemed to be looking straight through me, and I shrank into my father's side.

The owl flew out. Without a sound, it glided straight over our heads. I held my breath, watching it go. In the darkness, its feathers looked ruddy red, and its wingspan was wider than mine. We watched it fly into a cluster of oak trees, and we ran after it, my father never letting go of my hand.

That was the bravest I had been.

Sitting on the bus, I closed my eyes tight and knew I would have to, somehow, be a thousand times braver now. I pictured Isabel holding Roo's cell phone and how she had said we had to tell my mother.

Emotional blackmail from my sister's best friend. Isabel had thrown so much guilt and worry at me, I still felt sick. But that wasn't the worst of it. Getting in trouble for what I'd done was so much easier to face than the fact of Roo in a coma.

Slater's words filled my mind: *Rise up, don't sink down.* These days I felt anything but brave, and most of the time I wished I could sink down into the mud, where Isabel found the phone. But just then, on the bus, I knew what I had to do: go see Roo and tell her everything. Not my mother but Roo, even if she couldn't hear me, whether I was being rational or not.

"What's the matter?" Em asked. "You look pale."

"I'm fine," I said. My phone was burning a hole in my pocket. It was crazy, but I wanted to text my sister, tell her I was coming. Instead, I started to text Newton: *Can you give me a ride to the hospital?* I hesitated before sending.

I didn't want him there when I talked to Roo. But how else would I get to the hospital? My mother had spent the morning there, and I knew she had plans to meet with an insurance person about the bills later this afternoon.

So I hit SEND.

"Who are you texting?" Nona asked.

Newton wrote back immediately: *Sure I'm tutoring but will be done in an hour pick you up then.*

Thanks, I write.

"She's got a secret boyfriend. Who is it, Slater?" Nona asked.

"What?" I asked, glancing over just as Em leaned forward to read my screen.

"You're texting Newton?" she asked.

"He's taking me to the hospital," I said quickly.

"Sorry, didn't mean to pry," Em said, giving me a quick hug. "Let's go to Foley's. We can wait for him there."

I texted him back: *I'll be @ Foley's.*

K.

"TEN, TEN, together again, like old times," Em said.

Foley's was a big barn, the general store for Hubbard's Point, with a café in back. Almost every beach kid worked there at some time or other, bagging, stocking shelves, serving grilled cheese and tomato soup and iced tea and the best lemonade on the Connecticut shoreline. TEN loved to sit at the small round tables where generations of lovers had carved their initials. It was our tradition.

I had found my parents' initials on one table: TM + ML. Tom McCabe + Maggie Laughton. Nona's parents' were on another. Emily's parents hadn't grown up together, and it was odd and a little embarrassing that her mother's initials were linked with another boy's, not Em's father's. Newton had carved his and Roo's. I had felt a little jealous of that.

We ordered lemonade, and as we waited for it, I touched the scarred wood and wondered if my initials would ever be there, immortalized with some boy's.

"It's been a while since we all came to Foley's," Nona said.

I nodded. I felt my friends gazing at me, half-nervous and half-hopeful. It was hard, because I couldn't really talk about Roo. I wanted to tell them, *You really haven't lived until you've watched someone clean your sister's feeding tube. Oh, and by the way, she's like this because I texted her while she was driving.* How could I say any of that?

"So where's Newton looking at for college?" Em asked after a while.

I nearly laughed, it was such a normal question.

"You don't know where?" Em asked.

"Nope."

"'Cause you're texting him and stuff."

"Well, we have other things on our minds," I said, checking my watch.

"Trinity," Nona said.

"What?" I asked.

"That's where he wants to go."

"How do you know?" I asked.

"He told me."

"But why were you talking to him?"

Nona laughed, sounding anxious. She glanced at Emily as if for support, which struck me as hugely weird. Even in this short amount of time, they had definitely gotten closer since I'd been so preoccupied with Roo. My heart had always felt closer to Emily; her kindness drew me in. But I had an abrasive, Velcro-like need to be close to Nona, edginess and all.

"Why were you and Newton talking?" I pressed, and I knew I was being crazy. Emily and Nona had known Newton forever; he was like a big brother to all of us. But my emotions were nothing close to logical right now.

"Why wouldn't I?" Nona asked.

"Because he's Roo's boyfriend."

Nona took a very deep breath, gazed at me as if summoning infinite patience from deep inside. "He and I are friends, Mathilda," she said. "Like since forever? Did you somehow forget that?"

"No," I said. So why did it bother me so much? My heart was skittering inside my chest.

"You two are making way more of this than you should," Emily said. "People are allowed to have friends, right? He needs all of us right now."

"He needs Roo," I said in a low voice.

"What's your problem?" Nona asked. "I know you're upset, but I'm on your side, okay? Newton's going through hell, too. Everyone loved Roo."

"*Loved?*"

"Loved, loves. Loved her the way she was, I mean."

I jumped up. "She's still alive, Nona."

"I know, but everything is changing. I see what it's doing to you and yes—to Newton, too. You punched him, Tilly. You know how crazy that is?"

"How do you even know that?" I asked, shocked. I hadn't told anyone.

"Um, he shows up at school with a swollen lip?"

"He *told* you?"

"No," Nona said. "Actually, Isabel told me."

"You were just holding it inside to spring on me today?" I asked, thinking of what a traitor Isabel was.

"In case you haven't noticed, everyone is walking on eggshells around you," Nona said. "No one wants to upset you."

"It's true," Emily said gently. "You've been through so much."

Their words sliced through me. I'd gone through nothing compared to Roo, and whatever bad things I was feeling, I'd brought them on myself.

"It's good to get this out in the open," Nona said. "Em's right—we're all tiptoeing around you and it's not good for anyone. Maybe that's why Newton is mad at you."

"He's not mad at me!"

"Whether he's 'mad' or not, you hit him in the face, and he's been like family to you," Nona said. "I have, too—I know

I'm just your 'quasi best friend,' which sucks, if you want to know. You and Roo have always been like this," she said, crossing her fingers and holding them up. "Okay, I get that Roo's your big sister and your true best friend. But I'm your friend, and practically your sister, too. And you're not letting me be."

"I HAVE ONE SISTER," I yelled, and everyone in Folcy's turned to look at me.

"No one's saying otherwise," Em said, trying to reassure me.

But she didn't know about the cell phone and texts; she didn't know what it was like to see Roo suffering so horribly. I wanted to tell them everything, and I also wanted to lock it inside forever. I couldn't say a word, so I just grabbed my things and rushed out.

"Tilly!" Em called, but neither she nor Nona followed me.

I could barely see through my tears. Everything was crashing in on me. The texts, Isabel, Miss Muirhead, Nona possibly getting closer to Newton, me needing to talk to Roo, my own guilty feelings. Stumbling down the back steps, I teetered into the trash cans, balancing for one cool second before losing it.

Newton pulled into the parking lot, just in time to see me pitch face-first into the garbage. He jumped out of the car and helped me up, picking nasty slimy old lettuce and lemon rinds off my shoulder.

His hands felt steady and strong. I closed my eyes and leaned into him for a second. He braced me, and when I looked up, I saw him gazing into my eyes; we were standing so close I felt his warm breath on my forehead, and I lurched away before he could see me blush.

"You okay?" he asked.

"I lost my balance. Just take me to Roo, all right?" I asked.

"Yeah, Tilly," he said.

"You want to go to *Trinity*?" I asked, once we'd gotten into his car and were heading under the train trestle, onto Shore Road.

"I'll probably apply. Why?" he asked.

"Never mind."

"Why do you sound so harsh?"

"Why'd you tell Nona?"

"We were just talking. I told her I want to go to a college in Connecticut, to be near Roo."

"Why didn't you talk to me about it?" I kind of shocked myself by how jealous I was sounding. And why was that? He was Roo's boyfriend, not mine. But still, my chest felt tight, upset at the idea of him confiding in Nona. And I knew it was nuts—Nona would never go after him. My reaction was all me, and all crazy.

He laughed nervously. "I'm sure I'd have gotten around to it."

"Yeah, well, next time tell me, not her."

"Whoa, Tilly."

"We have to keep it in the family, Newton," I said. "For Roo's sake."

"Obviously," he said.

"Will you do me a favor?" I asked. "When we get to the hospital, will you let me go into her room first?"

"Alone?"

"Yeah," I said.

"Sure. If you need to," he said. And he didn't ask why. That made my eyes sting again. He got me, he trusted me. I didn't deserve the trust, considering what I had to tell Roo. But it felt so good to be understood.

Right then he did the strangest thing: He reached across the seat and grabbed my hand. It was awkward, the way his fingers clasped with mine, holding on for just a second, then letting go. My skin tingled from his touch, and I wished he'd held on longer, and that made me feel worse than ever. I yanked away, hard.

We headed out of Black Hall toward the bridge, passing the accident site. I looked for Miss Muirhead, but she wasn't there. My mouth was so dry, I couldn't have spoken even if I'd known what to say. I felt churned up over Newton helping me out of the garbage and the way he'd grabbed my hand just now. I couldn't stop thinking about the way his hand had felt on my shoulder, the way his fingers had brushed against mine.

It was crazy, that's for sure. He was the only person who got what I felt for Roo, and I understood his feelings, too. Our worry for Roo brought us closer to each other in a way that felt thrilling and dangerous. That's all it was. I felt him glance across the seat to look at me; my cheeks burned as I blushed.

We couldn't get to the hospital soon enough for me.

Roo

Tilly came tearing into the room. I thought I spotted Newton behind her, but then my view of the door was blocked by Raccoon—the petite young nurse who wears thick mascara, the one who ties with Indifferent for being my least favorite, the one who seems so put-upon by having to wipe my drool and change my catheter and adjust the splints on my hands.

"You know you're not supposed to be here without your mother," Raccoon said, following Tilly over to my bed. "You get too upset."

"I'm fine."

"I'm not trying to be mean, but my job is to look out for your sister."

As if, I thought.

"Okay, fine, but I'm not leaving," Tilly said.

"Do you want me to call security?"

Tilly completely ignored her. It was as if the nurse wasn't there at all. It was just us, Tilly and me, and she pulled that ugly turquoise vinyl chair up to my bed rail, leaned over, and took my hand.

"Rooey," she said.

I was answering her in my mind, telling her *I am here, I am alive inside, I can hear everything! Just see me!* I wanted that so badly. I wanted her to talk to me for once, to know I was here and not feel the way we had when talking to our dad's grave, when we knew he was gone, that he wasn't really there.

I saw her searching my face, my eyes, my mouth for a sign. I wanted to blink at her, but I couldn't move my eyelids. I wanted to laugh, or groan, or say her name. I wanted to tell her, *I love you, we're sisters, trust yourself—you know I'm here.*

"Rooey," she said again, squeezing my hand.

Raccoon stormed out of the room, and I heard her saying in a loud voice that she needed help, the patient's sister was here, could someone please call security to defuse a dangerous situation. Her voice finally faded away, and Tilly and I were alone.

"I love you," Tilly said. "I think of you every minute. I can't stand seeing you like this, Roo. I'm a mess. I feel so guilty."

She gulped on a big sob, and I saw the tears rolling down her cheeks. My eyes filled, too.

"I have something to tell you. Something awful."

I didn't care what it was. I just concentrated with all my might on getting her to look, really look, at me and see me.

"I did something," she said. "I am the reason you're here. I hate myself."

Don't hate yourself, I wanted to say. *Just figure this out!*

"Okay, I'm going to tell you something about the day of your accident. Two things, actually. One thing is good. Lucan, that's the dog, is fine."

My mother had told me that early on, but I hadn't heard a word about the dog since. I had been worried that she might have been lying to me, or maybe he had taken a turn for the worse. In any case, the news distracted me, momentarily, from my obsession to get Tilly to see that I was in here. I knew Tilly wouldn't lie to me about this, and I felt a sense of relief, an unbelievable, momentary blip of semi-lifting of worry and stress.

"He has a broken leg, but it's healing well. I saw him. He limps, but he's going to be fine. Okay." A deep breath. "The rest isn't so great. I wish you could hear me. I wish you could just blink and let me know you know what I'm saying."

I can't blink, but I know what you're saying! I wanted to shout. The stress was back, stronger than before. I needed her to get this; I didn't have it in me to go on much longer. *I can't move my eyelids at all. Can you ask me something else? Can you look into my eyes and see I'm here?*

"Can you please just," she began, and I must have been exasperated, because all I could do was look up at the ceiling, a heaven-help-me moment. My eyeball flicked up and down. Tilly stopped mid-sentence, mouth dropping open. And then . . .

"Roo?"

I'm here!

"Oh, God," she said. "Did you just look up? Did you just move your left eyeball? If you did, and you hear me, do it again."

I did it again.

"You hear me?"

My left eye flicked up, then down. I had a very narrow field of vision: Tilly and the ceiling.

"Roo, is this real?"

I looked up.

"You know who I am?"

Duh, Tilly. I looked up.

"You understand what I'm saying?"

I looked up.

She grabbed my other hand, she was holding both my hands now, and she did a happy, screaming dance. We were doing a jig, only I was in my hospital bed. Still, I was doing it in my mind, and it felt real. A few moments passed while she hooted and danced like crazy and discharged energy for both of us.

Then she settled down, and I saw that Newton was there, too, summoned by her shrieks.

"What's going on?" he asked.

"Newton," Tilly said. "She hears me. She's in there! Roo!"

I looked up.

"See that?" she asked.

"What? See what?"

"She moved her eyeball!"

I did it again.

"Roo?" Newton said.

I looked up.

Tilly plopped down on the chair, heavily and with new gravity in her eyes, and peered at me more closely, as if she were trying to read tarot cards in my pupils.

"Okay," she said. "I might be losing my mind, and I want to make sure. You can't speak, and you can't blink, but you understand everything I am saying?"

I looked up.

"Bear with me. Don't look up until I say a true statement. I'm starting now. We live in France."

I didn't look up.

"My name is Henrietta and I hate owls."

I didn't look up.

"We do NOT love the beach."

I didn't look up.

"We are sisters."

I looked up.

"Oh my God, oh my God," she said, taking my hands and starting to dance again. I wished I could smile because, for the first time since I got here, I would actually grin. I wished I could dance because I would whirl Tilly around. Newton was frozen in place. I wanted to grab his hands and have him hold me and kiss me and dance me all the way to the stars.

"You can move your eye," he said. "You can move your left eye!"

Yes, I can.

"If you can move that much," Tilly said, "why not more? That must mean you're going to be okay, the stroke was bad, but you're going to get better!"

I believe you! I want that, too, and why not? My mind is fine, I'm all here or all there, I am dying to get out of here, and now that you know I am the same inside, you can tell the doctors and I can really get better.

Just then, Raccoon charged in with two security guards and one of them approached Tilly as if she was a hardened criminal, but she stopped him with her smile, and she stood on her tiptoes and raised her arms into the air.

"My sister!" she cried out. "My sister is here! Get Dr. Danforth! My sister is awake; she can hear and understand us! She's out of the coma!"

Then she leaned over, threw her arms around me, and so did Newton, and we were all holding one another, and that was all that mattered, and I forgot all about the fact that Tilly came here to tell me something terrible.

Tilly

I held Roo so hard, and suddenly that look on her face, the frozen glacier grimace that had seemed foreboding, now seemed beautiful to me. My eyes were an inch away from hers, so close that when I blinked I felt my eyelashes mesh with hers. Newton was part of the hug, too, the three of us crushed together. I gripped my sister's hand, pressed it between us; instead of feeling inert, it now felt warm and full of life.

Behind us, the security guards and nurse stood in their own knot, and I could hear them talking. Given my recent misbehaviors, I had expected to be hauled off. But that didn't happen. I heard the nurse say she was going to page Dr. Danforth, as I had asked.

When Newton and I broke away from hugging Roo, he leaned into her, trying to see what I had seen. And he took over the questions.

"Roo, can you hear me?"

Her left eye flicked upward.

"You saw, right?" I asked him.

He paused, studying her face for other signals of intelligence and life within, watching for the subtleties that would indicate her essential Roo-ness. No one but me knew her better, so I trusted him, didn't interrupt, just sat back and texted my mother: *Mom, come NOW. ROO IS AWAKE!*

"We've been so worried," he said, stroking the back of her hand. "We've thought you were gone, that you'd left us. I want to believe that we've been wrong. And I want to believe that Tilly is onto something. But how can we know for sure? Can you tell me more?"

She looked up.

"You can move your left eye in a vertical track?"

Up: yes. She might as well have said, "Uh: duh."

"When you look up, with your left eye, you're communicating with us, right?"

Upward glance.

I half wanted to shove him away. Newton is such a scientist, so into empirical evidence, he wouldn't be convinced by a few eye movements and emotion alone—but I knew for sure, and I swear I could feel Roo almost laughing with me, yet at the same time, so in love with Newton and his methods. So I calmed myself down and watched him rummage in his book bag.

He pulled out a notebook and wrote the alphabet in block capitals. It seemed to take forever. He held the paper up in front of her face, black pen poised just beneath the row of letters.

"Spell your name," he said, then began slowly moving the pen from left to right, pausing momentarily beneath each letter. Roo's left eye flicked up once for *R* and twice for *O*:

Roo.

"Who is your favorite poet?"

Rilke. At that, my heart began to pound; she wasn't just awake and aware, her mind was still sharp.

"It's March, Roo," Newton said, sounding as excited as I felt. "April's coming soon. What meteor shower will we see?"

"You gotta be kidding me," the security guard said out loud. Until now, Roo had been known as the vegetable in room 413, and if questions were going to be asked, shouldn't they be simple, such as how many fingers am I holding up? I was grinning and couldn't tell them how perfect this was, how incredibly *Roo & Newton* it was as I watched his pen move geek-ily and patiently along the alphabet, and Roo spell out the answer:

Lyrids.

Didn't these guys know this was a love song, this was Newton's way of reconnecting us to Roo and her intelligence— and her to him and me, and to this exact world instead of the drifting-away, brain-damaged one we'd all consigned her to?

It was getting late, and outside the window the sun had set and the amber sky was darkening. Streetlights and parking lot lights hadn't yet come on, and in the violet night, I swear I saw a shooting star. I caught my sister's eye, and realized she was looking past Newton, straight at me. I felt her gaze, and I shivered because I knew she had seen the star, too.

My mother and Dr. Danforth entered the room at the same time. I went to the door and threw myself into my mom's arms. We walked to the bed, and I eased her down by Roo's side. Dr. Danforth stood back; she was holding her breath. Newton held the paper in front of Roo. He held the pen ready, just under the letters. My mother clutched my hand hard, and I could feel that hers was shaking.

"Roo, who is sitting beside you?" Newton asked.

The pen moved, and Roo's left eye flicked up at *M, O, M.* But she didn't stop there:

Mommy.

My mother began to cry. She let go of my hand and buried her face in Roo's neck. She stroked Roo's hair, her face.

"My girl, beautiful girl," she said.

Newton and I stepped away. My mother held my sister and rocked her the way she had when we were young, when we were sick or couldn't sleep, when she would hold us on her lap and comfort us and tell us we would feel better soon. My mother did that to Roo, and as I watched Dr. Danforth lean close, I had the feeling that she was observing not so much as a doctor but as a woman who had come to care very, very much about this incredibly special girl.

And as Newton and I stood by the window, letting my mother and the doctor have their time with Roo, we did the most natural thing: We held hands. We were practically family, after all, and this was one of the greatest moments in our family's life.

Chapter Six

Roo

*T*aylor Swift, whose real name was Nan, brushed my hair, getting me ready. It was early in the morning—the day I was to leave the hospital in New London for a new one in Boston.

My mom, Tilly, Newton, and Isabel were out in the hall, waiting to give me a big send-off. I could hardly believe it had been just four days since my breakthrough with Tilly. So much had happened—the entire world had changed. The way people looked at me, talked to me was different, brighter. They were taking care of a person now, not a ruined lump lying in a bed.

Taylor/Nan used a pink plastic brush, sweeping tendrils off my forehead, pinning them back from my face with a small gold barrette.

"We have to keep your hair out of those beautiful eyes," she said.

"That's right," Pearl said, rubbing my hands with some new lavender-scented lotion she had brought from home. "We don't want anything blocking your ability to speak your mind; we want you to be able to tell those doctors in Boston what's what."

"I cannot believe she was in there the whole time, and none of us noticed," Nan said.

"Talk to *her*," Pearl said, calm and wise as always. "Right, Roo?"

I looked up.

Pearl smiled, shook her head; it felt as if she was proud of me. Although I had heard the other nurses calling her Etta, to me she would always be Pearl—precious, and old-fashioned, and as deep as the sea.

Because Tilly had figured out I was conscious, I was now considered to be a good prospect for treatment. Dr. Danforth had secured me a bed at Boston Medical Center, one of the top places for patients with complicated neurological conditions. Leaving this floor was hard; I had really gotten used to the nurses, and they were all coming into my room to say good-bye. I felt sad; in such a short, intense time, this had become my world. I wanted to be excited, but I was incredibly nervous and scared about the trip.

"Stay strong," Indifferent said, giving me a big squeeze.

I coughed and wheezed, and she dabbed my mouth because of course I couldn't do it myself. Getting emotional made my nose run, and that wasn't good for anyone.

Just then, Dr. Danforth walked in. Other than Pearl, my doctor was hardest to say good-bye to. She had kept me alive. She had never talked down to me, never used baby talk, never ignored me.

Even the kindest nurses like Pearl and Nan had treated me, at least slightly, as if I were an object, not really here. But not Dr. Danforth. She had always treated me as a smart girl who had had a bad accident. Her eyes, the compassion in them, had always let me know she knew I had suffered a tragedy, had lost so much. She'd let me know I was still of value. I still mattered.

"Here's what I think," she'd said last night. "It's rare, but I think you have locked-in syndrome. I want to keep you here, and treat you myself, but I honestly feel Boston is the best place. My colleague Dan Hill leads the field here in the US, and he will be calling in another specialist from London. Roo, I am so sorry I missed it for so long."

She spoke to me as if I understood more about medicine than I could, but I followed her, appreciating her words. She spoke about brain injury and the difficulties in assessing consciousness, how my scores on the Glasgow Coma Scale—my verbal, eye, and motor responses—had caused her to classify me in the severe range, and how locked-in syndrome is rare and mimics coma so thoroughly as to be referred to, in some literature, as "the coma that's not a coma."

"Roo, they will learn so much more about you in Boston, and be able to help you in a way I can't here. The tests are extremely advanced, and Dan has worked with other locked-in patients."

My condition had a name. I wasn't crazy. All these weeks when I had heard everything, understood every word, ached with longing for Newton and the beach and the stars, for school, for being at home with Tilly and my mother, for life with my dad—and no one had known I was there. When I had wept, they'd thought my eyes were running; when I had screamed, they'd assumed the sound was just noise escaping an unconscious lump that used to be me.

I'm locked in. My body is paralyzed, but my mind isn't.

Now, after Indifferent's hug, I felt even more tearful as Dr. Danforth prepared me for my journey. She did her normal exam, and I knew it would be our last time. She listened to my heart and lungs, shined her light into my pupils, examined the color and tone of my skin, the rate of my swallows. The orderlies had arrived with the gurney, ready to take me downstairs to the ambulance, and although Dr. Danforth could have said good-bye to me in my room, or on the floor, she rode the elevator with me.

My mother, Tilly, Newton, and Isabel rode down with us, too. I knew that only one could ride in the ambulance with me; as much as Tilly wanted it to be her, my mother had insisted. In fact, after they said good-bye, Tilly, Newton, and Isabel would go back to school. My mother would get me settled in Boston, then take the train home.

We were on the loading dock, behind the emergency room. The day was bright, and for the first time in over a month I felt sunlight on my skin. A breeze ruffled my hair. The ambulance was a van, and as it backed up to the platform where I lay on my stretcher, I heard the beep-beeping of a vehicle in reverse. That triggered a memory of emergency vehicles arriving soon after my accident, when I'd been lying bloody and broken in the car, having to be cut out of my seat belt by EMTs.

The accident was fresh in my mind. The idea of being on

the road made me feel terrified. Dr. Danforth tucked an extra blanket around me, then crouched down by the stretcher. Her soft fingers encircled my wrist as she took my pulse.

"Your heart rate is higher than it was upstairs, Roo," she said.

I looked up.

"Are you nervous?"

I looked up.

She moved her face so close to mine; the expression in her eyes was gentle, concerned, and she gave me a reassuring smile.

"That's normal," she said. "You have a long ride ahead of you. But you are in good hands, and your mother will be with you. Boston Medical is excellent, there is nowhere better. I will be following your case closely. I won't lose track of you, I promise."

There was so much I wanted to say to her. Thank you for everything, don't forget me, please help me get better, help me get back to where I was. And questions: Is there any hope for me? Will I be able to go to school again? Will I walk, will I ever be able to talk again, will Newton and I be able to go out on the beach and look at summer constellations?

I felt her lips touch my forehead, a good-bye kiss. And when she stood up, to let the orderlies push me into the back of the ambulance, my field of vision enlarged and I saw that everyone from the floor had come down to see me off: Pearl, Nan, Indifferent, the woman who delivered food trays, the blood technician, and Dr. Quiet. Some were smiling, some were crying.

Then my family surrounded me. My mother, Tilly, Newton, and Isabel all hugged and kissed me, and said they'd see me in Boston.

"*Bendiciones en su viaje*," Isabel said. "Blessings on your journey. That's what *mi abuela*, my grandmother, said to us when my mother and I left Mexico to come to the States. She gave this to me, to keep me safe, and Roo, it will keep you safe on your way to Boston."

She slipped off the necklace with the tiny gold cross she always wore, mingled in with her chains of milagros—I had never seen her without it—and attached it around my neck. I knew it had belonged to her grandmother, who she hadn't seen since leaving Mexico, and I knew it meant the world to her.

"You know I love you, *amiga*," Isabel said. "Take a little part of me with you."

I looked up. *I love you, too.*

"Okay, it's time now," Tilly said, angling herself between me and Isabel. She said it so sharply, I wondered if something was going on between my friend and my sister. "You've got to get Roo to Boston!"

My impatient sister. But we did have to go; I was tense and already tired, and the emotion of leaving was getting to me. Tilly wedged close to me. She looked so worried, her brow furrowed, and her eyes red as if she hadn't slept.

"I have to tell you something," she said.

I waited, remembering that she'd mentioned this on the day of my breakthrough, something so terrible she thought I'd despise her for it.

"I texted you," she said. "The day you crashed, you and I were texting."

I looked up. Yes, we were. I was an idiot to do that. I brought this on myself, but did we have to talk about it now?

"You knew, you remembered?"

I looked up.

"All this time you've known?"

Left eye, vertical movement, what do you want me to say?

"Roo, I have been so worried you hate me for it!"

If I could have rolled my eyes I would have. *Hate you? Never. Hate myself? Not so clear.* From the time I picked up my cell phone to the moment I hit SEND: three seconds, maybe four. That was all it had taken to destroy my life.

Tilly hovered, as if she wanted more from me. I realized this confession had been tormenting her. Had she thought I didn't remember? Had she really been afraid I would blame her? I wanted to reassure her but didn't know how. Besides, I hadn't even gotten into the ambulance, and my strength was waning.

I looked beyond Tilly, to make sure Newton was there. He was, standing back, behind the rest of the crowd. Everything between us had flipped. Before the accident, I had been the one seeking distance, but now I worried so much that he would pull away, especially since we would be so far apart. The ride to Boston took at least two hours. How would we survive this?

Maybe he read my mind. He had been known to do that. He stepped forward, and it was just us. Face-to-face. He smiled. His heavy black glasses were crooked on his long nose. The tiny screws that held the earpieces to the temples always got loose, and I had been the one to carry a tiny screwdriver in my backpack and tighten them for him. Without me to help, his glasses were a mess.

"I'm going to see you up there as often as I can," he said. "I can't drive up every day, even though I want to. You know I want to, right?"

I didn't know how to reply to that. I was so full of doubt. How could he want to stay with me?

"Exams are coming, and I'm lining up college visits. But a hundred miles and one day, one week apart, are nothing to us."

Did I believe it? I wanted to.

"You know all those stars up there? Behind the daylight, waiting for the night? They are just like us, Roo. Infinity." He whispered so no one but I could hear him. The breeze blew, ruffling his brown hair and blowing a few strands of mine free of the barrette Nan had clipped on. They tickled my nose and cheeks, and I wanted to push them back.

"We're forever," he said.

I looked up, wanting to say, *Yes, we are.* But he didn't see, because my hair was in my eyes. And then my mother climbed onto the ambulance, and the orderly pushed my stretcher inside, locked the wheels into place, and made sure the monitors were attached and the straps across my body were fixed tight.

As the doors closed, I heard everyone clapping and shouting, cheering for me, telling me to have a good voyage, a safe trip, a wonderful life, telling me to come back and visit, telling me they loved me and would miss me. Tilly's voice was loudest of all, followed by Isabel's, calling out my name.

And my mother held my hand, and as soon as the ambulance began to move, I fell asleep, exhausted by the journey ahead and by so much love, more than I thought the world could hold.

Tilly

*T*hat night should have been great. I was all set to make one of my famous pizzas. Mom had gone shopping, and our refrigerator was full with fresh crust from Bagatto's, frozen tomato sauce that Mom had put up from our garden, and extra mozzarella. Mom had told me what time she'd be home from Boston, and I had the oven preheated and ready. I threw in some garlic bread and made a salad, just to get started.

Any word from your mother? Newton texted me, and I felt my heart jump to see his name on my screen. What was that about?

Yay, Roo made it to Boston a-ok, I replied.

Great. Let me know if u hear anything else.

K. Ttyl

And the totally psycho thing was, I *wanted* to talk to him later.

I kept walking to the window to look for my mother. She had taken a train from Boston, and I figured she'd catch a cab from the station to our house.

I wanted to hear all about Roo, how she'd done on the trip, and what her new hospital room was like, all of it. At the same time, I was fantasizing about Newton. I pictured us driving up together, many times in the future. Every time we got good news, would he hold my hand in the car like he'd done on some of the recent drives to New London?

I shook those thoughts off. How bizarre were they, and how messed up was I to be dreaming of my paralyzed sister's boyfriend? But the feeling of his hand kept jolting me, and the way his eyes looked behind his glasses, staring at me as if he liked me. Not like Roo's sister, the way he always had, but as something more. Was I wrong? I hoped so, and I hoped not.

The sound of car doors slamming made me shut off the fantasies and run to the kitchen door. Expecting to see my mother paying a cab driver, I felt shocked to see both her and Isabel getting out of Isabel's family's Toyota.

"Hi, sweetheart," my mother said, kissing me. "What smells so good?"

"I'm making pizza and garlic bread. How's Roo?"

"It's going to be a long haul, but she is in the right place," my mother said. "The hospital is so big—I got lost trying to find my way from her floor to the lobby. She has a private room there, too, I'm so relieved, and it's fancy. The equipment—it's like being in a lab. Your father . . . well, he would have loved it. And I know it's going to help Roo."

"How come you're here?" I asked, half ignoring my mother's words, only aware of Isabel.

"Tilly, how rude!" my mother said, laughing but sounding embarrassed for my bad manners.

"I picked her up at the train station," Isabel said.

"It was so sweet of you to call and ask my train time. You'll stay for supper, right?" my mother asked.

Isabel stared at me. She had little circles under her big brown eyes, and she was frowning. I raised my hands in front of me, as if I could push her away.

"No," I said.

"I told you to tell her," Isabel said. My mother had walked into the front hall to hang up her coat and put on her fuzzy slippers. I heard coat hangers jangle and the thump of one shoe, then the other.

"I told Roo!" I whispered. "And she understands and forgives me! It's just going to upset Mom."

Isabel jostled my arm. "I was texting Roo, too," she said. "I know she didn't crash answering me, but I can't sleep, Tilly. I feel I played a role in what happened to her, and even if you don't feel guilty today, it will build up and get worse. We have to tell your mother."

"Tell me what?" my mother asked. She walked into the kitchen, wearing her ratty black house sweater over the clothes she'd worn to Boston, and her scuffed-up old Uggs slippers. She looked a little tired from the long day, but so much happier than she had since Roo's accident.

"Could we sit down, Mrs. McCabe?" Isabel asked.

"Okay, what is this?" my mother asked. She stood rooted in place, feet stuck to the floor, as if she couldn't take one more bit of bad news.

"Mom, I didn't mean to do it," I said, shaking so hard inside, feeling my face turn bright red.

"Tilly . . ."

Isabel reached into her jacket pocket, pulled out Roo's phone.

"Where did you get that?" my mother asked, reaching for it.

"By the creek. It was wedged into the bank, all caked with mud, but I cleaned it up and charged it. I wanted to save it for Roo—I knew there would be pictures she'd want. But there was another reason. I'd been texting her."

"When she crashed?" my mother asked. Her voice sounded hollow.

I couldn't take it anymore. I grabbed the phone from her hand, clicked the little green message icon in the upper left screen, and showed my mother the last text Roo had sent. To me.

"I did it, Mom," I said. "I was waiting for her at the museum, and she was late, and I just kept texting her. I didn't mean for her to . . ."

My mother's expression changed from sad to disappointed to furious in about three seconds.

"You didn't mean for her to take her eyes off the road and roll the car into a ditch?" my mother asked, her voice sharp. "Is that what you didn't mean?"

"Yes," I said, shrinking, feeling my shoulders hunch so hard I thought they'd meet in front of my face.

"Mrs. McCabe," Isabel said. "Tilly would never have hurt Roo, and neither would I. You'll see texts from me in there, too."

My mother stared at the phone, squeezing it in a tight fist as if it were her enemy. "You both should have known better."

"I realize that," Isabel said. She put her hand on my shoulder. "I take responsibility. And so does Tilly. We wanted to be honest and up-front. I can't sleep, knowing what happened. Tilly feels as bad as I do."

Worse, I felt like saying. Everyone texted, all the time. I didn't have my license yet, and I thought I'd never text while driving, but hadn't Roo thought that, too? All those good intentions, yet I'd caused my sister total disaster. And it was ten times more horrible, having my mother know.

"Okay, girls," my mother said. "I'm going to go upstairs now."

"But the pizza . . ." I said.

"I'm not hungry," my mother said.

She left us standing there and went up to her room. Isabel started to hug me, but I backed away.

"You think I'm a traitor?" she asked.

I didn't answer, but I was seething inside. The look on my mother's face, the fury in her voice, were now seared in my brain along with the rest of the nightmare.

"Well, I'm glad I told her," Isabel said. "You will be, too, eventually. You might not believe this, but I did it as much for you as for me."

"It must be nice to be so sure of what's right," I said.

She looked at me sadly. "*¿Crees?* That's what you think? That I'm so sure?"

"You seem it."

"No. Not true. I question everything, Tilly."

"Right and wrong, that's you," I said.

She gazed at me sadly, and her big brown eyes welled up. "You're right; there's a moral choice in everything. I know the choice exists, but I don't always make it. I just try." She wiped her eyes. "I'll finally be able to sleep tonight. I hope you will, too. Good-bye, Tilly. See you at school."

She left, and I turned off the oven and threw all the pizza ingredients into the garbage. My stomach growled—it was hungry, even if my mind was not. I wished Roo were there. She understood and forgave me.

I thought about Isabel's words. I was surprised to know she had doubts about things, but I still wished she hadn't told my mother. I felt like an owl pellet, slimy and gross and full of tiny bones and beaks. And I knew I wouldn't be able to sleep that night.

I glanced at my phone and considered texting Newton. But why? That would just be further proof of the fact I was a revolting person. I could have called Nona or Emily, but after what had just happened, it would only feel like small talk. So I stepped onto the back porch to smell the salt air and hear the spring peepers and wish the night would hurry up and pass so I could stop thinking of the way my mother had looked, seeing those texts from me.

I remembered standing in the marsh with Isabel, looking at Roo's phone. I had a soft, sweet memory of dog smell, putting my arm around Lucan and hugging his neck, realizing he was really okay. But once again I felt the same shock as the minute when Isabel had first shown me the phone, when I'd realized what my text had done.

There was one person who might make it better, but I'd have to wait until the next day to see her.

I think I'm going to die.

The Boston hospital was unfamiliar and my room was freezing cold. Was this a panic attack or was I having another stroke?

A nurse was checking my vital signs, but she didn't speak or smile—it was late at night; maybe she thought I was asleep.

I feel so far from home. I'm not in Connecticut anymore. My mother was here, but she left. What will happen to me?

Newton said he was going to look at colleges. Visit schools, book informational interviews with alums. His life was going to go on, and mine was going to be stuck right here, in a hospital bed.

Where will he go? Why can't I go with him?

After all my grand plans, I would have given up Yale in a second, just to stay close to him.

I tried to breathe more deeply, because I was going over the edge.

Is it possible the ambulance ride was too much, and I'm going to die?

I was hooked up to a monitor, and I could it hear it beeping quickly.

Now the nurse paid attention. She shined a light in my eyes. She watched the digital screen, the jagged line that showed my heartbeat.

"Hi, Roo," she said. "I'm Nina. You're awake, aren't you? You're at Boston Medical now; we're going to take good care of you."

Am I dying? I asked, but she didn't reply, of course. She couldn't hear me. She didn't know me. But she sat beside me now, holding my wrist and taking my pulse with her fingers in a way that felt more reassuring than the machine.

"You're okay," she said. "The doctor prescribed something for anxiety, and I'm going to give it to you now. You've had a big day."

She left the half-dark room, then returned, and she injected a syringe into the IV line, and I felt an instant sense of relief—but it was upsetting, because beneath the medication, my emotions jumped and slithered. The drug didn't stop them, just drove them deeper. They were like snakes under the floor of a tent, writhing around.

I slept, then woke up again. A new nurse was on. She said her name was Christina. I wanted to ask her to call Newton for me. She hit me with more medication, and it kicked in hard, and I drifted from my hospital room, through the early spring night, south down the highway I just traveled, reversing direction, back to Hubbard's Point.

Newton and I were sitting at the kitchen table, working on college applications. Tilly's pizza smelled great—it was her only specialty, but a good one. There was a fire in the fireplace, and the logs crackled. Newton's legs were so long, his knees touched mine under the table.

We'd both lived for this—the spring of junior year when we'd really get serious about college guidebooks. It didn't matter that I already knew where I wanted to go and had visited a hundred times with my dad. While Newton tried to figure out his next move, I could spend hours reading descriptions of Yale's residential colleges, different libraries, courses of study.

It was our shared geekitude. Other kids might look forward to actually attending college, but this part of the process was exciting to me. Thinking carefully about each answer, writing an essay that would express who I was, what I needed. With my father gone, I wanted Newton to be proud of me. I wanted to be proud of myself. I wanted to excel, and so did Newton.

When we were twelve and in sixth grade he got a B in science, and his father made him stay up all night memorizing the periodic table of elements, wouldn't let him go to bed until he'd mastered it. I swung by his house the next morning, to pick him up so we could walk to the bus together, and he was still wearing the exact same clothes he had worn to school the day before.

"Um, did you sleep in those?" I asked.

"Didn't sleep," he said.

"How come?"

"My report card," he said. I knew he'd been afraid to show his father the B. I stood there not knowing what to say. My dad would never have gotten angry about a grade—he'd have offered to help me improve. But Newton's father was different, and without being told, I knew he'd given Newton a hard time that night. I'd hated his dad at that moment.

It was our first year of middle school, and kids would have teased him for showing up in yesterday's clothes. Since Tilly wasn't waiting for me—she was only in fourth grade, at our old school, and my parents drove her—I helped him change. I went right up to his room with him and picked out clean pants and a maroon sweater.

Then, waiting in the hall, I could hear him chanting under his breath, "Hydrogen, helium, lithium, beryllium, boron . . ."

His father walked out of the bathroom in his pajamas and jumped to see me standing outside Newton's bedroom.

"You startled me, Roo. What are you doing?"

"Walking Newton to the bus."

"Be precise, Roo. If you are walking Newton to the bus, you can't also be standing in the upstairs hall, can you?" He walked away chuckling. I clenched my fists with anger. Not because he'd been mean to me, but because Newton had a father like that instead of one like mine. Yes, my dad liked me to get good grades, but he'd never punish me, or shame one of my friends.

I had known Newton for two years by then, since we were ten, and I felt this overwhelming emotion I'd never known before. My face felt hot, and I wanted to bundle him out of his house forever and keep him safe.

When he walked out of his room, I grabbed his hand.

"What is it?" Newton asked, looking startled.

"Just, I don't know."

He laughed nervously, his eyes flicking toward his father's door. I could tell he was worried his father would come back, but the longer I held his hand, the bigger his smile got. Mine too. We stood there in the upstairs hall, beaming like crazy.

That was the moment we'd changed from just being friends to starting to love each other.

Lying in my new hospital room, my dreams wove back and forth between childhood and now, between Newton's hallway and my kitchen.

That's right, now I'm at the table in our house, working on my college essay, my knees touching Newton's. Sitting there with him, hearing my mother and Tilly talk in the next room, I write about the ecology of our little spit of land jutting into Long Island Sound, the blue crabs in the tidal marsh and the piping plovers nesting at Little Beach. I lost my father when he died, but I write about finding him every day in the world of nature he taught me to love. I feel the warmth and certainty of being exactly where I am supposed to be at this moment in time.

Then the snakes wriggled under the tent, and my heart fluttered because I wasn't home, not at all. I was paralyzed, and medicated, and locked in, and immobile in a bed in Boston while my family and Newton were a hundred miles away.

And I texted with Tilly, and that's why I was here, that's why everything changed. I screamed as loud as I could, but no one heard. A nurse came in eventually, not Nina and not Christina but someone else, someone I hadn't seen before. She took my vital signs and shined her little flashlight in my face, gazing at my eyes as if wondering if there really was anyone inside.

Chapter Seven

Tilly

I sabel had been wrong, and I had been right: The night took forever, and I couldn't sleep at all.

I rode my bike to school instead of taking the bus. It was early April, and tree branches were turning pink. Hermit thrushes and warblers on their spring migration north sang from thickets along the road.

I made it through classes and avoided Emily and Nona at lunch, eating in the library. I managed not to see Isabel or Newton, either, and I was grateful for that.

On the way home, I sought out Slater. I found him walking north on Shore Road, and I slowed down to ride alongside him.

"Hey," he said.

"Hey. Are you going to work right now?" I asked.

"How'd you guess?"

"I was hoping. Can I head to Miss Muirhead's with you?"

"Sure," he said.

I got off my bike and pushed it so we could walk together. The day was warm, and he wore a navy blue T-shirt with the entwined letters NY, NEW YORK YANKEES.

"How's your mom?" I asked.

"She's having a good week," he said.

"Week?" I asked.

"Yeah. We figured it's better to keep our sights on the day, maybe the week," he said. "Better not to get as far as the month."

"Why not?"

"Things change," he said.

My face drained, and he saw.

"Sometimes for the better. I think it's good not to get too ahead of yourself. Keep it in the day."

"Everything is different," I said. "Before my sister got paralyzed, she was the smartest girl in school. And the prettiest, the nicest, the most popular."

"She's the same person."

"You haven't seen her."

"Inside she's the same," he said. "She's probably going through a ton of stuff, and that's shaking her. But don't fall into the trap of thinking just because she's disabled, she's lost who she is. You've got to help her."

"Help her how?"

We walked along, and he seemed to think about it. "Like, to hold on to herself," he said. "If you're doubting who she is now, after the accident, think what it's like for *her*."

"I know. She was—is—the most special girl in the world. It's weird to think of me helping her. She's my big sister.

She always looked out for me. I can't imagine what I can do for her."

"Yeah," he said. "But I think you can. She's your family, so you sort of have to, right? Maybe it's not even a choice."

I glanced down and away so he wouldn't see my face turning red. No, maybe it wasn't a choice. Especially considering that I had put her in this position.

The road meandered along the tidal creek, where I saw tiny silver bait fish glinting under the surface. We were a hundred yards away from the spot Roo had crashed.

If Slater knew what I'd done, how I had texted her, he might not even be talking to me. If he had any idea that I was the cause of her condition, he wouldn't be saying I could help her.

We cut through a field and headed down Ferry Road, following the narrow creek toward the wide and bright-blue Connecticut River. The lane twisted and turned, and rose and fell, following the contours of the glacier-scored land. Granite walls, their stones covered with silver-sage lichens, bisected meadows and defined yards. Roo loved to photograph our town's stone walls; some of them dated back to the 1600s. It seemed so unfair that she was stuck in a hospital bed, unable to do what she loved, while I walked along. As much as I'd wished I had a talent like hers, right now I knew I didn't deserve one.

Slater led me down a driveway made of finely crushed clamshells, toward a rambling blue Victorian house. It had ornate white gingerbread decorating the porch and rooflines, a coral-pink door and shutters with starfish and scallop shell cutouts, a cozy herb garden and two grape arbors, a ramshackle gazebo overgrown with honeysuckle and bittersweet vines, and a carved sign over the front door: CASA MAGICA.

" 'Magic house'?" I asked.

"That's right," he said.

It was Spanish and made me think uncomfortably of Isabel.

Lucan came limping to the door, Miss Muirhead right behind him. Her white hair was piled on top of her head, held in place by two crisscrossed ebony sticks. She wore a simple black dress with a tiny amulet pinned to it, intricately carved from wood and mother-of-pearl. I remember Nona's story about Miss Muirhead trying to heal her sister, and I wondered what the amulet contained.

"Hi, Miss Muirhead. I hope you don't mind, but I brought—" Slater began.

"Tilly! What a nice surprise. Slater, I'm so glad you invited her."

"Well, I invited myself," I said. "I hope that's okay."

"It's more than okay," Miss Muirhead said.

"Good," Slater said. "I'm going to get to work. You want me to start with the ones in the music room today, right?"

"That would be great," Miss Muirhead said as I wondered what "the ones" were. "And we'll all take a tea break soon," she added.

"Sure thing," Slater said, disappearing through the front hall, Lucan wagging his tail after him.

"You came," Miss Muirhead said, beaming at me when we were alone. "I was hoping you would. How is your sister?"

"Well, she . . ." I began.

"She is improving, isn't she?"

"It's hard to say. But yes. In a way. They took her off the ventilator and moved her to Boston. A special hospital."

"That's wonderful."

"Miss Muirhead . . ."

"Please call me Martha," she said.

She was ancient, and it felt weird, but also, somehow, right. "Okay, I'll try. Martha."

"There, that was easy, right?"

I nodded. I looked around. Bronze statues of graceful girls, looking more like sprites or spirits than humans, danced in the hall. Bookcases everywhere were crammed to overflowing. Dark and formal portraits of somber-looking ancestor types shared wall space with delicate watercolors of local scenes of the river and marsh and churches and Long Island Sound, impressionistic oil paintings of the herb garden, house, and bouquets of day lilies. Tall windows were wide open and over-looked the garden and woods, with glimpses of the river beyond. Outdoors, more sculptures stood along the crunched-up clam-shell paths.

A crash of sudden discordant music drifted through the house. Lucan barked, muffled by rooms and walls and moth-eaten oriental rugs and tapestries and all those books. Slater called out, "Everything's okay!"

"What was that?" I asked.

"He's moving Althea's sculptures; he must have bumped the one by the piano. All these bronzes you see are from her Sisters Series. They're of us, when we were young. She had a forge and a kiln, out in the backyard, in one of the little buildings by the river. I was always so excited to see what she would do next."

Two shabby chairs of worn green velvet, with polished wood arms and claw feet, faced the hearth. The fireplace was made of small round stones, with a smoke-smudged wooden mantel. A hand-painted banner decorated the mantel: wildflowers, starfish, and scallop shells, and, in graceful script, the words:

Those who don't believe in magic will never find it.

"My sister painted that quote," Martha said. "It's from Roald Dahl."

"The author who wrote *James and the Giant Peach*?" I asked.

"And *Matilda*," she said, smiling. "Your namesake."

"But those are children's books."

"We were children once," she said. She stared at me a long time, and I had the feeling she was seeing straight into my troubled thoughts about Roo and my texts. I must have blushed, because she let me off the hook. Smiling, she led me into the kitchen.

She had baked sugar cookies earlier, and they were cooling on a rack by an enameled stove so old it looked as if it belonged in a museum. She handed me a pale-pink glass plate, and I arranged the cookies on it. Opening the refrigerator, which looked as antique as the stove, she removed a pitcher of iced tea. It contained slices of lemon and orange as well as sprigs of vegetation. She chuckled at the expression on my face.

"You don't like greenery in your tea?" she asked.

"I've never had it before," I said politely, vowing that the stuff would never cross my lips.

"I brew the tea fresh, with Earl Grey from Fortnum & Mason, their Piccadilly store in London, and then I add herbs from my garden to make it very local. Today we have white lavender, thyme, and rosemary."

I leaned over to smell, and then she poured me a glass over ice. I was thirsty from my bike ride, and I have to admit, it was delicious, like drinking the spicy-salty air itself.

We loaded up a big silver tray. Martha started to carry it, but I took it from her. She was quite tall, but stooped and slightly frail. When we walked down the hall, I glanced through an open door. A black cat lay curled up on a window seat. I saw a straight-backed chair positioned by a vintage brass telescope pointing up at the sky.

"For watching birds?" I asked.

"For watching stars," she said. "And the moon."

At that I thought of Newton. He would love this old scope. Instead of picturing the owls I might see gliding from the tall oaks to hunt along the riverbanks, I imagined Newton there by the window, gazing up at star clusters and nebulae. Martha walked over to the cat, seemed to whisper something to it. I felt shaken, to be thinking of Newton so vividly—instead of my stargazing sister.

"I did something horrible," I heard myself saying.

"Nothing could be that bad," she said.

"I texted my sister while she was driving," I said. "And that's why she nearly died. I'm not sure anything could be worse."

Martha took the tray out of my hands. She placed it on a nearby table and reached out, as if to touch my shoulder. Maybe she wanted to reassure me, but I couldn't stay to find out. I ran out the door and jumped onto my bike, and I rode as fast as I could away from Casa Magica with no idea of where I wanted to go.

*E*ugenie, one of my favorite nurses in Boston so far, was trying to get more circulation into my feet by massaging them. She grew up in Maine, and came to Boston when she got married, and always told me stories about her two daughters—we'd bonded over the two-girls-in-a-family dynamic, using my new letter board to talk.

Jen Whitaker, from the hospital's AAC department—augmentative and alternative communication—had delivered it to me my first day here, and we had had communication therapy every day since. The board contained all the letters of the alphabet, but instead of appearing in their regular ABC order, they were arranged by frequency of use. It also had space breaks, punctuation, and a button to start new paragraphs, or thoughts.

Last night, Eugenie told me her younger daughter, who is two, ate a fig for the first time, and the older one, who is six, read to her from *Owl Moon* by Jane Yolen. Then they played with the family cats and called it a kitten party. Then the older one cried because the younger one got scratched. Sisters, even toddlers, feel each other's pain. I wondered if the younger girl would grow up to be afraid of snow angels.

And *Owl Moon* had been one of Tilly's favorite books.

"Hello, Roo," a young doctor said in an English accent as he walked into my room. He was lanky and looked barely college age, with an angular face, wavy brown hair, and bright-blue eyes, and he was wearing a Franz Ferdinand T-shirt under his white lab coat. "I'm Dr. Howarth. Dr. Hill invited me from London to work with you."

"Roo, I will come back later, if that's okay," Eugenie said, closing the bottle of lotion.

"Don't leave on my account," Dr. Howarth said. "Perhaps you can help Roo and me get to know each other."

"Of course," Eugenie said. "Roo, Dr. Howarth is the absolute tops in the field of facilitated communication. We are very lucky to have him on your case."

Most of the doctors were my mother's age or older, but he was so young and cute, and I liked his English accent, I felt embarrassed having him see me this way. I wanted Eugenie to pull the covers up to my neck so he couldn't see my dry, scrawny, atrophied legs.

"Doctor, let me start by introducing you to Roo's photography. She took all of these photos," Eugenie said, gesturing at them displayed around the room.

"Brilliant," he said.

I watched him move slowly around the room, his back to me, as he took his time regarding my photographs. It surprised me that he would focus on them, especially if he was so important. The doctors here were busy, and although they were kind, they didn't slow down for pleasantries.

Dr. Hill, the much older neurologist, was so high up he rarely even made visits. His main work was studying the results of my tests. In the three weeks I had been here, I'd met him four times, and he intimidated me. He was as tall as Newton, and appeared so imposing, with his wavy white hair and dark wool suits, and the way people hushed when he spoke.

But Dr. Howarth seemed down-to-earth. Not just because of his T-shirt, but also the way he was taking his time studying each of my photos as if he was really interested.

"These are extraordinary," Dr. Howarth said. "The land-scapes in particular. They give me the feeling I am right there. The river, the beach, the driftwood log: beautiful. Where did you take the photos?"

"A lovely place called Hubbard's Point," Eugenie said. "Roo has told us all about it. It's the seaside section of Black Hall, Connecticut, where Roo is from."

"You capture people very well, too, Roo. This girl in the rowboat . . ."

Tilly.

"Her laughing eyes, that floppy yellow sun hat, the energy in her shoulders—I feel I know her, just looking at her picture. She looks as if she's about to row out into the bay and cause some kind of stir."

"That's Tilly, Roo's younger sister," Eugenie said. "I'm sure you'll meet her; she comes to visit often."

"And this fellow?"

"Roo's boyfriend, Newton. He is also a frequent visitor."

Always with Tilly. They carpooled to see me. I loved that they came and were supporting each other, but sometimes I wanted to see them each alone. I had secrets with each of them. Nothing deep and dark, but just the quiet private things that only you and the other person knew, that only you and the other person could understand.

"Wow, this shot needs to be in *National Geographic*," Dr. Howarth said, looking at the enlargement of "Star Trails," the time-lapse photo I had taken that night at Little Beach, when Newton and I had said *I love you*. I couldn't stand to think about how we'd kissed, how his arms had felt around me, how badly I wanted to go back to the beach with him.

When he turned, Dr. Howarth was beaming, as if with pride in me, his new patient. He looked directly into my face, and I saw him see something in that very second—as no one else, not even Tilly or Newton—had so far.

He saw my inner pain. The smile drained from his face, and he pulled a chair close to the side of my bed, even with my knee, because that is where my field of vision could take him in.

"I'm sorry, Roo," he said. Very naturally, as if we had known each other a long time, he took my hand.

I whimpered, hating the sound.

"She's very brave, Doctor," Eugenie said.

"Yes," he said, gazing into my eyes. "I know that. Brave girl."

My chest heaved with agony, thinking of that night with Newton, feeling so trapped, completely locked in, and knowing

I would never get there again. Dr. Howarth's blue eyes were full of sorrow.

"You miss those times, don't you?"

I looked up, and a tear slipped from my eye.

Dr. Howarth reached for a tissue, wiped the tear away. It was such a relief to be with someone who wasn't determinedly upbeat, wasn't just trying to cheer me up, tell me all would be well when it wouldn't, not ever again. My lungs exploded with air. I was sobbing, but I sounded like a whale, not a human being.

He stayed by my side.

Eugenie held my feet, as if anchoring them to the bed, as if I were a balloon that might float away. After a minute, she covered my legs with a white blanket and left the room.

"You have such talent," Dr. Howarth said after a long time, once my heart had slowed and settled a bit. "Your photos say so much about you, Roo. You have a beautiful soul and a brilliant eye. You capture the perfect instant of beauty and action, and somehow you translate that exact moment, and the feeling that goes with it, to the viewer."

He reached toward the shelf under the window and brought out the letter board, the more sophisticated version of the alphabet Newton had created back in Connecticut, the one that had first allowed me to spell out my thoughts.

"Would you like to talk?" Dr. Howarth asked.

My left eye flicked up. *Yes.*

He held up the board Jen and I had been working with, my lifeline to communicating with everyone.

"This is very rudimentary," he said, tapping the plastic surface. "It's effective, but we can do better."

I moved my eye, and he realized I wanted to speak. Like Newton, he used his pen as a pointer to indicate each letter, and I spelled out my question.

How?

"I'm going to build you a computer," he said. "My specific field of study is BCI—brain-computer interface. Your pupil response is very keen—that's why we've been measuring your eyes' response to light and movement. And you have binary function—one, two, your eye moved up and down. That switching is all an operating system needs to function. And it makes you a great candidate, Roo. We're going to help you communicate by using a computer."

He held the pen, waiting for my response; I could hardly bear to state the obvious.

My fingers do not work.

"You see, the computer works with brain power, not muscle movement. We will fit you with electrodes that will hook up to a laptop. Your brain waves will do the rest."

Sounds hard.

"It's the opposite," he said. "It's easy, especially for someone like you. You are so creative, intuitive. I only have to look at your photographs to know that. You see beyond what others see, Roo."

I do?

"Yes." He held my hand again. "You have a beautiful, unusual vision. I want to talk, really talk with you, and that will happen better once I rig up this system for you. I've already built the basics; we shall go to work in earnest tomorrow, and you will be communicating freely very soon. I promise you." He let go of my hand so he could work the board and get my response.

I had so many questions. How will this work, why am I a candidate, am I dreaming? Instead, because what he had described sounded like science fiction, and because all the other questions tumbling around in my mind seemed too complicated, I asked,

Promise how?

"It's what I do," he said. "Roo, in a case like yours, your mind is acute, but it has become disconnected from your body. Everyday things like conversation become impossible. But this computer—it's like a translator for your thoughts. The software will digitize your brain signals, and those neural spikes will transmit to the laptop and show up on the screen."

How?

"Just like what we are doing here. Only instead of your eye movement telling me which letter you want, your brain waves will speak directly to the laptop, and the words will appear."

Training?

He laughed. "Roo, training is the easy part. Once we implant the sensor and hook you up to the electrodes, you will get used to it very quickly. Within an hour or two, I promise—see, another promise! The hard part is finding a patient like you."

Really?

"Oh, yes. And I hope you will talk to me once we get to that point. I want to hear more about your photos, and why you love the night sky so much. And all about your life, what matters to you."

Thank you.

"I've never had a patient like you," he said. "LIS—locked-in syndrome—is so rare. When I was at medical school in the UK, I observed only one case, an elderly man who had had a stroke. It made me very happy to be on the team that helped him regain abilities to communicate with his wife, his son and grandchildren. I have worked with others since, and I've spent a long time developing software to help people. But you are different, Roo."

How?

"All human beings are valuable, deserving of help. But you are gifted." He glanced up at the wall, at my photos.

I thought, but did not spell out, *That's what my father used to say.* It filled me with emotion.

"I want the girl who took these pictures to get behind a camera again."

My eyes stung.

Not possible, I spelled out.

"If I have anything to do with it, it is."

I wanted to say, *Don't get my hopes up.* Instead, I spelled again, *How?*

"Your eye, and your pupil response, and the system I will build for you. I will find a way to connect the computer with your camera. The only thing is, I want to be with you when you take your first photo. Will you let me do that?"

Yes.

"We'll be spending a lot of time together. You're going to get tired of me." He held my hand again, and his blue eyes were full of warmth and humor.

My face felt hot, and I knew I had turned scarlet. Inside, my heart flipped, and I felt prickles racing into my face. I felt instantly guilty, as if I were betraying Newton.

"Do you think you'll get tired of me?" Dr. Howarth asked.

No.

"Wait and see," he said, and laughed. "I tend to be a bit obsessive when I get started on a project. But I am determined that you will be shooting photos again before summer."

I hope.

"Hope matters a lot," he said. "All the medicine, all the science in the world can't heal if you don't have hope. But I am talking to the girl who photographs the stars, who snapped those shots right there." He gestured at the wall. "And that girl knows hope. She knows the world beyond, and the possibilities. Dream of the possibilities, okay, Roo?"

Okay.

"Good." He squeezed my hand again. His blue eyes scoured mine, reading my emotions. They were all over the place: happiness, excitement, trepidation, fear. Then he winked, smiling.

In my mind I winked back. And I felt as if he knew, because his smile got wider.

Tilly

Right after English class I stopped by my locker and got slashed in the heart. Someone had taped an article from the morning paper to the gray metal door:

TEEN TEXTING CAUSE OF NEAR-FATAL ACCIDENT

New evidence has surfaced in the case of Black Hall honor student Ruth Ann McCabe and the accident that nearly took her life in February. Her mobile phone, assumed lost in the marsh where she crashed her family station wagon, has been found.

Police analysis revealed that texts had been sent between Ruth Ann and a family member just before she drove the car off the road into a tributary of the Connecticut River. Ruth Ann had been on her way to pick up her sister, Mathilda, at a nearby museum. A talented photographer, Ruth Ann, known to friends and family as

Roo, had stopped to take photos of the winter scene, and was running late.

"This is tragic," Black Hall High principal Chase Gordon said. "We cannot stress strongly enough the importance of never texting while driving. Our school has always been committed to this cause, and we have been proud of our student body for following it. Ruth Ann's accident has left us all heartbroken and unfortunately illustrates how serious this dangerous behavior can be."

"People don't realize how fast you can lose control of the vehicle," said Connecticut State Police spokesman Sgt. Mark Grandview. "And it's not just kids—adults are texting, too. A large percentage of our worst crashes involve cell phones. You take your eyes off the road for a second, and you can destroy your life—or someone else's."

Toxicology tests were determined to be negative for both drugs and alcohol, and police do not believe that speed was a factor in the single-car crash.

"It was texting, 100 percent, pure and simple," Sgt. Grandview said. "The message is clear: Don't text and drive."

Ruth Ann was recently moved to a Boston area hospital for specialized care. While previously this newspaper has withheld her name because she is a minor, we have decided to print it in the article because of a statement from her mother.

"My daughter's life hangs in the balance because of one bad decision. She texted. If even one family can be spared our heartache, then talking about it will be worth it."

Yes. My mother turned Roo's phone in to the state police so they could analyze it. She had told me about this interview, but seeing it in black and white made me feel she'd thrown me to the wolves. I wanted to be furious at her, and even more at Isabel for making me tell my mom, but mostly I hated myself.

"Who put this article here?" I asked Nona, who was rummaging in her locker beside mine. "What idiot would do this? Marlene, right? Who else?"

"What's the difference?" Nona asked, glaring at me.

"What, you too? You think I'm rotten?"

"You're obviously the family member mentioned in the article," she said. "You were texting with Roo?"

"You've never texted before?" I asked.

"Not to someone I know is driving."

"What makes you think I knew she was driving?" I asked, desperately grasping.

"She was on her way to pick you up. God, Tilly," Nona said. "And not only that, I had to hear about it in the newspaper, like everyone else. Couldn't you have told me about it?"

"You could have talked to us," Em said, walking over from her locker across the hall.

"What was there to say?" I asked, upset that even Em was lashing out at me.

"If you don't know that, I feel sorry for you." Nona shook her head and walked away. Em gave me a long look and followed her. I felt like crying.

Mr. Gordon had canceled second-period classes for an emergency assembly in the auditorium. I wanted to skip, but that would have made things even worse. I slunk in just as he was starting, and I sat in the last row, behind everyone. I could barely stay still, so nervous at what he was going to say. Kids were buzzing and everyone—including me—knew he was going to talk about the article.

About me and Roo.

The vice principal, Mrs. Lansing, stood onstage with Mr. Gordon, deathly looks on their faces. Teddy Messina stood behind the overhead projector, halfway down the middle aisle, while other kids from the AV club pulled down the big white screen above the stage. Usually, at assemblies like this, everyone was restless and noisy, happy to be out of class, hanging out with friends in the middle of the day.

But this morning, total silence.

I wanted to run out, leave school and never return. Slater was a few rows away; he turned around, scanning the crowd till he found me. He waved, inviting me to sit with him. I shook my head. I inched halfway out of my seat, but sat down again; bolting would only make it worse.

Newton sat off to the side, three-quarters of the way back, head down as if he didn't want to see what might appear on-screen. Nona and Em occupied our regular seats. I looked to see if they had saved one for me, and Em had—there was an empty chair next to her.

Marlene, Debbie, Allison, and the other Marlene-o-Matics were front and center. They weren't going to miss a minute of my takedown. I heard clicking and half turned: Isabel and friends of hers and Roo's from photography club and the school paper were behind me, photographing the assembly.

Isabel. My face turned into a knot, thinking of how she'd started this.

She caught my eye, and I looked away. Hard. I hope she knew she'd ruined my life. I found myself watching Newton. He couldn't even raise his head. I wondered if he had read the news article, and if so, how much he despised me. I slunk down in my seat.

Mr. Gordon tapped the microphone. A yowl of feedback fed through the speakers, and he cleared his throat. He wore his usual blue blazer and plaid tie. His round tortoiseshell glasses rested on the bridge of his hawk nose, and his friendly face looked not angry, as I would have expected, but full of mourning, as if someone he loved had just died.

"By now," he said, speaking into the microphone, "many of you have seen the news story. You might think it is, in a way, old news. Ruth Ann's accident took place in February. But this story focuses on new information. Ruth Ann had been texting with a family member. We will not divulge her name at this time."

A nervous buzz went up through the crowd. My muscles felt tight, poised to spring. Here it came: Whether he said my name or not, everyone knew. He was going to blame Roo, blame me. He was going to criticize us for something I already hated myself for.

Tilly, people whispered. *She was texting with Tilly. What other family member would it be?*

My mom was reliable Mrs. McCabe; half of them had had her in middle school. She wasn't someone who would text while her daughter was driving. The auditorium rustled, and it felt like every single person turned to look at me. I kept my eyes down.

"Ruth Ann is not the only one to do this," he said. "I could ask those of you in this room who have ever sent a text while driving to raise your hands—and I know, if you were being honest, most of your hands would go up. But I'm not going to ask."

Mrs. Lansing nodded to Teddy. He dimmed the auditorium lights.

A photo of Roo from last year's yearbook filled the screen. It was larger than life, and her huge smile touched her blue eyes, and her long, dark hair gleamed in the daylight, and you could almost feel her wanting to reach out, hug you, and invite you to go running on the beach with her.

"This is our friend, Ruth Ann McCabe," he said. "The way she looked last spring."

Mrs. Lansing nodded, and another photo took its place.

I gasped: It was Roo in her hospital bed. The shot was blurry, as if the person taking it had moved suddenly, as if maybe there had been too much emotion to hold the camera steady. But you could make out the fine shape of Roo's oval face, her perfect cheekbones, and her blue eyes—open and staring in that seemingly unfocused way. And you could see her cracked lips pulled back, her mouth wide open in that silent, glacial scream.

Students whispered, groaned, wept. The sounds of choking, sniffling, and pure and utter grief filled the auditorium.

"Ruth Ann's mother gave me that picture," Mr. Gordon said, his voice breaking. "She loves her daughter—both of her daughters—so much, she was thinking of all the parents, all the siblings, everyone who loves a friend or family member. And she wanted to make sure all of you know that this can happen if you text and drive."

Mrs. Lansing left the stage. I saw her shoulders shaking, as if she, too, was crying. She stood by Teddy, placed a steadying hand on his shoulder. He removed Roo's photo and the screen glowed garish and white and blank.

"You all know Ruth Ann was brilliant with a camera," Mr. Gordon said. "Taking pictures, especially of nature, was her passion. She planned to enter a prestigious photography contest, and she hoped to apply early decision to Yale University. Her academic record is so excellent, I can only believe she would have been admitted. There are two paths in life. The ones we take, and the ones we don't. I am going to leave you with a few minutes of silence." He bowed his head and took a long pause before looking up again. I saw his eyes were red. "Mrs. Lansing selected some of her favorite photos by Roo, including some that were taken the day she crashed. I would like you to watch them now, and realize that they represent Roo's other path— the one that is no longer available to her because she took her eyes off the road for three seconds to send a text. Please watch."

I had made it through okay, but him using her nickname pierced my heart, and I wasn't sure I could stay in my seat.

The screen filled with one of Roo's shots of a bright-red sunrise over the beach. Then a photo of the Black Hall marsh, deep green at dawn. Then a series of the full moon rising, getting higher and smaller in the sky with each shot, behind Hubbard's Point. Ice on the river. The streetlight at the end of a curving beach road. Gold light spreading like butterscotch across the snowy marsh. The bait shop boarded up for the winter. Then a screen shot of her last text: *5 mins away.*

People began to openly sob, and I couldn't take it anymore. I inched out of my row, then tore out the back door of the auditorium.

I wanted to escape, leave school and never return. The halls were empty. This had been Roo's school. She had been so excited for me to be a freshman and join her here. We had had just one semester and two months together before she crashed. She would never return, never be a student at Black Hall High again. I clamped my arms over my chest, trying to hold myself together. I ran past the office, out the door into the parking lot.

My bike was locked to the rack. Fumbling with the combination, I didn't hear footsteps. It wasn't until I felt hands on mine, and jumped a mile, that I realized I'd been followed out.

"Newton," I said.

"Where are you going?" he asked.

"I'm getting out of here."

"Roo wouldn't want you to run off. She'd tell you to stay and face it."

"Don't you hate me like everyone else?"

He glared at me.

"Didn't you read the article?" I asked, shoving him, waiting for him to blast me. "Didn't you see those pictures? The one of her in the hospital. And her photographs, 'the other path'?"

"Of course I saw them. And I was there when she took half the pictures. And of course I read the article."

"And? Did you figure out I'm the family member?"

"What do you think?" he shouted.

"I think you know," I said, shocked because I'd never heard him use that tone of voice before. "I'm the one she texted to. Three seconds that took everything she had. I did it."

His face turned red. It almost scared me because I'd never seen him that angry before. But he didn't move. He towered over me, a tall, skinny giant.

"I thought I had," he whispered.

"What?"

The world stopped dead. Then a flock of geese flew overhead. Trucks from I-95, just half a mile away, rumbled noisily. The interstate and birds and wind in the branches filled the air, drowning out the silence between Newton and me.

"I thought I had done it," he said finally.

"Done what?"

"Texted and made her crash. It's ironic; we loved her most, and we're the ones who sent the texts."

"Yours were way earlier. I looked."

"Yeah, well, I didn't know that, I didn't have the exact time. I only know that I sent them knowing she was in the car; I didn't care. I knew she was out working on her portfolio, then going to pick you up, but all I could think was, she wanted space, she wanted distance, she's leaving me, leaving us. I wanted reassurance from her."

"Space?" I asked.

"She was going to break up with me," he said.

I sat down hard on the ground, looking at my feet.

"So you saved me here, Tilly. I figured I was the one who sent her off the road."

"You weren't."

"I might as well have been. We don't know exactly what happened. She sent the text to you, but she'd been reading the ones from me."

"You're just trying to make me feel better."

"I don't know," he said. "Maybe I am."

I thought about what he had said. And remembered that one Saturday months back, when he had called our house, and Roo hadn't wanted to take the call. And I remembered him asking me something at the hospital in New London.

"Space, really? You two?" I asked.

"Yeah."

"I'm sorry," I said, feeling hoarse, my voice barely working.

"Thanks."

"Why, though?" I asked. "You two are . . . Newton and Roo."

He shook his head, a combination of sorrow and confusion. "She wanted it," he said. "College coming up, and I don't know. She didn't talk to you about it?"

"Not at all." Why hadn't I asked her why she hadn't wanted to talk to him that day? I suddenly felt hurt, that my sister had been considering something so big and hadn't confided in me.

Newton had come out to try to convince me to go back inside, but that wasn't going to happen. I saw something change in his eyes. He put his hand on my waist, steered me toward his car. I tingled just like the day he'd caught me tripping down the steps at Foley's, just like when we'd held hands the day Roo left Connecticut in the ambulance. We got into his car, and without a word, he drove out of the parking lot. He didn't have to tell me where we were going.

Chapter Eight

Tilly

We hit the highway heading north. It took two hours to get to the outskirts of Boston, and then we got stuck in traffic. My thoughts were swirling, trying to hold on to anything but the fact he had said "loved": *We loved her most.* Was loving Roo seriously the past tense for him? My gaze slid his way.

He was as awkward and gawky as ever, and his heavy glasses still slid down his nose, but looking at him this time, I felt more tenderness than I'd ever felt. His bony wrists poked out of his threadbare navy sweater, and his big stainless steel watch, a chronometer Roo had given him for his sixteenth birthday, looked gigantic on him. His Adam's apple protruded, but instead of wanting to make fun of him and call him Ichabod Crane, as I had so often since childhood, I kind of loved it, because it was such a distinctive part of Newton.

I had a shocking thought: *What would it feel like to kiss him?*

I'd only been kissed one time, when I was twelve, by a summer boy at Hubbard's Point. I barely knew him—his family had

been renting a cottage for July. He lived in Hartford and was a
year younger and an inch shorter than me, and we'd met flying
kites after a storm. His name was Jimmy, and he was cute in a
super-freckly way.

We'd gone crabbing at the end of the beach and had bluefish
heads for bait, a bucket full of rock crabs, and sandy hands. We
were balanced on a seaweed-covered rock, and he burped. I
looked over to laugh at him, and he swooped in for the kiss.

It shocked me so much, and his sandy hand scraped my
sunburned shoulder so hard it felt like sandpaper, I toppled
straight into a bed of wet seaweed and accidently pulled him
in with me, and barnacles scraped our legs, and he came so
close to crying, his lower lip wobbled. The whole situation
smelled like crabs and bluefish heads, and it wasn't exactly
romantic.

When I got home, I told Roo the whole thing. She had listened sympathetically. But as a big sister, part of her role was
letting me know that as kisses went, my first didn't pass mus-
ter. So, any time she wanted to get me going, all she had to do
was say, "Jimmy." And we'd be lost for five minutes in a combination of embarrassed and hysterical laughter. If she said
"bluefish," it could go on for five more.

Looking at Newton, I found myself imagining a much different kind of kiss. The thoughts terrified me, so I turned away,
my face to the side window, watching the Boston skyline come
into view. We passed Fenway Park. Baseball season had started,
and there was a game scheduled that night. People had started
to arrive; I tried to concentrate on memories of going to see the
Red Sox with my parents and Roo, how my father had bought

us hats and pennants, and how Roo and I had worn our baseball mitts, hoping to catch a foul ball.

All this way from Black Hall, we still hadn't said a word to
each other. We found a parking spot and marched into the medical center, through the lobby to the west wing, and up the
elevator to the fourth floor.

We walked down the corridor, which had already become
familiar. It was lined with private and semiprivate rooms, all
filled with patients who had complex neurological conditions.
When we got to Roo's room, I was expecting the usual
gut-clenching moment of guilt and regret.

Instead, I found laughter and bubbling-over joy.

My mother was there. She was still on leave of absence
from school and came nearly every day; I could barely look at
her, considering that newspaper interview and the fact that
she'd handed over a disgusting photo of Roo to be shown at
school.

"Hi, honey," my mother said. "Hi, Newton." She came to
hug us. I hoped she noticed the major cold shoulder I was giving her, but she just gave me a harder squeeze and went back
to Roo.

My sister's bed had been cranked to a forty-five-degree
angle, and she was more upright than I had seen her since the
crash. She looked like a character in a futuristic movie, wearing
a black cap that fit tightly over her head, almost like a Mouse-
keteer hat without the ears. From it ran a bundle of wires that
connected to a laptop open on the tray table in front of her.
Several nurses and doctors, including the austere Dr. Hill, tall

and imposing with a lion's mane of wild white hair, were clustered around Roo.

"You see, Roo—it will be as streamlined as thinking a thought and having it appear on the screen," a young man exclaimed in an English accent, grabbing Roo's hand. He looked about the age of a college kid, and he wore a doctor's coat over a bright-red T-shirt with black writing on it. He had long, brown hair that waved over his eye and reminded me of a tragic English poet.

"I can't believe it!" my mother said.

"Tim has pioneered this technology," Dr. Hill said. "His lab is at the very forefront."

Newton and I stood in the doorway, watching.

"She'll be a master, right off the bat," the young doctor, who I assume was Tim, said. "Once we get started, we'll be on to robotics and she'll be reaching for that camera."

"The camera?" my mother said, sounding nervous and protective. "I'm not sure we should get her hopes up for that."

"Roo and I have discussed it," the Tim doctor said. "And our girl is all about hopes. Right, Roo?"

He held up the board, and Roo spelled out,

Yes.

I drifted over to the bed, feeling invisible. Suddenly people noticed me. The nurses who knew me said hello, Dr. Hill shook my hand and Newton's, and my mother gave me a big smile. I couldn't believe she wasn't picking up on my iciness.

"Tilly, Newton, this is Roo's new doctor. Dr. Tim Howarth," my mother said, and we shook hands. His coat fell open enough to reveal his T-shirt said ROYAL BLOOD, one of my favorite bands.

"Tim is why Dr. Danforth allowed Roo to come here," Dr. Hill said in his deep, authoritative rumbling voice. "Dr. Danforth knew that we had a grant to invite him to our hospital to further his research—brilliant projects, changing the world for people with brain injuries—and then Roo came to us. Essentially, he arrived straight from London to help Roo."

Dr. Howarth's eyes were on Roo, and she and he were communicating on the letter board:

You came just for me?

Was she *flirting*?

Dr. Howarth squeezed her hand and nodded.

"I certainly did, Roo," he said.

Major recoil and *ewww*. The look in his eyes was so fake, acting all interested and staring at Roo as if the rest of us weren't even here.

"I've been reading about BCI," Newton said. "Brain-computer interface, right? That's the technology? I wondered if you would be trying it with Roo; I hoped, but I know it's so new, and with the expense, it seems a lot of patients are missing out."

"Forget the money, we'll pay it!" I said. "Just make her better!"

"Tilly," my mother said. "Slow down."

"The concept is actually rather simple," Dr. Howarth said. "Roo has heard this before, so forgive me, Roo . . ."

You are forgiven.

He laughed, enjoying her humor, and again I felt a twinge.
"Right, then. In severe brain injuries, such as stroke, where the
pathways from the brain have been badly damaged, we teach
patients to bypass the compromised nervous system by sending
brain waves directly to the outside world. So instead of using
her brain to send messages to her fingers to type on a keyboard,
she will learn to send them straight to the computer itself. Or,
eventually, a robotic arm."

"Can she do it right now, with all that on?" I asked, gesturing at the weird little hat and wires.

"I'm not sure Roo likes being referred to as 'she' when she's
right here," Dr. Howarth said.

He said it lightly, with amusement in his charming English
voice, but it felt like a slap in the face.

"Whoa," I said. "Don't tell me how to talk to her. She's my
sister!"

"All the more reason. And there's that 'she' again," Dr.
Howarth said.

I looked to my mother for support, but she was dabbing
drool from Roo's mouth.

"Tilly asked a good question," Newton said, and I felt proud
and grateful that he had my back. "How do the signals get from
the brain to the computer?"

"A sensor," Dr. Howarth said, finally half-turning from
Roo to answer Newton. "A tiny chip implanted on the surface
of her brain's motor cortex."

"Mission control for body movements," Dr. Hill said, making notes on Roo's chart.

"Brain activity recorded by the chip is relayed through gold wires to the computer," Dr. Howarth said. "My software records the signals—thoughts, actually—decodes them and sends them to the computer. By thinking, *Hello, world, how are you today?* the words will appear on the screen. I, for one, am anxious to hear your thoughts, Roo."

Thank you, she spelled out, and Dr. Howard gave a little bow of acknowledgment, making me seriously want to throw up.

"As if she would ever say 'Hello, world.' Lame!" I muttered. My head was down, my hair falling in my face, so no one would see my expression of disgust.

"Oh, honey," my mother said, hugging Roo. "It's so exciting."

"How will she be able to use a camera?" Newton asked.

"Ask *her*, please," Dr. Howarth said.

Newton flinched, looking as offended as I felt. Who was this British jerk to act as if he cared and knew more about Roo than we did? Newton clammed up. His mouth was a hard line.

"Roo," Dr. Howarth said. "Are you ready to take some pictures for me? As soon as we get the system operating."

Yes, Roo said.

I rolled my eyes. I really couldn't stand this guy.

"There you have it," Dr. Howarth said. "And now I think it's time for all of us to let you rest. I'd like to do the surgery as soon as possible."

"Surgery?" I asked.

"To implant the sensor," my mother said. "You heard Dr. Howarth, didn't you, Tilly? Roo wants it, and I've given my consent."

It wasn't as if Roo hadn't had several surgeries immediately after the accident and stroke, but I was shaking at the idea of Dr. Tim Whoever-He-Was cutting into her head.

"You've done this before?" I asked. "This surgery?"

"Yes," he said.

"It's a clinical trial," Dr. Hill said, and the words scared me to death.

"Experimenting on Roo?" I asked. "Mom, are they kidding?"

"It's her best hope," my mother said, her voice thick with tears, and I could tell she was trying to disguise the despair that was obviously competing with her optimism. "Be positive, Tilly."

"But it's her brain!" My teeth were practically chattering, I was so terrified.

"Talk to your sister," Dr. Howarth said, more loudly than before.

"Tilly, calm down," Newton said, seeing that I was about to lose it. My pulse was so speedy I thought I might pass out. Then I felt Newton's hand on my back, and I took a deep breath and tried to control myself.

"Okay," I said, looking the doctor straight in the eye. "You've done this surgery?"

"Yes, I have," he said. "Many times on monkeys, with great success. And more recently on several patients—again, with excellent results."

"Monkeys!" Oh, that was all I needed to hear. I pounded my hands on the tray table, rattling the water pitcher and plastic cup resting there. "Leave my sister alone! Does she even know you're experimenting?"

My mother strong-armed me away from the tray table, and I heard Newton say my name loudly and firmly: "TILLY!"

"It's not precisely experimenting, but yes, it is a clinical trial," Dr. Howarth said unflappably, as if I hadn't reacted at all.

"Could things go wrong?"

"In any surgery, there are risks: of infection, of her body rejecting the sensor, and, because Roo has already had a stroke, there is a higher risk for a cardiac event."

"Stop!" I said, shaking so hard I thought my legs would give out. "What does *cardiac event* even mean? I don't want her to die! Mom, Newton, help! We're so lucky to have her the way she is. Right now. Able to talk to us. So what if we have to use the board? We don't care!"

"Maybe Roo cares," Dr. Howarth said. "In any case, talk to Roo about it. Ask what *she* wants. Right, Roo?"

Right. TY, she spelled.

WHAT? They were chatting away as if they were old friends, he was defending her from us. And she even had little spelling shortcuts with him, *TY*, *thank you*, when I happened to know that part of her communications therapy included spelling all the words out fully so she would gain mastery over the board.

"You should really spell the whole word," I said pointedly to Roo.

She didn't even answer me.

It felt as if these new doctors had swept in and were taking Roo away from me, as if they were using their scalpels on my skin and bones. And it embarrassed me for Roo, the way she was swooning over Dr. Howarth. He was just a doctor, and she was just a case. I knew my sister so well, and as much as I couldn't believe it, and wouldn't have if Newton hadn't mentioned that she wanted "space," she obviously had a crush on this doctor, and was about to put her life into his hands.

"Go ahead," Dr. Howarth said. "Ask Roo how she feels about the surgery."

I edged between my mother and the doctor, put my face close to Roo's. I leaned my forehead against hers, closed my eyes, felt her eyelashes against my cheek. For the first time since I'd entered the room today, I felt almost calm and right.

"Roo," I whispered. The sound of her name soothed me. How many times had I said it during the course of our lives? A million times? A billion times? Her skin felt smooth and cool against mine, and my breathing slowed to match hers.

We were sisters. We came out of the same womb. There had been times we'd read each other's minds. She was older than me, and she had always taken care of everything. Everyone at school might think I'm horrible, but she understood and held nothing against me. She was my girl.

"Roo," I said. "Rooey."

Tilting my head back, I looked into her eyes.

"You know I'm with you?"

Her eye flicked up: *Yes.*

But what was she thinking? Really thinking? What did she want? Why was she flirting with this dumb doctor when Newton was right here? Didn't she know he was just patronizing her? I didn't want her to make a fool of herself.

"I miss you," I whispered. "There's too much happening, and we haven't been able to be together. Do you really want this?"

Yes.

"A piece of metal in your brain," I whispered. "Why am I so scared? Are you?"

She didn't look up. Did that mean no, she wasn't?

"Clinical trials," I said. "Experimental brain surgery?"

She looked up. *Yes.*

"You honest and truly want it?"

Yes.

"There you go," Dr. Howarth said approvingly. "You're talking to her, spot on."

"I might kill you," I growled.

"Sweetheart," my mother said warningly.

"Tilly," Newton said, putting his hand on my back again, making my legs feel wobbly. "Don't, okay?"

"Okay," I said.

Dr. Howarth gently put the white plastic communications board into my hand. "Here," he said. "This might help you two talk."

But I couldn't, not with everyone right there. Especially him. I felt raw from the day's events: the news article, the assembly, and now this doctor telling me how to talk to my sister.

Roo had taught me to read when she was five and I was three. She had protected me from bad dreams, from snow angels. She had told me I had the poetry of owls inside me, and she had let me choose the lines from T. S. Eliot for our dad when she'd so much rather have had Rilke's about falling stars. She was my big sister.

But right now, as I pressed my cheek to hers, she stared right past me, looking at him. At the pompous jerk, this brand-new doctor.

"I can't," I said, backing off.

"Tilly?" my mother asked.

"We've got to go," I said, bolting away from the bed. I caught Newton's eye, and he was already halfway out the door.

"The girls are very close," I heard my mother say, making excuses for me. "This has been hard on Tilly. But she's grateful, as I am. For Roo's treatment. For deciding she qualifies."

Qualifies. For the clinical trial. We wouldn't have been able to afford the best care in this special hospital for Roo, unless she was about to be an experiment.

They were giving her the top treatment possible, with the finest hospital accommodations, and all the latest technology, because the surgery had rarely been done before.

Newton and I waited in the lobby for my mother; when she didn't come downstairs right away, I knew I couldn't stay in the building another minute. Newton must have felt the same way, because he grabbed my arm, led me out the sliding doors and down the side street to his car.

I gulped fresh air, felt late afternoon sun on my face, felt free and tried not to think of Roo. She was locked in, entombed in her own body, stuck in that room upstairs.

We sat inside the car, not starting it, not speaking, just sitting, for a long time. The day had begun with that news article taped to my locker, and here we were in Boston learning that Roo was going to have a computer chip and a whole lot of gold wires connected to her brain.

"It's good news," Newton said slowly, eventually.

"How can you say that?"

"From a scientific standpoint, which is how Roo will be looking at it, it's pretty cool. I have been reading up on this stuff, figuring it would be an option for her. It's ethically weird, because most disabled persons won't be able afford it, but as long as Roo's the one who gets it, I am all in."

"Well, I'm not. Did you hear what he said about her being at higher risk for another stroke? Remember what that was like, when we thought she was brain-dead? That could happen here, Newton!"

"She wants it, Tilly. That's the bottom line. And from all I've read about BCI, it's been very successful."

"In monkeys. The poor things! I'm against lab research on animals."

"I know, it's intense. You know my dad does pharmaceutical research, and believe me, I never want to go near that field. But this might really help Roo."

"I hate that doctor," I said slowly, testing Newton. Had he noticed the flirting? Had it hurt him?

"But she likes him," Newton said.

"I don't trust him. I wanted to clock him, didn't you?"

"Yeah, it crossed my mind." So he had noticed!

"Jerk."

"But he's taking care of her, Tilly."

"For some kind of warped glory!" I said.

"I don't know," Newton said, gazing up at Boston Medical Center's dark redbrick edifice as if he could look straight into Roo's room four floors up. He felt crushed; I could see it. Newton and Roo had been together since childhood, and even though he was trying to hold them together, they were falling apart.

I didn't want that. I stared at him and felt the pain coming through his skin.

"I'm scared of the surgery," I said, my lip trembling. "Of what might happen to her."

"So am I," he said.

He reached for me, and I fumbled my way into his arms. Tears made me blind. We sat there on the Boston side street in the shadow of that huge hospital where Roo was about to have new surgery. Newton held me for a long time. His sweater smelled like Hubbard's Point: salt air, pine trees, wild thyme and sage, and Roo. *Roo*, I thought. *He smells like Roo.* And I told myself that that made holding him okay.

Chapter Nine

Roo

$\mathcal{I}$ heard the razor buzzing, scraping my scull when they shaved my head. I felt wisps of hair falling past my ears, and my bare head felt cold. What would I look like without hair? Back in Connecticut they had cut it, shaved patches, but now it was all gone.

Christina gave me a preanesthetic tranquilizer. Waiting for the chip implant surgery, even under medication, I wanted to jump out of my skin. Tilly was right; it was experimental, and I was terrified. I wanted to reach up, touch my smooth scalp to see what it felt like, but I couldn't move my arm. Being both bald and incapacitated made me want to shriek.

Drugs zoomed through my veins. They didn't drive the grief and rage away but made me feel like I was floating on them.

Dr. Howarth came into the operating room, dressed in blue scrubs. He had a small blue cap covering his long hair and a mask over his warm smile—but I could see it in his blue eyes, the way they crinkled at the corners.

I fought the drugs. I didn't want to go under. What if I didn't wake up? Or what if I did and everything was worse? I wanted to claw the tubes out of my body, run from the operating room.

"It's going to be okay, Roo," he said. "I've got you."

No, you don't, I wanted to say. *No one does. I'm alone and it's horrible.*

Somehow he knew. He crouched down so he was eye level with me. I had to fight to stay alert, to see what he was trying to say with his eyes. I saw them asking me to relax, to trust him.

"Beautiful girl," he said.

I'm quadriplegic and I'm bald! I wanted to scream.

"So lovely and brilliant. I can't wait to be able to talk to you. And this operation will allow it."

I don't want it! Stop! Make everything go back to the way it was, make me whole, make me real again. I shouted with all I had. But then something weird happened—the longer I stared into his eyes, the more I saw the smile, the patience. He was waiting for me to calm down. He knew I was wrecked inside, and he was giving me a chance to pull it together.

Will I die? I wanted to ask.

"You're going to wake up in a few hours," he said. "And I'll be right here with you. I am going to do everything I can for you. Everything. Okay?"

I looked up.

"Usually, I have my patients count backward from one hundred," he said. "But I'm going to ask you to count the f-stops on your camera, all right?"

I tried to look up in assent, but I was so drowsy.

"I'll see you when you wake up," he said. "And no more Dr. Howarth. I want you to call me Tim."

Tim, I tried to say, forgetting my voice didn't work, but the anesthesiologist had injected more and stronger drugs into my IV line, and I was out.

When I came to, I was alone. Well, I wasn't, but I didn't know that. I was in the recovery room being attended by nurses and video cameras. The temperature was nearly freezing—to prevent swelling, I learned later—and my head felt as if a truck had parked on it. I was on a respirator, and I heard the monstrous sound of air being forced into and out of my lungs.

No sign of Dr. Howarth, I mean Tim. Or had the anesthesia made me imagine he'd asked me to call him that? Had I merely wished that he had said he would be here with me when I woke up?

I went back to sleep and had many dreams. In one, Newton was giving Tilly a ride on his shoulders. They were on the beach at Hubbard's Point. I was underwater, a giant blob without arms or legs, but I could see everything. She flew like a bird, and he caught her. They kissed, and no matter how loudly I screamed, they couldn't see me under the waves.

When I woke up again, I was in my hospital room. My head hurt worse than before. My eyes were so swollen I could barely see, but the tube wasn't in my throat and I was breathing on my own. It felt as if I had swallowed a hot poker, straight from the fire.

I must have groaned, because within a second, Dr. Howarth was at my side. He read the monitors, shined a light in my eyes. My stomach heaved with nausea; he held the basin by my mouth, the way the nurses usually did.

"You did wonderfully well," he said. "You are a trouper, a champion, Roo."

Is it normal to have such a terrible headache? I wanted to ask. He didn't offer the board; I was too exhausted to talk anyway. With him sitting there, stroking my forehead with a cool washcloth, I dropped off again.

Another dream: on the beach, walking as if I were whole again, as if nothing had ever happened. It was dawn, and the sun was rising. Far ahead, I saw two little girls building a sand castle. It was Tilly and me, decorating the intricate sand structure with kelp, sea glass, and scallop shells. My heart ached, because I loved that little Tilly so much.

"But if you're me, who am I?" I asked the little girl who looked like me.

"You're dead," she said.

"No I'm not, I'm here."

"Guess again," she said.

And then I disappeared.

And I woke up. My head was bandaged. The nurses kept the incision clean. Dr. Hill came every day, more than I had ever seen him. Dr. Howarth sat with me for hours. We watched the Nat Geo Channel on television, and he set up a chessboard and said we would play when I was better.

Every time my mother came, she started off cheerful and smiling, but at some point during the visit, she cried. It got so I expected it, and was even comforted, oddly, by the sound of her soft sobbing. When I was little, the sight of an adult's tears terrified me. I wanted to believe grown-ups could never get that sad, because they knew how to control the bad things in the world.

But now I would have told her, *It's okay, I know it means you love me and are sad for the way things are. But*, I would have said to her, *this is our life now. This is the way it is. Are you going to cry through it?*

A couple of days after my surgery, Tilly and Newton came.

Tilly hugged and kissed me, and I had my usual big-sister reaction to her, wanting to reassure her that all those fears she'd had about the surgery hadn't come to pass—*Here I am, still alive, getting better.* I saw the worry in her eyes and wished I could wipe it away.

Then Newton. Oh, the way he rested his head on my shoulder. I smelled his shampoo, wanted to reach up and touch his face, feel his skin with my fingers. I'd been worried about him seeing me with my head completely shaved, but he didn't even mention it.

"You came through so beautifully, as always," he whispered. I felt his breath on my ear.

"You did," Tilly said.

Give us a minute alone, I wanted to say to her. And I expected Newton to ignore her, but he didn't.

"She's amazing, isn't she?" he said to her, not to me.

"Dude, she's incredible," Tilly said. She put up her palm, and he gave her a high five. They both laughed. He drifted away from my bedside. I saw that the high five had turned to a handclasp— their fingers entwined. And they stood there smiling at each other. Not letting go.

The handclasp and their smiles went on and on. *Am I seeing this?* I cried out, but no one heard.

My boyfriend and my sister? My mind tried to push the possibility away. I was still dreaming from before. But I heard them talking, their voices real.

"Are you feeling better?" Newton asked Tilly.

Is she feeling better? What about me?

"Yeah. Seeing her calms me down. That stupid assembly really got me going. But she loves me, she's not mad at me," Tilly said.

What assembly, and think again, Tilly—love? Not right now. I am furious at you. Back off from Newton!

They were my most important people. But now, paralyzed, I could see something developing between them, and it made me feel seasick. I began thinking back, little moments since I'd had the accident. That day when Tilly had blown up at Dr. Howarth, I'd glimpsed them touching, reassuring each other. It had bothered me a little at the time, but now it was making me insane.

By the time they left, I wasn't speaking to them, but they didn't even know. Big hugs, big kisses, see you soon. I felt crazed and jealous, imagining them in the car on the way home.

And then Isabel arrived.

"*Hola, preciosa,*" Isabel said, approaching my bed, dropping a bunch of packages on the table, holding my two hands in hers. "*¿Cómo estás?*"

No tan bien, I wanted to say to her. Not too good. *¿Y tú?* And you? How do you say *I hate my sister* in Spanish? *Did you see them in the hallway?* I wanted to ask.

"What's wrong?" she asked, sitting on the edge of my bed. She was sensitive and could always pick up my mood.

The chip wasn't online yet, I hadn't been trained, so we resorted to the good old letter board. She moved the pointer and I spelled out:

Tilly.

"I just saw her and Newton leaving the hospital," Isabel said.

Together?

"*Sí.* They drove up to Boston together."

That's not what I meant. My heart was beating so fast, and I heard the monitor starting to beep. I was in the red zone.

"You okay?" she asked, frowning with worry. She wore a rose-red angora sweater, her milagros and the pressed violets, and moonstone earrings I'd given her last Christmas.

No, I spelled on the board. *Upset about Tilly and*

But before I finished, she grabbed my hand. "I know about it," she said. "In a way, I've made it worse. I told your mother, and since the assembly, Tilly isn't speaking to me. But I had to, Roo. It was eating Tilly up, and honestly, me too."

Isabel knew about Tilly and Newton flirting? Or was there way more? What assembly? She offered the board again, and I spelled out:

???????

Nina came in to check on my heart monitor and vitals, and Isabel spent the time decorating my room with things she had brought from home. She plugged in the plastic Virgin Mary so she glowed, draped Christmas lights from fixtures hanging from the ceiling. The room felt warmer than before, less fluorescent. She gazed at my photos, especially the ones I had taken for the Serena Kader Barrois Foundation Photography Contest. When Nina left, Isabel returned to my bedside and placed the photo album and newspaper on my lap.

Dr. Howarth walked in. He nodded to Isabel but came straight to me. Leaning down, he squeezed my hand, looked into my face. I felt shocking relief to see him. He gazed into my eyes for a long time, and he saw that I was an emotional wreck.

"What is it, Roo?" he asked, handing me the board.

Everything wrong, I spelled.

"Can you tell me why? Perhaps introduce me to your friend?"

"I'm Isabel," she said. "Roo's best friend."

"I'm Dr. Howarth," he said, glancing at the album and newspaper. "Are these what's bothering you, Roo?"

"I haven't even shown her yet," Isabel said.

"May I look?" he asked.

"Yes," she said. They held the album so I could see. "It's my portfolio, for the photography contest Roo and I are entering."

The portfolios were required to have a unifying theme. Mine had been nature in the coastal environment. Isabel's had been her family's immigrant experience, including injustice at her mother's job. Shots of her mother in her waitress uniform, unsafe conditions in the kitchen, such as towels hanging by an open flame, family shots of Day of the Dead skeletons and flowers at her cousin Melanie's house, Isabel's mother's specialty mole poblano, Melanie and her sister Ana in festive pink dresses at Isabel's *quinceañera*, her uncle's new silver truck. But those photographs were gone, and her project had been redone.

Every photo was of me. Starting when we were thirteen, the year we got our first cameras and fell in love with photography together: at the beach, riding Newton's bike with Tilly balanced on the crossbar, studying at Isabel's house, accepting the science prize at eighth-grade graduation, and shots of me with my family and Newton all through high school.

When she turned the next page I gasped, nearly choked.

Me on a ventilator in my hospital bed back in New London, head bandaged, tubes everywhere. It must have been shortly after the seizure, because I was on the ventilator. My face was swollen and bruised, with stitched-up cuts on my scalp and forehead. And my eyes were open, a monster staring horribly into the void.

Is this how I look?

Next was a shot of me in this bed, here in Boston, taken from the doorway. My eyes were still open and staring, my gaze still unfocused and unintelligible.

I had to admit I admired the way Isabel had caught the daylight glinting through the clear IV tubes running from clear bottles of saline and glucose solutions hanging above my head; I cringed at the sight of my catheter flowing into the bag of brownish-yellow pee, affixed to the bed rail.

"My portfolio is dedicated to you, *mi amiga*," she said, her voice thick. "Without you, my best friend, I wouldn't even be a photographer."

"How do you feel about it, Roo?" Dr. Howarth asked.

Kind of shocked, I answered.

"Is it an intrusion, too much?" Isabel said. "I love you no matter where you are or how you look, and I want to tell the story of you. But if you say you prefer I leave these out, that is what I do."

I couldn't reply yet. I turned to the very last photo, a shot of the school auditorium. I felt a pang of nostalgia to see that old place, and tried to spot my friends, especially Newton. There he was, sitting by himself near the far-left aisle. I stared at him for a long time. Mr. Gordon and Mrs. Lansing stood onstage; behind them, on the projection screen, was a photo of me in the hospital.

What is this? I spelled.

"School assembly," Isabel said. "The day the news article came out."

"Which article?" Dr. Howarth asked.

She handed him the paper. "About texting and driving."

He read it, frowning.

What does it say? I asked.

"That you were texting with a family member," he said in a low, quiet voice.

My body felt cold, as if my blood had turned to ice. I knew what had happened, and so did Tilly, but did the whole world have to hear about it?

"I texted you, too, that day," Isabel said. "I swear I stopped once I knew you were on the way to Tilly. I would never put you in danger."

"But Tilly did?" Dr. Howarth asked.

"Yes, she did," Isabel said, head up high and sounding ferocious. "It was the last text before Roo went off the road."

Her words hung in the air, and I heard Dr. Howarth exhale a long breath.

My ice-cold blood had turned to poison. I could taste it in my mouth. My schoolmates had gathered in the auditorium to talk about me, to blame me for my own mistakes. For the first time in weeks, I pictured the old lady and her dog; I had come so close to killing them. If I hadn't texted Tilly back, that wouldn't have happened; and if Tilly hadn't barraged me with a thousand impatient texts, I never would have reached for my phone.

"Well," Dr. Howarth said after a few seconds of quiet.

"I found the phone," Isabel said.

"Right now I'm thinking of the article. It's brilliant, really," Dr. Howarth said in his British accent. "As much as it hurts, Roo, this story will help others, keep them from texting behind the wheel. You have to know that. People's lives will be saved because of you."

"It's true," Isabel said. "Everyone at school has promised to turn off their phones as soon as they get into their cars."

"Roo, you are healing from the surgery," he said. "We'll begin working on the computer in just a day or two. Everything will look brighter, dear girl. I promise it will."

"Roo?" Isabel asked, holding up the board of letters. "Please talk to me?"

I couldn't think about the article anymore, or her photo essay. My thoughts turned to something even more painful.

Tilly and Newton? I asked.

"What about them?" she asked.

Together? I asked.

"What are you talking about?" she said, sounding shocked. *Nothing.*

And she relaxed and smiled. But I knew what I'd seen. Not even the school assembly or Isabel's pictures of me looking horrible bothered me as much the memory of Tilly and Newton, right here in my hospital room, clasping hands, not letting go, as if I weren't even here.

Tilly had nearly killed me, and now she was stealing my boyfriend.

For the first time since my accident, I really thought about giving up. I thought it would be easier to just die.

Tilly

The minute I got off the school bus, I felt I'd stepped into one of those scenes you see on the news, usually at the site of a school tragedy. There were rows of TV trucks with gigantic satellite dishes and hordes of reporters with microphones.

I tried to skirt around where they were all clustered. Nona and Em got off the bus behind me. We'd kept our distance from one another since the article. But then we started texting, then seeing each other on the bus, and now we were back together. That was the TEN way.

"What happened?" I asked them.

"Uh, it's about you," Nona said, pressing even closer to me as a whole bunch of reporters came running toward me all at once. I wasn't totally sure whether Nona wanted to protect me or get into the picture. But I appreciated her being my human shield, and let her block me from them. It seemed there was an invisible line just outside the school driveway, and the reporters all stopped there.

"Mathilda!" one of them called.

"Look over here, Mathilda!" a man with a camera crew behind him shouted at me.

"Just a few questions!" called the blond reporter I remembered from the hospital.

"Have you talked to your sister about what happened? How does she feel about it?" said a woman I recognized from TV, one of the tabloid shows that Roo and I used to watch and laugh about.

"Did you mean to text her?" asked the blond reporter.

"NO!" I screamed to all of them.

Em put her arm around me. So did Nona. It felt so good to be embraced by TEN again. Then Newton walked around the news trucks from the school parking lot.

"Good thing they don't know he's Roo's boyfriend," Nona whispered. "Or they'd be all over him, too."

"Look, there's Isabel," Em said.

Isabel and her cousin Melanie were on their way into school from the parking lot, but Isabel veered toward the TV trucks. My stomach clenched as I saw her talking to the blond reporter. The woman gestured for her cameraman, and he stood behind her, a handheld camera balanced on her shoulder, shooting Isabel being interviewed.

"What's she doing?" Nona asked.

"Typical Isabel. I'm sure she thinks she's doing a public service," I said. I knew I sounded bitter, but her talking to reporters about our private pain kind of made me sick.

"Well," Em said gently, taking my hand as if to soften her words, "it is an important story, and we do want others to know the dangers of what can happen."

Even if that was true, I really couldn't take hearing it just then. A big semicircle of students had formed just outside the double doors, and I put my head down and walked right past Marlene and Andy. I expected some snarky nastiness, but no one said anything. Somehow the silence hurt even more than mean words, and I felt myself choke up.

But I had to get through this day. My first class was computer arts. I stopped at my locker without talking to anyone, went straight to the computer lab, and took a seat as far from the windows as I could. I didn't want to hear or see anything that might remind me of the TV trucks outside.

I was the first one there, early for once. I logged on, and even though we weren't supposed to check social media, I figured I'd kill a little time on Facebook. One glance at my home page made me gasp.

5 mins away

Roo's last text to me! It was all over my newsfeed, posted by lots of my friends, and as I scrolled through the site, I realized EVERYONE was sharing it. I couldn't believe it. I just stared at the screen.

We had gone viral.

The signs were all over school. I noticed them walking between classes, while I was still numb thinking about the Facebook post.

FULL MOON DANCE

Come celebrate and raise money for our friend
Roo McCabe
Sponsored by the Black Hall High Science Club

SATURDAY NIGHT,
BLACK HALL TOWN BEACH, 8 PM
Dress: Beach formal

The signs all featured photos by Roo, provided by my mother, who had given them permission to promote the fundraiser. The photos showed the moon at Hubbard's Point, in all its phases, throughout the seasons: a silver crescent glowing in rose-and-lavender twilight as the sun set over Little Beach; a half-moon caught in the bare branches of trees where owls roosted near our father's grave; the full moon shining a golden path on the snow-covered beach.

At lunchtime, I saw that a bunch of kids had set up a stand in the cafeteria, for people to make donations, buy tickets, and sign a card for Roo. Isabel was front and center; that didn't surprise me. I looked around for Newton, copresident of the science club, but he wasn't there. For some weird reason, Marlene was hanging around, selling tickets as if she cared.

"Why are you here?" I asked her.

"Because I feel really sorry for Roo," Marlene said.

"Yeah, right."

"Everyone who saw that picture in assembly cares about her, Tilly."

"I'm sure she wouldn't want the pity of someone who would smash birds' eggs."

"That's like a hundred years ago," Marlene said. "At least I didn't text my sister off the road. Did you see all the news vans outside? You're like the poster child for teen texting. And Mr. Gordon wants them there. He said it was fine as long as they don't come on school property. It's a story everyone should hear!"

I glared at her and hoped she felt my total derision. She probably hoped to get on TV.

Then I walked away, not feeling like myself at all. I went to the table where Em was already sitting.

"Hey, Tilly. They're looking for you," Slater said, coming over. "Out there, by the satellite trucks. You're the interview they want."

"I'm not talking to anyone," I said.

"It might be good," Em said. "You could tell your side of the story."

"The only person whose opinion matters is Roo," I said.

"It makes our school look so bad," Em said. "As if we're Texting Central."

"Exactly," I said. "As if Roo texting me back is the only moment in her life that counts. They should interview people about her photographs, about what a great person she is."

Em stared at me so sadly, I felt my face turn beet red. I was being a little pathetic. But it made me sick that every single thing you'd done in life could get erased in a second: And from then on, you'd be remembered for that one instant of bad judgment. Like Roo. From now on, she would be known worldwide as the Texting Teen. And I might as well have been wearing a sign, TEXTING MONSTER, around my neck.

Roo would get it. That was the crazy part. She would look at Marlene with her flat-ironed hair and fake tan, her bright-red, inch-long nails, and she'd know she was OBVIOUSLY just trying to get on TV.

Slater stood up to go sit with some of his guy friends. "Keep your head up," he said to me.

"You think I should talk to them?"

"It's up to you. Only if you have something you want to say."

He left, and Nona walked in. TEN was at our usual table. Sitting between them, I stared out the window. The trees behind school were leafing in, tiny green leaves everywhere. Roo and I had grown up sensitive to the rhythms of nature. This was the first year my father wasn't here to take us looking for signs of spring. I thought of Roo in that hermetically sealed hospital room, and knew she couldn't feel the season changing. My heart shrank down to the size of a walnut.

"What are you wearing to the dance?" Nona asked.

"The *dance*?" I asked, as if I'd never heard a more foreign term.

"Yeah, that's what I said." She rowed on the crew team, and her asymmetrical hair was turning platinum blond again, from the sun and maybe a little help from some bleach. She wore dangling owl earrings I'd given her for Christmas, and their blue-green eyes matched hers.

"My mother's sewing me a long skirt," Emily said, making a face.

"Yeah, but she's awesome," Nona said. It was true. Emily's mother was a seamstress; she had a shop called the Golden Scissors, and she made dresses for the wealthy women in town.

"I know, but homemade clothes?" Em asked.

"Well, mine will be homemade, too, sort of," Nona said. "When Althea died, Martha gave my mother a bunch of her dresses. They're gorgeous, satin trimmed with velvet and lace, all black. A couple had slips to go underneath, black and slinky with rustling petticoats. Old-school but amazing."

I nodded. She'd look stunning, like an alluring witch, with an old-fashioned black gown setting off her white-blond hair.

"How about you, Miss Tilly Mae?" Nona asked. "What are you going to wear?"

"Me? I'm not going." The words came out so fast, I barely had time to think over the possibilities. What if Newton was there? What if he asked me to dance? I could still feel him holding my hand. It was my favorite thing to think about. I'd barely been able to sleep last night, thinking about him, and losing sleep with guilt, and thinking about him again: an endless cycle of fantasy and shame.

"Get out! You have to," Nona said.

"Nope," I said.

"Tilly, first of all and mainly, it's to benefit Roo. So you have to go," Nona said, typical and bossy. "Second of all, this will cheer you up."

"It's been horrible for you," Em said.

"Yeah, slightly," I said, choking on tears. I tried to breathe, to pull myself together. "And besides, as if a dance could cheer me up."

"Oh, Tilly," Nona said, patting my back.

I folded my arms, put my head down on the table. Peeking under my elbow, I spotted Newton walk into the room, sit alone at a table by the wall. I wanted to go over, see if he was okay. What if he reached across the table, touched my fingers the way he did when were alone in the car? Would the whole school see? My body felt warm just thinking about it, and that made me feel even more horrible.

"Come with us after school," Emily said.

"I'm going straight home."

"We need a little excursion."

I didn't say yes, I didn't say no. I was thinking of how I could use a little excursion, a break from hospitals and guilt.

So after school, TEN skipped getting on the bus. We walked in a big half circle around the parking lot to avoid the TV trucks and cut through the woods into town. Black Hall had a charming main street lined with sea captains' houses and a few quirky boutiques.

We went to Ruby's for lemonade and homemade granola bars, to fortify ourselves. Then we stopped into the Golden Scissors to say hi to Emily's mom and eventually headed to Looking East, a store with lots of cool things.

Em and Nona tried on dresses, bracelets, necklaces, and hats. Shopping felt wrong and dumb to me. What did clothes matter when my sister was paralyzed?

Emily always went for the proper, preppy stuff—pink, yellow, and green, with stripes or checks or big bright flowers. Nona liked anything black, especially leather. She found a vintage motorcycle jacket and tried it on.

"This would look pretty cool over Althea's dress," she said, studying herself in the mirror.

"It's totally you," I said.

"And this is so *you*," she said, lunging for the rack and grabbing an off-white slip dress to hold up in front of me. It had skinny straps with delicate amber-colored lace and tiny copper seed-pearl rosettes embroidered around the hem and down the deep V in front. It was really beautiful, and I felt a little faint to imagine Newton seeing me in it.

"I'm not getting anything. I told you, I'm not going," I said, pushing it away. "Besides, it looks like underwear."

"That's the point!" Nona said.

"It's a little racy," Emily said, doubt in her voice.

"Tilly, it's pretty. Come on."

"I'm waiting outside," I said, feeling sick to my stomach. I sat on a bench till they finished. I didn't feel like part of TEN anymore. The things they did barely concerned me. My world had changed so drastically, and Newton was the only one who really understood.

Even worse, I found myself having almost constant fantasies about him—my sister's boyfriend.

I was officially the world's worst person.

Chapter Ten

*C*hristina moved me from my bed to the wheelchair with a tall, straight back. I felt like such a lump, unable to help at all, and I was afraid she would drop me.

"I've got you, I've got you, don't worry," she said. She was small, but very strong. She tied me in with straps; I felt them compress my chest, and heard the buckles clink.

She pushed me around the halls, no particular destination. My heart raced; I felt anxious being out of my room for the first time. I was both thrilled to leave those familiar four walls and anxious to return to my only sanctuary. I'd felt safe in there.

We passed the nurses' station and other patients' rooms. It was hard to see because I had no peripheral vision, but Christina tilted my chair each way so I could get as full a picture as possible of my corridor.

When we got to the solarium, Christina pushed me over to a table. She pulled a chair up next to me, then went to get herself a glass of water from the fountain. Because my range of vision wasn't great, I was stuck staring at an empty table. But when Christina returned, she pointed me toward two other disabled patients, in wheelchairs across the room.

"They're really nice," Christina said. "I want to introduce you. Is that okay?"

I very purposely did not look up. Christina raised the board, but I made no indication that I wanted to talk.

"Morgan is twenty-four years old, Christina said. "She had a stroke in her eighth month of pregnancy. And Dani, the woman she's sitting with, is thirty-one. She's in the army and suffered severe burns and a traumatic brain injury in Afghanistan."

I stared at the two women in wheelchairs, my eyes flooding. *Get me out of here,* I thought. *I am not ready for this.* I looked at Morgan's slumped-over posture, and all I could think about was *Did she have the baby? Was it okay? Will she recover?* And Dani looked almost as if she were wearing a mask. Her entire face had been rebuilt. She had no hair.

How could Christina think that I'd want to hang out with these poor women? How could she assume we'd have so much in common just because we'd had brain injuries? I could barely handle my own situation. I felt horrible, but I couldn't bear seeing them anymore, and I wanted to get back to my room.

"So you're not ready to meet them?" Christina asked gently, watching my face.

I stared straight ahead, cold as stone.

After a while, she wheeled me back to my room and put me back to bed. She held up the board, and I asked,

Morgan's baby?

"A little girl, Chloe. She's perfectly fine, and Morgan's husband brings her in often."

Dani?

"She is a wonderful person, Roo. It's taking time, but she is getting better. It's hard after what she's been through, but she's moving forward. She has a very positive attitude."

I felt so down, so unable to see the good. I wondered, could you only be a wonderful person if you had a positive attitude? Because just then that felt impossible to me. If I could have closed my eyes, to shut Christina and the world out, I would have.

Finally, Christina got the hint. She covered me up, gave my shoulders a gentle *You can do it* shake, and left the room.

I felt more depressed than ever. I got confused by time in here; it was hard to keep track of the hours and days, without school, work, schedules, deadlines, and plans. It was easier to just sleep.

I drifted in and out, dreaming of my father. We were sailing, in search of deeply diving humpback whales. I held the tiller with both hands, to keep the boat from heeling over, capsizing in the wild wind. I felt so strong and powerful. My father sat across the cockpit, scanning the ocean for danger.

We had been seeing whales, bright-blue mammals, not the realistic gray with white flukes, but azure as a September sky. They had disappeared, and now the sea was writhing with orange sea monsters. They had beady black eyes and fangs, and my father was gesturing, trying to help me steer through them.

I tried to call out to him, but my voice wouldn't work. No matter how loudly I yelled, he couldn't hear me because the words were trapped in my throat. I looked down into the waves and saw one of the monsters looked like Tilly.

I woke up, panicked. And Newton was sitting by my bed. Alone. No sign of Tilly, or my mother, or anyone. The machines beeped. Light streamed through the window, letting me know it was still daytime.

"Hi," he said, leaning toward me to offer the letter board.

I just stared from my bed. I didn't want to talk to him. I felt shaken by my dream; having bad thoughts about Tilly upset me.

"I needed to be alone with you," he said. "There's always someone here."

I listened, quivering inside.

"It's hard," he said. "And I feel like an idiot, saying that. I look at you, all you're going through. Who am I to complain about anything?"

My mouth made that awful wide-open yawning sound that came from nowhere; I had no control over most of the noises emanating from my body. But I saw Newton stop, frown, try to decipher the meaning, the expression on my face.

"I'm sorry, Roo. Did you say something? Could you try again, could we use the board?"

He waited for me to say something, but I felt too frozen and furious, too betrayed. My chest hurt, as if someone were standing on it. After the way he was acting with Tilly, how could I trust him? Only Dr. Howarth, Tim, knew how I really felt.

"You don't want to talk to me?" he asked, offering the board.

Tired, I spelled.

"Okay," he said. We sat in silence. Christina came in to check my IV and replenish the saline solution.

"You're Newton, right?" she asked.

"Yes, nice to meet you."

"I'm Christina. I recognize you from the pictures." She gestured at the wall, a photo of Newton in a kayak, wearing sunglasses and a big khaki canvas hat, holding up the ten-pound bluefish he'd just caught, smiling like the happiest boy in the world. "I like that one best. Looks like you ate well that night."

"It was a great day," he said, looking at me.

"I can tell," she said. "Okay, good night, you two. See you Sunday, Roo. I'm off the next two days."

She left, partly closing the door behind her. Sounds from the hall were muffled. Newton and I were alone again.

"Do you remember that day?" he asked. "How we cleaned the fish, and cooked it over a fire, and how we said we were going to go camping together this summer? And how we were going to have beach picnics together for the rest of our lives?"

I looked up. *Yes.* But I wanted to say: *Don't do this.*

"Things have changed. It's obvious," he said. "And we have to figure it out. We have to adjust, Roo. I'm the same as I was before."

I'm not.

"And inside, you are. I know you must be upset, scared, frustrated. All those things and a million more. I didn't feel too great meeting Dr. Whatever-His-Name; he seemed a little possessive of you. But he's helping you, and I can't wait for that computer to be online. I can't wait to sit here and talk for hours, the way we did out there. The important things don't change, Roo." He stopped, so choked up he couldn't go on.

I was, too. Just hearing him talk this way was beautiful, but it also broke my heart. We had been so great.

"I know you wanted to break up," he said.

He stared at me, waiting for me to look up, to agree with him. But I didn't. I just listened.

"I DON'T want to break up, Roo," he said slowly. "We've seen a lot of meteor showers, and I want us to see more. As long as there are shooting stars in the sky, I'll be here with you. We're going to cook on the beach until we get old, I swear we will. You're my life, Roo."

I couldn't let his words in. They were too painful, because they reminded me of how we were, how I was. I couldn't stand thinking of myself that way, because it was over.

You shouldn't have, I said.

"Shouldn't have what?" he asked.

Tilly!

"I don't know what you're talking about," he said. "What about her?"

Was he serious? I scoured his face for signs of a guilty conscience, but he really looked confused. He had never lied to me, tried to trick me before. But nothing in this world seemed trustworthy anymore.

I saw you holding hands.

"You're being ridiculous."

Just say you don't want me.

"Roo, that's crazy. Weren't you listening to everything I just said? I think it's you who doesn't want me!"

Besides, his name is Dr. Howarth.

"Dr. Howarth?" he asked. "Excuse me?"

You said whatever his name. It's Howarth.

"Really, Roo? Is this a bad joke? What do Tilly and Dr. Howarth have to do with us? Didn't you hear what I said about you, about how I feel?"

The door opened, and Dr. Howarth walked in.

"Was someone taking my name in vain?" he asked, then laughed and approached my bed. "Hello, Newton. How are you doing, Roo?"

Fine, I spelled.

"I don't mean to interrupt," he said. "But we are getting so close to hooking you up to the computer, Roo. I'd like to run some tests on the sensor, if you can spare the time."

"I'll leave," Newton said.

"Sorry, Newton," Dr. Howarth said. "I know it's a long drive back to Connecticut for you. If I didn't absolutely need her right this minute, I would postpone the test."

"Roo comes first," Newton said, his voice flat. "Whatever she needs."

He unfolded himself and stood, gathered his jacket and backpack together. He paused by my bedside, gazed into my face. I had the feeling he could look right into my eyes and see that I was beyond hurt, furious. I was done with him, it was time to break up—if he wouldn't do it, I would.

But here's the paradox: When he walked out the door, I wanted to call him back. I wished I could undo the knot in my mind, in my heart. I felt like a tangled ball of nerve endings. I wanted everything bad to disappear, and the magical threads that had always held Newton and me together to come back.

"That was lovely, what he said about cooking on the beach," Dr. Howarth said.

I felt startled to know he had overheard us, upset that our privacy had been invaded.

You're my life, Newton had said.

For so long I had known that was true, and he had been mine. But I wasn't an idiot. One thing about loving science: It makes a person practical. Newton was saying he loved me, but love was a feeling, not an immutable fact, and I'd seen him and Tilly. She was my sister, the closest he could come to being with the old me, the way I used to be.

Dr. Howarth stood beside my bed, removing my bandage and examining the incision that hid the chip buried in my skull. I felt the heat of the bright lamp on my scalp. A tear squeezed from my eye, and Dr. Howarth wiped it away with his fingers.

"It's okay to cry, Roo," he said. "It's very hard to let go of things we love most, to accept that life changes."

He held up the board for me.

But I do not want to let go.

"I know," he said, sounding sad. "I wish you didn't have to."

Have to? I asked.

"It makes things easier, my darling. In the long run."

My darling, Dr. Howarth had called me. Two hours ago, that would have made my heart leap. I had a crush on my doctor. He was used to seeing patients like me, girls with shaved heads and zigzag scars, who made grotesque body sounds, who couldn't speak or move, who lay in one place until their skin festered with pressure sores.

My doctor held my hand, but there was only one person on earth I had ever wanted to call me darling.

Rilke wrote: *We need, in love, to practice only this: letting each other go. For holding on comes easily; we do not need to learn it.*

Letting each other go. I had learned that lesson with my father, less than a year ago. I hadn't thought I would have to face it again so soon, or ever, with Newton. Lying in my hospital bed with Dr. Howarth holding my hand, I trembled inside, an earthquake in my chest, thinking of Newton, all the beach picnics we would miss, all the shooting stars we would never see.

As long as there are shooting stars in the sky, I'll be there.

Except he wouldn't.

And neither would I.

Tilly

*T*illy," my mother called. Lying on my bed, doing algebra, I stayed very still so she wouldn't come into my room. She was so mad at me, so disappointed in me. I couldn't stand the expression in her eyes when she looked at me. But she knocked on the door to my room, walked in, and handed me a bag. "This is for you."

"What is it?"

"It's what you're going to wear to the dance tonight."

"I'm not going," I said.

"Tonight's the full moon. It's the Full Moon Dance. You're going."

"Mom, forget it. I can't show my face there." And not only that, even worse, I was having seriously dangerous thoughts about dancing with Newton. I had to make sure that didn't happen.

She sat beside me. She pushed my book aside, saving my place with scrap paper. Crinkling open the bag, she pulled out the cream-colored slip dress TEN had picked out for me at Looking East.

"Nona called to tell me she had had the store hold it, and I stopped to pick it up for you."

"You shouldn't have done that. We don't have the money, and I am not going to the dance."

"Honey, this has been a nightmare for all of us. And I know the articles and interviews have been hard on you."

"So what?" I muttered. Ever since that first day with the news vans at school, it seemed like there had been a never-ending stream of news stories, blogs, Facebook posts. I stayed offline and away from the TV. "I don't care. I deserve it."

My stomach ached. Mom started playing with my hair the way she used to when I was little, and the way Roo always did. I closed my eyes and felt the tingles on my scalp. The feeling brought back floods of good memories. I wanted to go back in time and have Dad be alive and Roo be in the next room. The windows were open, and I heard birds in the thicket, waves breaking on the beach.

When I opened my eyes, I looked at my shelves of creatures and owl pellets, and the sight of them made me feel faint. I snuggled closer to my mother, wanting to be innocent again. Of everything.

"Are you mad at me?" I asked after a while.

"Oh, Tilly."

"I know how you must feel about me; you probably hate me," I said. I paused for her to answer, but I was terrified that she'd say yes, she did hate me. When she didn't speak, I talked faster, my words tripping over each other. "She was the good daughter, the smart one, the great one. And look what I did to her!"

My mother stopped playing with my hair. She gazed out the window, toward the beach, as if seeing our family all together on the sand, back when we were whole and happy.

"She did it to herself as much as you did," she said. "You both made a big mistake. I wish I could take it away from both of you."

"You can't."

"No, I can't."

"You gave those pictures to Mr. Gordon. And the reporters," I said, unable to keep my voice from shaking.

"I love you and Roo more than my own life, but keeping secrets isn't going to help anybody. I'm sure it felt awful to have your friends find out about the texts, but I'm glad they did. And I'm glad it's in the news. The truth might save someone's else's child."

I cringed. Maybe she was right, but didn't she know how it made me feel, how the guilt was eating me up?

"So get dressed."

"I really don't want to, Mom."

"It's a benefit to help your sister, honey. Hold your head high—you made a mistake, and you're facing it. Picking yourself up and moving forward is the right thing. It's what Roo's doing, learning how to talk a new way. I'm proud of her. Make me proud of you, too, okay?"

"By going to a *dance*?"

"Yes. Exactly because it *is* so hard to show your face, and live your life at school, that's just what you have to do. And I'm not taking no for an answer."

So my mother helped me fix my hair, pin it up in a French twist. We stood by the bathroom mirror, and she hugged me from behind. How many times had Roo stood at this very mirror, looked at her reflection? Why should I be getting ready for the Full Moon Dance and not her?

I had tried; I really had. Now I saw myself in the mirror, all dressed up. My hair looked fancy, up like this. You could see that I actually had cheekbones—who knew? I felt weird thinking it, but I looked, well, pretty. And that made my thoughts jump to Newton. Would he notice me?

My mom dropped me off at Town Beach, where a DJ had set up equipment under a gazebo decorated with tiny white lights. Janey Burke and Jeremy Stanton manned the science club donation table. The photography club had supplied refreshments, and Isabel presided over the food table. Her mother had made a huge batch of tamales; the steam rising from the cornhusk wrappers smelled good.

The night was warm, almost like summer. A light breeze blew off the Sound, pressing my cream-and-black silk lace dress against my body. Em and Nona stood by the science club booth, and I walked straight over. Nona hadn't gotten the leather jacket after all. The black dress made her look so delicate, not half as tough as she would have liked, as if she'd stepped straight out of a vintage photo. Emily looked ethereal in a shimmering white halter dress.

"Hey," Nona said to me. "You look great."

"You told my mom about the dress," I said.

"She didn't mean to upset..." Emily began, sounding nervous.

But I gave them both a big hug, pulling them close. "Thanks, Nona. Both of you."

"We never know how you're going to react these days," Nona said. "But even if you got mad, it was worth it to get you here."

"You had to come," Em said. Her gaze slid to the kids behind the science booth, especially Jeremy, her crush. Like most of the boys, he had done his best with the dress code, beach formal: He wore his father's tuxedo jacket, a white shirt, no tie, and board shorts.

Then I spotted Newton. He and Roo were copresidents of the science club; he sat in the back of the booth. He hadn't bothered to get dressed up at all. He wore the same blue shirt I could swear he'd been wearing at school yesterday, jeans, and topsiders. I waved, but he didn't see me. He faced away from the dance floor, looking out at Long Island Sound.

He wasn't going to dance. He wouldn't be asking me or anyone else. So I wouldn't dance either.

I found myself thinking of Roo.

She would have been the most beautiful girl here, bubbling over with enthusiasm, helping Isabel at the food stand, dancing with Newton and everyone else, including me. She and I had started off dancing to "Baby Beluga" when we were tiny, and we'd danced together ever since. The sound track to *The Little Mermaid*, graduating quickly to music by our parents' favorite, Bruce Springsteen, with Roo loving "Thunder Road" while I was more of a "Badlands" girl. At Christmas, we pretended we were snowflakes, twirling to music from *The Nutcracker.*

"Hey," Slater said, holding out his hand. "Will you dance with me?"

I had been thinking so powerfully about my sister, I forgot to say no. Instead, I nodded.

Slater wore a white jacket and black shirt, tie, and pants. I took his hand, and he led me to the dance floor. His arm around me felt sure and strong as we moved to a Katy Perry song. He didn't know I was numb, only half-there. My eyes kept darting to Newton.

"You look beautiful," Slater said.

"No, I don't," I said.

"You're not big on taking compliments, are you?"

"I'm okay at it," I said. "Sometimes."

He laughed, and we just danced. Out by the beach road, the fleet of media trucks had parked, wheels in the sand. Their lights were bright.

"Looks as if they don't want to miss the big event," I said.

"Don't think about them," Slater said. "This is for Roo. We're all here for her, Tilly."

The music changed and a slow dance began to play. Kids drifted on and off the floor. Isabel waved us over, served us cups of lemonade. She looked beautiful in a copper-colored silk blouse and long black skirt, and ornately tooled silver disc earrings, and I felt the lemonade was meant as a peace offering.

"Did you hear, someone from town has offered to match whatever science club raises for Roo?" she asked. "Mr. Gordon got a call on Friday."

"Who is it?" I asked.

"I don't know. The donor wants to stay anonymous," Isabel said.

"I'm sure it will help," Slater said. "Her treatment must be expensive. My mom's costs a fortune." ·

"It is, but her hospital expenses seem to be covered," I said, thinking of Dr. Howarth and his clinical trial.

"Really, how?" Isabel asked.

"Dr. Howarth has his ways," I said.

"Oh, he is wonderful," Isabel said. "I met him last time I visited, and he was so supportive of Roo, and even of me. My photography."

"I hope he doesn't hurt her," I said.

"How would he?" Isabel asked.

"She thinks they're really close. Friends. But he's just being professional."

"Hey, she loves Newton. End of story. But if bonding with her doctor gets her through, it's okay with me. He's the best there is." ·

"Yes, we're so lucky," I said sarcastically.

Isabel laughed and pulled me close. "Tilly, you are something else, you know that?"

She kissed the top of my head, but I flinched away. I couldn't help it; I wasn't ready. I didn't doubt that she loved Roo, but things had changed between us, and I wasn't sure they'd ever go back to the way they were.

A fast song came on and the DJ cranked it, and people got all excited. Isabel began to dance with Slater and, really not getting the hint, gestured for me to join in. As if I would.

I backed a few steps away.

"Come on, Tilly," Slater said, holding out his hand.

"Not my music," I said.

"Swim, I dare you!" someone yelled from down the beach, and I was glad for the distraction, because both Isabel and Slater turned to look.

"Sharks come at night!" someone called back.

"Skinny-dip!" Nona shouted.

"You wouldn't!" Em said.

"Yeah, I would; *you* wouldn't," Jeremy said.

"The moon hasn't come up yet—let's wait for it."

"I'll moon you!"

"Bite me!"

"Sharks are gonna bite you."

Squeals and cheers, and a whole group of kids—ones I liked, mainly, with Marlene and her prissy crew standing back, lest their mascara run—tore down to the water's edge where the gazebo lights didn't reach and began peeling off their clothes to splash into the cold Sound in their underwear. *Roo would love this*, I thought. We both adored swimming at night, had grown up doing it the way other kids go skateboarding—edgy, slightly dangerous, but thrilling.

"Shark," Teddy Messina yelled.

"Great white or tiger?" Janey Burke called.

"You're not being funny," Emily called. "If you want me to come in, you'd better stop saying shark."

Nona whooped and tackled her from behind, and she and Jeremy threw her in and dove after her. Emily laughed, splashing them both, swimming away and making Jeremy follow.

I saw Newton leave the science booth, as if he felt as apart from the fun as I did. He walked down to the tide line but instead of heading left, toward the pack of swimmers, he began to run, fast, in the opposite direction, toward the wilder nature-refuge end of the beach.

My heart skipped; I had the sudden feeling he was going to do something desperate. I began to follow him.

"Tilly!" Slater called after me.

Isabel said something to him, but I didn't hear, and I was glad they didn't come after me. I kicked off my shoes and walked barefoot onto the sand. Newton was moving so fast, he was almost out of sight. I ran along the tide line, my feet hitting pebbles, sharp shells, and slippery trails of wet seaweed. The sand was hard and packed, so I picked up speed.

The tide was rising, and the waves' front edges splashed my legs and the hem of my dress. The farther I went, the more the music and gazebo lights faded in the distance. The moon still hadn't risen; the beach was very dark.

Growing up at Hubbard's Point, five miles down the coastline, I rarely came to Town Beach, so the terrain was unfamiliar. I vaguely remembered that a bight ran south from the inland marshes down to the water's edge, cutting a sharp, deep trench in the beach; it would widen with tonight's incoming, spring tide—one of the highest of the year because of the full moon—but I was pretty sure it was another half mile ahead.

I stubbed my toe on a rock, and yelped. Stopping to check the damage, I saw my big left toe bleeding like crazy. I had nothing to wrap around it, so I limped along on my heel, trying to keep my toe out of the sand. I felt really unsteady.

Where was Newton? My nerves were jumping. Where had he gone? I already felt responsible for one tragedy, my sister, and I wasn't sure I could live with another.

I scanned the beach, the white sand a little brighter than the upland grasses and scrub oaks and pines that grew along the berm, but I didn't see him. I could no longer make out the music playing back at the dance, but the thumping bass merged with the sound of surf. My foot was killing me, but I didn't care—I started to run. And I decided I couldn't take the chance of something happening to him, so I called out.

"Newton!"

No answer, so I picked up speed. What if he'd gone into the water, started swimming straight out; what if he needed help?

"Newton?"

Nothing, but then, "Tilly, watch out!"

I felt the sand beneath my feet give way, and I slid downhill into rushing, cold water. I went under once, twice, grabbed a breath, went down again, falling straight into the bight. Then I was treading water, gasping for breath and trying to figure how to climb up the sandy bank that had given way. I had misjudged the distance, fallen into the tidal bight.

Something splashed beside me and grazed my leg. I thought of my friends yelling shark and blindly struck out at the dark shape, gulping with panic. Strong arms held me, pushing me up to the surface so I could catch my breath and find my own strength. Treading water, I came face-to-face with Newton.

Hair dripping, fully dressed, he half held me.

"What were you doing?" he asked.

"Chasing you! I was worried."

"Tilly," he said, shaking his head, hitting me in the eye with his wet hair.

"Hey," I said, pushing him under.

"Hey yourself," he said, returning the favor.

I gasped, and suddenly we were having a wrestling match, teasing and dunking each other the way we had a thousand times, my left leg hooked around his right, so relieved he was okay, I accidentally swallowed a big mouthful of water. I coughed, and he pounded me on the back, and our bodies were pressed against each other, and my arms went around him. And we kissed.

I'm not sure whether he kissed me or I kissed him, but his lips tasted salty and hot, and my body turned inside out, and I gripped his arms so hard I think I bruised him. His body blazed against mine in the rushing tide; we were lost in nature, grief, and the night. We rode the current just off the beach, and I could imagine letting the ocean take us all the way out.

I pulled away from him. Looking east, I saw an orange glow on the horizon. The light seemed to float on the water, then spread across the waves, ripples of gold. It was the full moon rising out of the sea. It always looked gigantic upon rising, and Roo had explained to me why: It was known as the moon illusion and had to do with refraction and apparent distance. I could have asked Newton more details, he would know, but suddenly I'd been struck silent.

We swam to shore. I crawled up on the sand, my hair dripping and my new dress ruined. He inched his way along, stood up and shook like a wet dog.

"You lost your glasses," I said.

"They fell off when I tried to pull you out," he said. "It's not too deep in there. I'll find them."

"I'll help you look," I said.

He reached for my hand. We clasped fingers.

We stood staring at each other. The moon had turned from gold to silver, and its path was so bright, I felt I could turn and run across the waves, escape from both Newton and what had just happened. But I didn't want to.

"Oh, Tilly," he said.

"I fell in. I wasn't being careful," I said.

"I got so worried," he said. His face was an inch away from mine. "I thought you could have drowned."

"I thought that about you."

Our lips brushed. His nose bumped mine. He was a foot taller, and had to bend down to rest his forehead against mine.

My heart, my blood, every inch of my body was tingling. Our hands were still clasped. I realized I'd been wanting this to happen for weeks, since right after Roo's accident, when we'd started getting close.

"You're the only one who gets it," I said.

"Same with you," he said.

"But Roo."

"She doesn't love me anymore," he said.

"I don't believe that."

"I saw her two days ago, and she's changed. Not the outside part, the way she looks. That's obvious, and not what I'm talking about. But inside. She's pulled away from me."

"You don't have to let her," I said. And I meant it. But I also wanted Newton to hold on to me, to kiss me again, to want to be with me.

"It's her choice," he said. "She deserves to have this one, she has so few others. She wants to leave me."

There was nothing I could say to that. It felt like she wanted to leave all of us. And that made everything so confusing. I wanted to feel Newton's arms around me, to lie next to him in the sand and get warm. And that made me feel so guilty, I shook my head like a wet dog, drops flying everywhere.

"Whoa," he said. "You okay?"

"I messed up," I said.

"With the text?"

"For sure. And maybe with this?"

"This?"

"You know," I said. Did I have to spell the kiss out for him?

"Yeah, I do. Maybe we've both messed up."

My heart dropped. I half wanted him to contradict me, to say this was just what he wanted. But the idea of that made me slightly sick. Being with Newton behind Roo's back was just wrong. Even though I knew that, I wanted him to hold me again. What was the matter with me?

He hugged me then. Held me tight so my body was pressed against his, our clothes soaking wet but our skin burning hot. We stayed that way for a few seconds, and then he let me go.

"Want me to help you find your glasses?" I asked.

"I think you'd better go," he said.

"Yeah," I said. "Me too."

He touched my cheek and walked away, toward the bight, to dive in and look for his glasses. He was right to tell me to go. But I couldn't leave him searching in rushing water, after dark, by himself. Standing there, I swear there were two of me. The part that wanted to be a good sister, to be loyal to Roo. And the part that wanted more kisses from Newton, more everything.

So as the moon rose higher and flooded the beach with white light, I sat on the cold sand by the narrow stream, arms around my knees drawn up to my chin, shivering so hard I felt I might shake apart. And I watched over my sister's boyfriend as he dove and dove for his glasses, and tried not to think about our kiss, yet unable to think of anything else.

Once I saw that he was safe, that he had found his glasses and wasn't going to drown, I left the beach. I started walking home along the sandy lane. But when I got to the main road, I knew I couldn't face my mother. I still tasted Newton's kiss on my lips, felt the pressure of his arms around my shoulders, and I couldn't bear to walk into the house where I'd grown up with Roo.

So I went left and stayed along the road's shoulder, ducking out of the streetlight when the occasional car drove by. I passed the bait shop and dock, the fish market, and Paradise Ice Cream. It was past ten p.m., and the businesses were long closed. My curfew was one, but even if I didn't make it home by then, my mother would assume, or at least hope, that I was having fun at the dance.

I'm not sure I had a plan, but my feet seemed to know where they were going. I tried not to think about Newton. Or how the only other time I'd been kissed I'd also wound up falling into salt water.

How different tonight had been. I suddenly, confusingly, knew what the word *passionate* meant.

I passed the graceful, white Episcopal church set back from the road, and a few hundred yards north, I passed the thrift shop. The turnoff to town came next, but I stayed on Shore Road and headed up the rise that overlooked the skein of tributaries and marshes coming off the Connecticut River.

When I got to the creek where Roo had had her accident, I sat on the bank. I heard the water gently rushing in, and saw it sparkling in moonlight. Roo's shattered glass and taillights glinted, embedded in the silt. I looked up and saw a shape gliding overhead: an owl hunting the marsh. The sight eased the pressure in my chest and connected me to my father and Roo: *Wait for the early owl.*

I sat there a long time. My dress glittered with beach sand, but mostly it had dried. My mind was pretty empty, and I wanted it that way. There wasn't much I could bear to think about. And I definitely didn't want to go home.

Eventually, I began to walk again. Instead of heading back toward Hubbard's Point, I went down Ferry Road. Some houses were dark, but the blue one with the coral pink door had a few lights on. The barking began as soon as I stepped foot on the driveway.

Martha opened the door even before I climbed the front

steps. Lucan bounded out, greeted me, thumping my legs with his tail.

"Hello, Tilly," Martha said.

"I know it's really late," I said. "I'm sorry to intrude."

"You wouldn't be here if it wasn't important," she said.

"My sister," I said, my voice starting to shake. "You were with her after she crashed. Yours was the face she saw and the voice she heard."

Martha nodded, looking at me with a steady gaze.

"I wanted to thank you. For being with her. When she needed someone. It should have been me."

"You mean you should have been the person to find her?"

"The wrong sister got hurt," I said, my voice breaking. "I'm horrible. I should have been the one."

"Come inside," she said, putting her arm around my shoulders.

We walked through her big house, spookily lit by flame-shaped bulbs in Victorian brass sconces, blackened by time and salt air. In spite of the spring night, she had a fire burning in the library, where the two threadbare velvet chairs faced the hearth, and she settled me in one, wrapped a plaid shawl around my shoulders, and went to get tea.

I stared at the flames, letting their quick dance quiet my mind. Lucan stayed beside me, his big noble head resting on crossed paws, and together we watched the fire. Martha soon returned with a tray.

She had made tea in a brown English teapot, and poured it into two bone china cups with violets on them. Shortbread was stacked on one plate, and two dog biscuits for Lucan were on another.

"Thank you, it's delicious," I said, sipping the tea.

"I'm glad you like it. It's from the herbs in our garden. This mixture is called Maytime—chamomile, bee balm, peppermint, and rosemary. Althea was the best gardener I ever knew. When I drink this tea, I remember how much she loved it here, all the tender care she showed her plants, and Lucan . . . and me."

"Your sister," I said.

"Yes," she said. "From the minute I met you, I knew we were kindred spirits."

"Because we have sisters?"

"And because we feel responsible for what happened to them."

I glanced up, over the rim of my cup. She was staring at the fire through her wire-rimmed glasses. She must have been getting ready for bed when I arrived; she wore a flowing white nightdress with a black shawl wrapped around her shoulders; her long, white hair cascaded down her back. She looked so sweet. What would she think of me if she knew I'd kissed Newton?

"You took care of Althea," I said. "Nona told me."

"I did. I wouldn't have missed a minute of it."

"I wish I could take care of Roo."

"Maybe someday you can. For now, I'm sure your visits give her a lot of hope."

"I don't think so," I said, my heart twisting.

"How is she doing?"

"In some ways better. You mentioned hope—she has a doctor she likes, and he says maybe she'll even take photographs again."

"Oh, that would be wonderful!"

"I can't see how she'd do it—she can't move a muscle."

"The doctor wouldn't have told her if there wasn't a chance—he wouldn't do that to her. She must have a talent."

"She does! She's amazing."

"Then she has to take pictures. In order to heal and thrive, she must. When we were young, Althea and I loved to sing. We went to a harmony workshop in the mountains of West Virginia. It was right in the heart of Appalachia, and our teacher grew up singing with her sisters. She told us that singers have to sing, or they get sick. A person has to use her talents, Tilly."

I listened, thinking about that.

"Althea did. She loved to sculpt. Even when she got older and wasn't able to do as much, we made sure she got into her studio every day. We hired two students to take her piece to the forge."

"And did you sing?" I asked.

"Yes. Every night before bed—you saw the piano. I'd play, and we'd both sing, in the harmony we learned in those mountains. It was our secret language: song."

"You helped her," I said. "Why did you say you felt responsible?"

"We can have the best intentions," she said. "And still hurt the person we love so much. I saw what I wanted to see—that Althea was getting better, recovering from pneumonia—a complication from her illness. Then, one night, she begged me to take her into the herb garden. It was a night just like this—warm, bright with the moon."

"She wanted to see it rise?"

"Yes." She tilted her head back, looking through the window at the sky. "Sometimes it's hard to believe that's the same moon. The very same one Althea saw that night, the one we used to watch as girls. But it is—the moon never changes."

"What happened to her?"

"We stayed out for an hour," Martha said. "We sang songs about the moon, every single one we could think of."

"It sounds wonderful. She must have been happy," I said, my throat aching with tears

"Oh, she was. We both were. But her lungs were very frail. She'd been sick for a year, and her respiratory system was compromised. The air felt balmy, so I thought she would be fine. But in fact, it was the worst weather for her; clear and cold would have been better. The humidity made it hard for her to breathe. It was like damp cotton filling her lungs. She died in my arms, right outside, on the terrace, before the ambulance arrived."

"I'm so sorry, Martha," I said. I tried to imagine how it must have felt, and my heart broke for her.

"I thought I was helping her, giving her what she wanted, the chance to be in our beloved garden and see the moon. She seemed fine one moment—but she was dying the next."

"You didn't know!"

"No, I didn't."

We sat still for a long time, thinking of our sisters. Moonlight slanted through the mullioned windows, casting shadows on the faded rug. I glanced over at Martha and knew that I was sitting in Althea's chair; I wondered how often the two Muirhead sisters had sat here, how many moonrises they had watched over their decades together.

"I kissed my sister's boyfriend tonight," I blurted out.

"You did?"

I nodded. "He was rescuing me because I fell into the bight—" I stopped myself. "I don't want to give excuses, it doesn't matter how it happened, it just did."

"Do you love him?"

I thought about that. I pictured all of us together over the years: running on the beach with Roo and Newton, riding in the car with them, taking the bus to school with them, swimming in Long Island Sound with them. Them. I loved them together, and I loved Newton as a part of them.

But I also loved him separately.

"I do, sort of," I said. "I'm just not sure how."

"You don't want him to disappear from your life," Martha said.

"No."

"Maybe you feel that if you keep him close, it will bring her back."

I gave that some thought. Martha refilled our teacups and passed me a piece of shortbread. It tasted delicious, with an unusual flavor. I saw a tiny lavender flower baked into the dough and realized she put herbs in everything, even sweets.

Maybe this was her way of keeping Althea close, using her herbs all through the day, in everything she did.

"Could you tell me something?" I asked.

"What?" she asked.

"What exactly happened after Roo's crash?" It took all my courage to ask. Martha took a deep breath, closed her eyes as if remembering—or maybe pulling up the strength it would take to tell me.

"I saw the car coming, and heard it hit Lucan," she said.

I saw her watching for my reaction, and I steeled myself not to flinch so she would go on.

"My first thought was for him," she said. "He'd been thrown clear, and was trying to run. I grabbed him, held him, so he wouldn't hurt his leg more. But the car had flipped. I heard the metal crunch, and the glass break, and I thought there was no way anyone inside had survived."

"But she had."

"Yes. I heard her cry out, so I ran over, looked in, and she was hanging upside down, held in place by her seat belt. And she asked for Lucan. She was so injured, but her thoughts were for him."

"That's Roo. That's who she is."

"She mentioned someone else," Martha said. "You."

"Me? Why me?"

Martha leaned forward, looked at me with the gentlest gaze ever. It made my heart seize, and I was afraid to hear.

"She thought she was dying. She was bleeding hard, and the trauma was obviously great. She told me, 'Tell Tilly it's not her fault.'"

"Oh my God," I said.

"She believed she didn't have long—and honestly, neither did I."

"Everything is so broken between us now."

"No," she said. "It's not."

"You haven't seen her. You don't know, Martha."

"I know one thing, Tilly. When it comes to sisters, there's no such thing as broken."

"I can't face her again."

"You can, Tilly. She needs you. And . . ." Martha bit her lip, looked into the fire, then back into my face. "Even more, you need her. Your sister is strong—I can still see the purpose I saw in her eyes that terrible day, hear the resolve in her voice. You are the tender one here. I know you don't believe that, but it's true. You need her."

"I don't deserve her," I whispered.

Then Lucan barked, and the doorbell rang. It was my mother—Martha had called her while she was making tea. I stood up from my seat by the fire, and sand trickled from my drying dress onto the floor. My mother thanked Martha, and I suppose I did, too, and we said good night and walked out into the brilliant light of the full moon.

Chapter Eleven

Roo

r. Howarth connected the tiny gold wires leading from the electrode planted in my brain to a bundle of connections attached to the laptop and the computer-brain interface program he had designed just for me. Yes, wires in my brain. The idea terrified me so much I could barely think.

"Picture the cursor moving, Roo," he said. "Watch it on the screen and tell it where to go on the keyboard. Thought into action, that's what CBI is all about."

I was propped up in bed, and the computer was set up on a tray table in front of me. The screen was open and blank except for a cursor. He told me a lot about how CBI relies on signal acquisition and signal translation, device output and operating protocol, but the basic idea was for me to picture moving the cursor across the keyboard, typing out my thoughts.

I tried.

Move, cursor!

It didn't budge.

I felt like a blocked magician, trying to pull a rabbit out of a hat, or attempting to push a vase off a table, using only mind control. And I felt total panic, because if this didn't work, what would I do?

"Your only job is to move the cursor," he said. "You don't have to think about your brain, or electrical impulses, or how it works. It's just between you and the cursor."

I tried, I concentrated, I talked to the cursor. Beads of sweat popped out on my forehead, rolled into my eyes. I heard embarrassing little *eek*s of frustration emanating from my mouth.

"Let's take a break," he said.

I didn't want to, but I felt exhausted.

"As a little girl, you learned to read," he said. "And you tried so hard. Every letter, every word took enormous concentration. Perhaps your teacher asked you to 'sound out' the words. And you did. And as you grew up, and you loved to read, it became second nature. You didn't think about how to do it—you just did it. Your mother told me you would read all night if she let you. It became easy, a joy. That's what will happen here, Roo."

Nina came in to check on a pressure sore on my hip that had become infected. She was one of my favorite nurses, with shoulder-length dark hair and big brown eyes, a wide smile that always lifted my spirits.

"Oh, you're busy," she said. "I'll come back later."

"That's okay, we're taking a break," Dr. Howarth said. He stepped away while she swept the curtains around my bed for privacy.

"You're doing great," she said to me. "Don't get discouraged—the first part is always the hardest, but then it will become second nature—it really will. Are you using mindfulness on this? Your deep breathing?"

One day last week, Nina had come into my room and pulled a chair right up to my bed.

"Roo," she'd said. "You know I'm mainly an RN. I'm also a meditation teacher. Dr. Hill asked me to see if you might like to try it. Do you want to hear about it?"

I was curious, and I loved Nina, so I looked up.

"Okay," she said. "It's simple. It's called mindfulness. It helps with 'monkey mind'—the way our thoughts are constantly jumping around, up and down, like a monkey swinging through a tree."

Now I was really interested—my mind did exactly that, all the time.

"The idea is not to stop the thoughts—they will come, that's normal. But we can stop following them, and learn to let them go. So instead of worrying everything to death, chewing it over and over, we allow the thoughts to come and go. But our mind needs somewhere peaceful to land—our breath." She paused and took a breath herself. "That's right— so simple, and right here, wherever we are, in this very moment. So you breathe in and you breathe out. And you feel the breath coming into your body, and you feel it leave; your chest rises, then falls. And that's where you put your attention. Okay?"

I looked up.

"Let's do it a few times," Nina said. "Bring your attention to your breath, and let it whisk gently through your mind. Notice if it's a deep or shallow breath."

At first I wanted to tell her it was stupid; what good could it do? I must have sputtered, because she gave me a small smile of encouragement.

"That's okay," she said. "Stay with it. Let your thoughts and feelings in your heart come up, and let them go. Don't follow them. Stay with your breath."

I focused on the feeling of air coming in and out of my nose. Hurriedly at first, then a little calmer. My breath became steadier. And you know what? My thoughts weren't so brutal. Instead of feeling total despair, that I would be in this condition, this exact place, feeling so betrayed and brokenhearted, I felt myself right here with Nina, alive and breathing. And for that moment I was okay. I was fine. The thoughts weren't so overwhelming. They were like monkeys, but this time high in a canopy of tree branches overhead.

Now, while Dr. Howarth waited outside, Nina removed my dressing, cleaned the sore, applied Silvadene ointment, and taped on a clean bandage. I took the time to breathe deeply, and I knew Nina was doing it with me. Somehow I had the feeling she had come in on purpose, knowing I needed her. By the time she'd finished changing the dressing, I was calm, and my thoughts of despair and frustration weren't dominating me.

I was ready to start again and signaled Nina by looking up.

"Good girl," she whispered, kissing my forehead. "You can do it."

Thank you, I wanted to say. I really did have a team here, and as I prepared for this big step, I felt them with me.

Nina pulled back the curtain, and I saw Dr. Howarth sitting in the chair by the window, checking his phone. He was unguarded, looking away for a second, and my heart skipped at the sight of him. My mom had stuck by my side, and Isabel, but with the other important people in my life disappointing me, leaving me, he was my rock. He was so steady and patient, and he understood me, and I knew I could count on him.

He beamed when he saw me, moved closer to my bed. That shock of brown hair fell into his startling blue eyes; I would have liked to brush it back for him.

"Is this too much for today, Roo?" he asked. "Should we stop for now and start up again tomorrow?"

He held the letter board up for me, his pen ready to point to the letters.

No, I spelled. *I want to do it now.*

"That's my girl," he said. "I love your determination."

Nina gave me a big smile and a thumbs-up and left the room.

Okay, I am ready, I said.

"You'll be expressing yourself with lightning speed; this computer will be an extension of your central nervous system," he said in the English accent I could have listened to all day. But I had a job to do; deep down, I wanted to make him proud, I wanted to see the pride in his eyes as I had once seen it in my father's. And I wanted to feel proud of myself, too.

He was still speaking, his words and phrases flashed through my mind: *electrocorticograph . . . don't hold your breath, it's important that you're breathing in and out, that's a girl . . .*

focused commands, Roo, not vague thoughts . . . cursor up, cursor down . . .

Dr. Howarth was right beside me, but I went deeply into myself, the quietest part of my being, and I breathed steadily. I felt my lungs expand and contract, and I let all my thoughts and worries go. I looked at the cursor on the screen, poised beneath the row of letters and words. Here I was, breathing. In and out, and I knew: *I can do this. And I can do it right now.* Then I told that little arrow on the blue screen to go up.

The cursor moved up.

Dr. Howarth leaned forward but did not speak—now he was holding *his* breath.

I told the cursor to move to the letter *I*, and then a space, and then the letter *a*, then *m*, a space, then *h*, easily to *e*, *r*, back to *e*.

I meant to spell *I am here*, but it came out *I sm neeerrr*.

"That's it, Roo. That's the way!"

No, it's not, I thought. *That's not what I'm trying to say.*

"Try again," he said. "What's your name?"

Eooo.

"Almost," he said. "Give it another try."

Roo.

"Oh my God," he said. "Oh, Roo! My wonderful Roo! Oh, let me lift you up and spin you around!"

He hugged me, long and hard. I smelled his sandalwood-scented shampoo. I wished I could move my arms so I could hold him. In this hug was a strange, terrible anger at Newton. Dr. Howarth's hair smelled different, his arms around me felt more muscular, he wasn't wearing glasses, and he wasn't looking at my sister, and he was proud of me.

Tilly. Inexplicably, my next thought was *Wait till Tilly finds out what I can do. We have so much to talk about.*

And then I just lay still, basking in the fact I had learned something new, something wonderful.

It took a few more sessions to get better with CBI. It was the hardest thing I'd ever done, one step forward, two steps back. I developed a fever. They were worried my brain would start to swell, so I had to stop working and try to get some rest. The fever and anti-inflammation drugs made me sick, so I had a whole day of doing nothing but throwing up. I was too tired to even think about CBI.

Dr. H worked with me all day. And when he went home, I practiced meditation to keep from going crazy. The fact that I couldn't move gave me lots of time. And the more I focused on my breathing, the less tortured I felt about being paralyzed, about not knowing what the future would bring. It didn't work all the time, but it helped.

My mother visited, but I wasn't ready to try using the computer until I got better at it. Some days, mindfulness went out the window, and my frustration was killing me. I kept making mistakes, and my heart rate would increase to the point of worrying everyone, including me. It was an awful feeling, having my pulse pound so hard I thought I'd explode. It helped when Nina sat with me, which she did nearly every shift when she could grab a few minutes.

"Let's talk some more," Dr. Howarth said one day in May. "Are you game?"

Yes.

"Ah. Wonderful."

What we talk booottt? I asked.

"Take your time," he said. "Concentrate on each letter."

So I corrected myself: *What should we talk aboot ahout?*

"So many possibilities," he said.

Possibilities, I spelled.

"That is excellent, Roo."

Thank you.

He beamed. "You're welcome."

Although I'd been working for days, the breakthrough happened all at once. I got the hang of it, and suddenly the ease and fluidity of moving the cursor to express my thoughts filled me with surprise and happiness. He had said this would happen, and quickly, but I suppose I hadn't really believed it.

"Tell me what you love about photography," he said.

The camera tells the story that's in my heart.

"Really? In what way?"

I photograph what is beautiful to me, and then I have a record of what I love.

"Marvelous!"

I had the feeling he meant not what I had said, but that I could say it, that I had found the ability, using his system, to express myself.

I would like to photograph you, I said.

"Would you, now?" he said, grinning. "I make a rather poor subject, don't I, compared to your lovely pictures of the seacoast and the night sky? And your family?"

You are important to me. I blushed, wondering if he would get the link about photography, my heart, love, and wanting to photograph him.

"Thank you, Roo. And you are important to me, my darling girl. Oh, look! Here's Dr. Hill!"

Dr. Hill walked in, tall and elegant with his hooked nose and white mane, the elder statesman of neurology, but even he couldn't hide his excitement.

"What's this I am hearing about Miss McCabe having a breakthrough?" he said in his stentorian voice. A woman wearing a lab coat trailed behind him. She looked about thirty and had curly reddish-brown hair that reminded me of Tilly's.

It's all because of Dr. Howarth, I said.

"No, it's you, Roo," Dr. Howarth said.

"Spectacular," Dr. Hill said.

We were discussing photography, I said.

But my two doctors and the third were deep in their own conversation; they moved out of my field of vision to examine the cap and electrodes I wore on my head. I felt someone prodding my scalp, and I heard them talking.

"Intensity of pulses?" Dr. Hill asked.

". . . stimulated with biphasic TMS, occipital cortex site . . ."

"You were right . . . binary information . . . I see you changed the electrode positions on the scalp sites . . ." the woman said.

"Spatial filter, F4, T7, C3 . . ." Dr. Howarth said, and the list went on.

I stared at the computer screen. I had so much to say—not just to Dr. Howarth, but to the world, and even to myself. I wondered if I could start a journal, keep it private. Reading poems had always eased my heart, but I was not a poet. When we were young, and my mother was in graduate school, getting her teaching certificate, she used Tilly and me as guinea pigs for her classes. For one of them, she decided to have us write haiku, and I had loved the simplicity.

The hospital bed
Is the river of blue
And I am the boat.

"What's that you say?" Dr. Howarth asked, reading over my shoulder.

A haiku.

"How wonderful," Dr. Hill said, then, "We are going to keep you busy, Roo. Measuring brain waves and cognition."

"I'm going to call your mother now," Dr. Howarth said. "To report on this new level of progress. And I'm sure she will tell the rest of Team Roo. Oh, by the way, we have another team member for you to meet. Roo, this is Dr. Amy Gold."

Hello, I said to the doctor with the Tilly-colored hair.

"Roo, it's a pleasure and honor to meet you. I've been hearing so much about you from everyone here, and I've had some long talks with Dr. Danforth in New London. She thinks the world of you, and she sends her best regards."

My heart skittered, thinking of Dr. Danforth, of how much I relied on her those first weeks. I pictured the warm look in her eyes, the little teddy bear pin she always wore.

Nice to meet you. And plaszze ell r sai hi.

I took a deep breath, remembered to keep breathing, focused on the cursor, and redid it: *Please tell her I say hi.*

"I will," Dr. Gold said.

"Roo, we have tired you out. It's normal to confuse letters and miss a few, especially at this phase. It's not a setback. Please don't worry. We are going to let you rest now. You should feel a tremendous sense of accomplishment," Dr. Howarth said. "I cannot tell you how proud I am. Just over the moon."

Im vrr th moon tooo.

"Good," he said. "That is what I want to hear. Rest now, and I'll see you later."

Okay. Thank you.

They left my room, and for the first time since I had first woken up in the hospital, I felt a sense of peace. Being heard and understood, knowing there was no limit to what I could say, made a difference. It made all the difference.

Just before I fell asleep, I remembered that tonight was the full moon. And the kids at Black Hall High were having a dance to raise money for my care. I'd felt both embarrassed and frustrated when I first heard about it. I hated that I needed help, and that I couldn't be there.

But tonight I felt okay. Things were getting better. Just a little, but better.

I let myself drift off, and I dreamed of my haiku, that small boat on a big sea. It was night, and the full moon traced a path on the sea. I was sailing, I could hear music from the dance and see harbor lights up ahead, but someone was missing.

I was alone in my boat, but there should have been two of us.

Tilly

I couldn't sleep all night. When I came down for Sunday breakfast, my mother was sitting at the table, drinking coffee. She wore one of my father's old flannel shirts over her nightgown, and she looked as if she hadn't slept either.

"Would you like to explain how you ended up at Martha Muirhead's house instead of the dance?" she asked.

"I told you last night."

"You told me you 'felt like taking a walk.' That didn't sound right."

I poured cereal and milk into a bowl, stirred it around, not eating it.

"You went swimming in your new dress?" she asked.

"I fell in, Mom. I feel horrible—I know it cost a lot, and I'll pay you back for it."

"The price of the dress is not the point," she said. "What happened last night? Were you drinking?"

"No."

"Both Nona and Em have called here this morning. They were worried about you, too."

"There is nothing for anyone to worry about," I said. "I have to go see Roo today."

"You can drive up with me." It was Sunday, and my mother always spent the entire day with Roo. She'd bring books, and lunch, and papers to correct and stay until dinnertime. But I didn't want her there today.

"I want to go alone."

My mother peered at me as if I'd said I wanted to swim to the Arctic.

"Just how are you going to do that? You're fourteen, two years till you can drive. If ever."

"The train. You can drop me off at the station."

"I don't think that's a good idea after what happened last night. You haven't been showing the best judgment lately. Besides, I want to see her, too."

"Mom . . ."

"If you want to come, get dressed and we'll leave soon. She'll be happy to see us—Dr. Howarth called last night to say she's getting really good on the computer. And he wants me to bring her camera."

Thirty minutes later, we were on our way. I stared out the window at landmarks that had become familiar. They reminded me of Newton, because most of my rides to see Roo had been with him: the view of Mystic Seaport, Mystic Aquarium, the WELCOME TO RHODE ISLAND sign, the big blue bug in Providence, the small pine forest just south of Boston. I closed my eyes so I wouldn't see them, and wouldn't think of last night.

We parked on the street and took the elevator up to the fourth floor.

Every time I saw Roo, I felt the same rush of love and dread. But today she was propped upright, with her wired-up cap on, laptop open on the table across her bed. Mom and I kissed her. I went into super-devious calculation mode, because I knew I had to talk to her alone and didn't see how it would be done.

"How are you today, sweetheart?" Mom asked.

Great, Mom!

"Oh, that's wonderful!"

Hi, Tilly.

"Hi, Roo."

I can speak in complete sentences now and ask questions, she said.

My mother laughed, glancing at me to make sure I was watching, feeling the wonder.

"That's cool," I said.

"Can you ask a question?" my mother said.

Did you bring my camera, Mom?

"Yes," Mom said, laughing again, rummaging in her book bag. She placed Roo's camera on the table beside the computer.

"What are you doing with the camera?" I asked, even as I took note of the fact words were showing up on the screen as fast, apparently, as Roo could think them.

Dr. Howarth's going to show me how to take pictures with the computer.

"Awesome," I said.

So is this. The words showed up on the screen, then she activated the unmute button, and the next words came out in a female computer-voice. *There's no end to what technology can do. I'm living in my own private science fiction movie.*

"Roo, that's so great!" Mom said.

Check this out. I've always wanted an English accent. And now she was speaking in one. *Isn't that jolly good?*

"Are you trying to sound like Dr. Howarth?" Mom asked.

He hasn't heard it yet. I'm just playing around with the computer. I can sound like a man, too. She clicked another option. *Like this,* she said in a deep male voice.

I cringed because she sounded like a robot.

"Oh, it's so good to see you having fun!" Mom said.

So much fun! Roo said, back to the non-British female voice.

I caught Roo's eye on that one. We could always read each other's mind when it came to our parents. It was so like Mom to grab on to a tiny nugget of optimism and run with it.

"Tilly, what do you think of your sister? Isn't it incredible to see her using the CBI this way?"

"It's pretty great," I said. "I really didn't know how it would work, but it's amazing."

You can use me as your science project.

"Ouch," I said. "That's not funny. As if I ever would."

Sorry. I was teasing.

"Get along, girls," Mom said.

Could you find Dr. Howarth? Roo asked. *Now that I have my camera, we can start taking pictures. I want to take some of you two. Did you bring the cables to connect it?*

"I did," Mom said, digging into her book bag, laying a neatly coiled cable on the table.

The tripod?

"Oh, dear," Mom said. "I forgot that."

It's okay. Please get him, Mom. Maybe he can find one; he has his ways. Just ask Christina, my nurse this morning. She'll call him.

"All right," Mom said, stifling a yawn. "I'm going to run down and get a coffee, too. There isn't enough coffee in the world for me today."

We watched her go; I heard her footsteps in the hall and checked to make sure she'd really gone.

"We have to talk," I said to Roo.

No kidding.

"Something weird happened last night."

Forget last night. This is the first time we've been able to talk, really, really, since the crash. There's so much I want to say to you, Tilly. I want to be all, I love you, I miss you, but I am really mad at you.

"Why?" I asked, and I swear I was surprised. "I thought you said you weren't—that you blamed yourself for the texts, too."

Newton, she said.

My heart stopped. How had she found out?

"Roo . . ."

The way you're always coming up here together. I'm surprised he's not with you right now. You talk more to each other when you're here than to me. Dr. Howarth was right—you need to talk to me.

"It was hard to get used to the board," I said. "I'm sorry, it was just so awkward."

A little awkward for me, too.

"I know."

But you and Newton.

"Yeah," I said.

You held hands here right in front of me.

My face scalded. She saw that?

"It wasn't anything."

Um, it seemed like something.

"We were just happy about you getting better." My blood was barreling through my veins and I felt the most terrible combination of guilty and defensive possible.

So you're saying there's nothing between you?

"You're between us! We both love you!"

That's all?

"He thinks you don't love him anymore. He said that last night."

He shouldn't be talking to you about us! When did you see him? You got together last night?

My mouth was dry, and I could barely swallow. "It was the Full Moon Dance. A fund-raiser for you, Roo. The science club put it on."

I know about it. But you went with Newton?

"No! Of course not. But I saw him there. He didn't even want to go; he was just working at the booth. He didn't get dressed up or anything."

But you talked to him? Did you dance with him?

"I only danced with Slater," I said.

Okay, she said. Then silence, and we were both thinking, and I wondered how soon our mother would be back, and I knew this was my only chance. My mouth was dry, and I was a nervous wreck.

"There is something I have to tell you," I said, just wanting to get it over with, get the words out. "It's weird, it's so hard to explain, it's going to sound worse than it was, but you have to believe me—it was nothing, honestly."

Silence from Roo.

"I was worried about him, about Newton. He looked so miserable, and I saw him run off down the beach, to the dark end. He'd been acting strange. I went after him. I thought he might do something desperate. Like drown himself, I swear. I couldn't have lived with myself knowing first you, then him. So I ran down the beach, and I couldn't see where I was going, and I fell into the bight. I just went down so hard."

Are you okay?

Her question made me feel even worse. "Not really," I said.

Why?

"I did a terrible thing. It was a mistake; I hate that I did it. But everything is so messed up and confused. I love you, and he loves you, and you're not there, so somehow when I fell in, he rescued me, and it was almost as if he was rescuing you, as if he could have that chance."

Oh, no. I don't want to hear this.

"I have to tell you, to get it out in the open, because it meant nothing—we've been in a nightmare, and this was part of it."

Tell me!

"We kissed."

Roo said nothing. I waited ten seconds, thirty seconds, a minute, and she said nothing. I inched around to look at the screen, to see if there was writing, if maybe the computer sound went awry, but the screen was not only blank, it was dead. The computer was off.

I sat there staring at my sister. I lifted her hand, pressed it to my cheek. It felt lifeless and cold. I thought of what Martha had said, that Roo didn't need me as much as I needed her, and I knew she was right.

"Roo, please?" I said. "I'm so sorry. I had to tell you so you'd know, and because you have to believe me that he was kissing YOU. It will never happen again."

But she didn't say anything. After a while my mother returned with a cup of coffee, and she began fussing with Roo, trying to figure out why the computer had gone off, and I left the room.

Chapter Twelve

Roo

*W*hy doesn't the computer have a SCREAM button? "My" voice comes out sounding so calm and measured, so robotic and digitalized, and when Tilly told me about the kiss, I wanted to yell, and scream, and wail.

My mother so innocently tried to check the computer's connections, trying to figure out why it went off, not realizing I did it myself because I would rather be locked inside my brain than try to express myself in a remotely reasonable tone of voice. I'll have to have a word with Dr. Howarth and his software designer. When it comes to emotion, this system is EPIC FAIL.

"Sweetheart, I'm afraid to fiddle with it too much, it's such a specialized machine, not like my good old desktop. I asked Christina to call Dr. Howarth, and he should be here soon."

Good, I thought. He's my guy, and he gets it. He knows how crazy it is, trying to merge the way I am now into the world of *normals*—that is how I think of everybody now, the people who can walk and talk and go to school and wonder whether they feel like having grilled cheese or strawberry yogurt for lunch. Dr. Howarth might be a normal, but he understands me almost as if he'd been through this himself.

It seemed to take forever. My insides were churning, my mind had hold of that image of Tilly and Newton kissing, and I couldn't stand it. No amount of meditation helped. Learning CBI was a million times easier than dealing with this. I wanted to obliterate, just block it all out. Maybe if Dr. Howarth showed up, touched my hair, called me darling, got started showing me how to use the camera—*Why had my mother forgotten the tripod?*—I just wanted to get lost in photography and Dr. Howarth and forget the two people I had loved most for so long.

"Hello. Good morning, Roo. And Mrs. McCabe."

Dr. Gold came into my line of vision. Where was Dr. Howarth?

"Hi, Dr. Gold," my mother said. "We seem to be having technical difficulties. Roo was speaking just fine—the audio, oh my God! I love it!—but suddenly it went off, the screen is blank, nothing."

"Hmm . . . okay. It's just a matter of pushing the 'on' key. Roo, did you try the switch? Dr. Howarth showed you, right?"

I didn't respond, so Dr. Gold hit the button manually, and the computer powered up.

As soon as it did, I asked, *Where is Dr. Howarth?*

"Roo, I'm glad your mother paged—I was planning to come up this morning to talk to you, but I had surgery first thing. Dr. Howarth asked me to tell you he had to leave late last night."

He left? I asked in shock. I couldn't believe it.

"He would have come to say good-bye, but he got the call when he was at home, and he didn't even stop at the hospital on his way to the airport."

"Where did he go?" my mother asked.

"He had an emergency, a new patient in Toronto. Roo, he knows you are well on your way, and he felt confident leaving you in my hands. Even though he developed this software, he trained me and several other doctors, and we'll be right with you every step of the way."

He said he would be here, I said, rocked with grief and emptiness.

"I know. He thinks the world of you, Roo, and if he could have stayed longer, he would have."

What about photography? He made me promise I would take my first photo with him.

"I am not up to speed on those plans, but I will be in touch with him as soon as he gets settled, and I'm sure he will tell me everything he's thought of, to get you up and running as a photographer again. Will you be a little patient with me, Roo?"

I couldn't respond. My eyes blurred with tears. He had left without even saying good-bye. All our time together had been just work for him. My mother pushed the camera closer to me. I saw the warmth and love in her face, but if I could have, I would have thrown my camera out the window.

"She'll be patient, Doctor," my mother said. "You have no idea what my daughter can do when she sets her mind to it."

"I am sure of that," Dr. Gold said. "She is a shining star, that's for sure."

Tilly had returned from her big dramatic exit, and she stood in the doorway. She heard everything that had gone on, and her expression sent a shiver of grief through me—she looked so sad, as upset as I felt, and I realized that with all my thoughts about them and me, the normals who walk among us, Tilly was still my sister.

She was my little sister, and she was right here, but she might as well have swum to the moon last night. She was too far away for me to reach. Or maybe I'm wrong about that: Maybe I was the one too far away.

I didn't want to see her now, or ever.

Ever again.

Tilly

I buried my face in *My Ántonia* and hid out in study hall.
It was quiet in here, and I really hoped no one would bother me.
Emily came to sit beside me, whispering about how she and
Jeremy were probably going to go hiking at Devil's Hopyard
that Saturday, but honestly, I didn't care. She was one of my
two best friends, and she was happy, but I was numb.

After school I waited for the buses to leave before I went
out to the bike rack. At least the TV trucks had gone back to
wherever they'd come from. I really didn't feel like seeing anyone at all, and I wasn't in the mood for that special brand of
torqued-up end-of-day energy. It was only the first week of June,
but already hot and humid. I heard locusts in the trees.

Unlocking my bike chain, I thought I was the only one left
in the parking lot. Then I saw that someone had been sitting in
the shade of the long row of trees: Newton. And he was coming
toward me.

I fumbled the combination, wanting to get on the bike

and ride away before he got close. But my hands were shaking too hard.

"Tilly, we can't keep avoiding each other."

"Gee, I think we can."

"We didn't mean it, what happened."

"We didn't?" I asked, looking at the ground.

"Well, we did, actually," he said. "But it was a mistake."

"Yeah. It was. We screwed up."

"Big-time," he said.

That hurt a tiny bit.

We stared at each other. It was weird, being this close to him for the first time since the beach. I hadn't been sure about how I was going to feel. I tensed up, ready for a flood of emotions, but they didn't come.

He smiled at me, and I found it pretty easy to smile back. The strange thing was, there was none of that fizziness that had been flooding my veins for weeks now, no wishing he'd come closer, none of the strange, delicious yet shameful feelings that had been there since Roo's accident. It was just Newton and me, a little but not totally like old times.

"You okay?" he asked.

"Getting there," I said. "You?"

"Not so great. She won't see me," he said. "I drove up yesterday, and the nurse said my name was off the list; she specifically told them not to let me in."

"I'm sure she feels the same way about me," I said. "I wanted to be honest with her, not have a big secret between us. So I told her about the kiss."

"You WHAT?" His mouth dropped wide open and his eyes got huge behind his glasses.

"Yeah, I did. I had to, Newton. We can't have secrets like that; she reads my mind, and I read hers. She'd have known. I had to tell her."

"No," he said.

"Think about it, Newton. Think about Roo. Can you imagine her not figuring it out? She knows me, and you, too well."

"Maybe you did," he said slowly, shaking his head with total regret even as he came around.

"Yeah," I said.

"Was it bad?"

"What do you think?"

"It had to be as bad as it gets. It would have been for me, if she'd been the one to kiss someone," he said. "God, that sounds horrible."

I nodded.

"It kills me, hurting her. And her not wanting to see me. She's probably falling in love with Dr. Howarth."

"Big news," I said. "He's gone. He just flew away, on to the next patient. Roo is devastated."

"He left?"

"Don't sound so happy. She needed him. He was going to help her figure out how to take photos again. I really thought she had a chance. I know it was a long shot, but if she had just been able to take another few pictures, she could have submitted her portfolio in time for the deadline."

"To the Serena Kader Barrois Foundation," Newton said. "What was he planning to do? I mean, how could she actually take photos? Literally, how would it work?"

"Some kind of robotics," I said. "They'll program an arm so she can reach for a book, or lift a glass to drink, or position the camera. Dr. Gold, his fill-in, was going to try to help her. But, Newton, Roo has stopped caring."

"She's hurt," he said quietly. "But she'll try again."

"No, you don't get it. She's not speaking."

"To me? To you?"

"At all," I said. "She's shutting down."

He stood there, stunned.

I finally got my bike unlocked, and climbed on.

"What did Howarth say about the camera, before he left?"

"He didn't say anything to me. All I know is that Roo was excited, and now she's not. She's giving up, Newton."

I rode away and left him standing there. The afternoon was so hot, I was sweating by the time I hit Shore Road. I didn't want to go home and face my mother; I found it hard to look her in the eye. Roo hadn't told her what I said about the kiss, so she had no idea why Roo didn't want to talk on the computer anymore. The fact that I was behind this latest disaster in my sister's life, too, was too much to face. Instead of riding home, I cruised down Ferry Road.

When I got to Martha's house, I felt oddly comforted. A breeze blew through the big trees; the leaves were bright green, still untouched by summer's dust. Lucan had been lying in the shade, but at the sight of me, he stood and limped over, his tongue hanging out in a friendly way.

"Hey, boy," I said, petting him. "Are you okay? Are you all better?"

"He's doing great," Slater said. He came out of the barn, carrying a fifty-pound bag of topsoil on his shoulder.

"Hi, Slater. How's it going?" I asked.

"Pretty good. I'm helping Martha restore the herb garden. Come on, I'll show you."

I followed him along the neatly manicured path around the corner of the house, to a circular garden enclosed by a knee-high boxwood hedge. In the very center was a sundial. There were two weathered teak benches opposite each other on the perimeter; between the benches were several of Althea's bronze statues: a young girl sitting cross-legged reading, another gazing up at the sky, and two more dancing.

Lucan sat beside me as I watched Slater slit the bag and dump the dirt into a pile. The garden was divided like a six-slice pie. Five had been planted already, and he was working on the sixth. After a while I felt like a slacker, so I pitched in, helping Slater plant flats of five varieties of thyme: English, silver, lemon, wooly, and juniper.

"What brings you to Martha's?" he asked.

"I like to talk to her," I said. "Is she home?"

"She's inside, arranging slides of all Althea's sculptures. She's going to have an art show here, coming up soon now. It's why she's in a rush to get the yard looking perfect."

"When is it?" I asked while we worked. The sun felt good on my back, and I liked shoveling the dirt, arranging the plants.

"The day of the summer solstice, June twenty-first. Back in New York, I wasn't so in tune with the seasons. Nature was basically Central Park. Now she's got me looking at birds, and the river, and figuring out which herbs like sun and which ones like shade. It's cool."

"Your family wasn't into nature?" I asked, wondering what it would be like to grow up without loving birds, clouds, the ocean.

"Not too much. I hung out in the park, but that was mostly playing ball, not looking at trees or anything."

"What about your parents?"

"My dad died when I was ten. My mom worked at the museum all the time, but she had to cut back when she got MS."

"How's she doing?"

He shrugged. "Ups and downs. We moved out here because her doctor said fresh air and less stress would be good. So her sister made room, but sometimes they fight, and that seems like even more stress than back in the city. Martha gave me some herbs to give her."

"Sisters fighting," I said, and I could relate. "Not awesome. Are the herbs helping?"

"She says yes. She makes tea, says it tastes really good."

"I've had it," I said. "It does."

Martha came out the French doors in a black dress, pink flowered sun hat, and a stark-looking streak of white zinc oxide on her nose. "Ah, hello, Tilly," she said. "Slater is helping me get the herb garden back on track, and I see you're getting your hands dirty, too."

"I like it," I said. It actually felt great. It distracted me from my worries, working out in the sun with Slater.

"There's no better feeling than dirt under the fingernails! Hands in the soil. And don't the plants smell wonderful?"

I nodded. "Slater said you're having an art show."

"Yes," she said. "I started thinking after our last talk, when you told me about Roo and her photography. I decided art needs to be seen, talent deserves to be appreciated. Lucan and I are privileged to see Althea's sculpture every day. I want others to enjoy it."

"So you're having an exhibition?" I asked.

"Yes," she said. "The night of June twenty-first, the summer solstice."

"Longest day of the year," Slater said.

"Will you come, Tilly?" Martha asked.

"Sure," I said, but I didn't feel certain at all. I didn't feel like seeing a lot of people, even to celebrate Martha's sister. But I knew I would probably do it for her.

"How is Roo's progress with the camera coming along?" Martha asked.

"It isn't," I said. "The doctor who was helping her got a new patient and flew to Canada."

"Man, that's rough," Slater said.

"That is rough," Martha agreed. She took off her glasses and frowned, looking very troubled. I remembered what she'd said the night of the dance: Singers have to sing or they will get sick. And photographers had to take pictures.

"I'm afraid," I said. My hands had been in the soil. I brushed tears from my eyes, and I felt grains of dirt sprinkle down my cheeks. Martha knelt beside me, creakily, leaning on Lucan for support. She held my hands.

"She is strong," Martha said.

"Maybe not enough for all of this," I said. "I told her what I did with her boyfriend."

"You did?" Martha asked.

"Yeah. I thought it would be better to get it out in the open. I was wrong."

"No, you weren't," Martha said. "She has the right to her feelings about it, but she'll realize you were mixed up. You both were." She leaned on my shoulder to get to her feet, touched the top of my head, and walked into the house.

I glanced at Slater, wondered what he was thinking of all this. His expression was steady, not giving anything away.

"You mean you and Newton?" he asked finally.

"What do you know about it?" I asked.

"The night of the dance, I followed you the way you followed him. I wanted to make sure you were okay."

"You *saw*?" I asked, feeling humiliated. I'd have felt bad if anyone saw, but *Slater*? I wanted to disappear.

"Yeah, I was worried about you," he said.

"Why didn't you say something?" I asked. "Give me a hard time?"

"It wasn't really my business," he said. "And why would I give you a hard time?" Then he gave a soft chuckle.

"What?" I asked, outraged that he'd laugh. "It isn't funny!"

"No, it's not," he said. "But, Tilly, no one can give you as hard a time as you give yourself. Not even close. You told your sister, that's what counts."

"Thanks," I said, and the weird thing was, his words calmed me down. And I realized: No one at school was talking about it, which meant Slater hadn't told anyone. He'd kept my secret, Newton's and mine.

Slater reached for the hose he'd been using to water the new plants. He soaked his T-shirt, then wrung it out. He leaned over and used it to wipe my face, clean the dirt and tears off my cheeks.

He held my gaze, and I stared into his warm brown eyes. He nodded, and I saw him smile. Until that moment, I never knew you could feel a smile, but just then I did, as real as the sun on my skin, the breeze in my hair. I felt Slater's smile go into my bones, and touch the fear, whisk it away as if it were a feather, and it had just come up against something much greater.

Chapter Thirteen

Roo

"*Y*ou're doing well, Roo. We're almost done," Dr. Gold said.

I stared straight ahead. The radiology department, where I had been brought to have a PET scan, was freezing cold.

I still couldn't use mindfulness on my sister and Newton, but it really helped when I was having long, boring tests, when my body felt uncomfortable. I lay on my back as the machine beeped and tilted and took images of my brain. In between scans, I followed the breath in and out of my chest.

"Funny to think of pictures in this sense, isn't it? You and I both, in different ways, rely on cameras. And don't think I've forgotten. Tim, Dr. Howarth, left good notes. The software is already in place; it's just a matter of rigging up the hardware for you to start taking photos again."

I couldn't blame her for not moving faster. I hadn't been excited about photography since that day Tilly had told me about the kiss, the same day I'd found out Dr. Howarth had left for Toronto. In fact, I'd hardly talked about anything.

"Girl, you've got to fight the plateau," Christina said later that day, after pushing me back to my room in the wheelchair, loading me into bed, and reconnecting my wire harness to the computer. "The plateau is your enemy."

I was hooked up to the laptop. Even though I rarely spoke, they kept me logged in, just in case the spirit moved me. Everyone wanted the spirit to move me, but I had lost something along the way. I didn't care. I used to want to make everyone happy, do things to please my family and the people around me, but those feelings had slipped away.

Christina's words made me curious, though. She was a thirty-three-year-old African American nurse who had joined the army when she was twenty-one. She'd served in Iraq and Afghanistan, and she was on this floor because she'd had a lot of experience with TBI—traumatic brain injury. I thought of those women Christina had shown me, Morgan and Dani. Dani had been in Afghanistan, too.

What is the plateau? I asked, the first sentence I'd spoken in three days.

"It's when things are 'good enough.' When you're treading water. Not going back, but not moving forward, either. You do your physical therapy, you do your eye exercises, whatever the protocol. But you're not into it."

I didn't respond. I knew what she was saying, but I didn't want to get into any discussion that might encourage a pep talk.

"You're *not* into it, are you?" she asked.

Not really.

"What can we do to change that?"

I'm okay.

She laughed, snorting air in exaggerated disbelief. "Right! And I'm Princess Kate. The difference is, you can change your status. I'm never going to be royal."

I'll call you Princess Christina if you want.

She squeezed my shoulder and chuckled. "That would be nice. But what are we going to do about you?"

I'm kind of tired.

"That's because you're down. I understand, Roo. But only you can bring yourself up. You know?"

Yes.

"One-word answer, that's great. You want to hear about this guy I knew in Fallujah? He hit an IED in his jeep, got thrown clear but hit his head. His brain got trashed, Roo. Mush in his skull. Not like you; you came out of your accident sharp as before. Now I know you're sick of hearing this, maybe, but that's a gift."

I know, I said, just to make her shut up. I didn't want to hear about it.

"'Disabled' doesn't have to mean down for the count," she said.

Okay, I said.

"Not okay," she said. "I'm going to piss you off right now, I hope. If I do, it means I've done my job. But you're throwing it away, Roo. That plateau you're on? It can change real fast. It can turn into downhill. I've seen it. You don't use it, you lose it. You've got to challenge yourself. Do the CBI games."

CBI games? I was going to get high honors this semester and shoot for the stars college-wise. Now my greatest challenge was playing glorified video games, because that's what they were. There was one like *Tetris*, only instead of using a keyboard, I used my mind. In another, I had to escape from zombies and try to capture them. The one I hated most had bright-pink birds that looked like nothing you'd ever find in nature, flying through a department store, filling baskets with as many products as they could collect in their beaks in as short a time as possible. I wouldn't have played it in real life, and I felt worse than disheartened to have to play it here.

"Use it or lose it, Roo," she said. "Remember that. You can hate me, but this is tough love."

I turned off my computer and disappeared into myself. Christina had been my friend, and now she was attacking me. Tough love, who needed it? A year ago I'd had all the love in the world: My father was still alive, my parents were together, I was madly in love with my boyfriend, and my sister was my best friend.

Now I had a nurse acting as if she was still in the army and I was just someone to be ordered around. I felt Christina's hand on my cheek. She stroked it gently, whispered in my ear.

"I'm sorry, honey. I don't always know when to stop. I saw some bad things, they stick in my head. I want only the best for you. I'm sorry for pushing."

Apology not accepted, I wanted to say. At the same time, I wished I could move my arm so I could hold her hand. Caress it, tell her she was a good nurse, she was making a difference, I could feel the love she had for me, and for the patients she had met in Iraq. She carried the war with her.

I fell asleep.

When I woke up, I felt a cold nose on my cheek, where Christina's hand had been. It was a dream of snow falling, maybe. But I opened my eyes and came face-to-face with a big, lolling tongue.

"Roo? Do you remember us?" came the voice of someone standing behind the big, friendly dog. "This is Lucan. I got permission to bring him to your room, to visit you. It's me, Martha Muirhead."

My heart sped up to see them, especially Lucan. He nuzzled against my arm in such a friendly way. I remembered the terrible thump when my car hit him, and I felt so grateful that he was up and walking, that he was still alive.

She might have been the only person in the world I wanted to talk to. I turned on my computer. While it went through the clicks and whirs of powering up, I felt Lucan lick my hand. Martha stood within my field of vision. She was fine-boned with pale skin, big blue eyes behind wire-rimmed glasses, and white hair pinned up in a bun. Her dress was dark indigo, and she wore a black shawl with scalloped edges draped over her shoulders.

"May I sit down?" Martha asked.

I looked up, and although I assume she didn't have experience with locked-in patients, she seemed to understand that I was saying yes, and she pulled the chair closer to my bedside and sat. Lucan stood alert, and now his head was rested on my knee.

"It is so good to see you," she said. "I have wanted to visit every single day, but I knew you needed time to heal."

Like Lucan, I said, now that the computer was up and running. The digital voice came through the speakers.

"Exactly like Lucan," she said easily, as if talking to a computer was the most natural thing.

How is he?

"He is doing so well. He had a broken leg, but the cast came off in April, and he is just fine now."

I am so sorry I hit him.

"I know you are, Roo. You said so that day. I knew then what a special, luminous girl you are. I'll never forget that moment when we talked."

I could picture it. I was hanging upside down in the mangled car, held in by my seat belt. I could hear the creek rushing below me, and feel hot blood running into my eyes. I had never hit an animal before, and my heart was broken because I thought I had killed Lucan. I saw Martha clamber down the snowy marsh bank, slog through the water to get to me.

"With all you were going through, you cared only about others."

Lucan.

"And your sister," Martha said.

Tilly. My heart closed at the mention of her name.

"Yes, dear. Tilly. She's come to visit me a few times. Has she told you?"

Not really.

"The two of you remind me of Althea and me. She was my younger sister. The way you were so concerned about Tilly, wanted to make sure she was okay, that she didn't blame herself. Oh, that touched me, Roo. It helped me."

Helped you, how?

"I felt responsible for my sister's death. She had been sick for a year, and on the last night of her life, she wanted to go into the garden to see the moon. She was an artist, like you, and I thought it would be so good for her. So I helped her to walk outside."

That sounds beautiful.

"The moon was magical. She gazed up at it; we both did. The moon always made us young again, Roo. It would cast a spell on us, and the years would fall away. We sang together, making up songs. We would remember childhood times, and growing up—dancing by the light of the moon, swimming in the moonlight, always singing. We even had nicknames: I was Luna, and she was Willoughby Moon."

She must have loved you taking her out that night.

"She did. But it was a mistake. The air was too humid, and she couldn't breathe. She was okay at first, but when her lungs failed, it happened all at once. It was terrible."

You didn't know. You tried to give her something she would love.

"Yes, that's true. I trained with a doctor. I learned principles of Tibetan medicine, the use of herbs. The way the body's organs work. I went to Tibet and learned acupressure. That's why I blamed myself for so long, Roo."

But why? You just wanted her to see the moon.

"I practiced healing. I helped many people, but I couldn't help my sister. Do you know what she told me just before she died?"

What?

" 'I'm so lucky to have spent my life with a sister like you.' "

She loved you, I said.

"Yes. Our mother used to say, 'You'll have many friends in life, but only one sister.' She was right. You know that, you feel the same way, don't you?"

Althea never hurt you.

"Oh, yes, she did. She married my first boyfriend."

WHAT?

"His name was Charles. We all went to Black Hall High together, just like you and Tilly and Newton."

My heart ached, hearing his name. How did she know about Newton?

"Charles invited me to the Hamburg Fair when I was fifteen. He was a year older. He picked me up in his parents' car, and we drove up the river to the fairgrounds. He bought me kettle corn, and we watched the horse pull and the wood-carving competition, and he won me a stuffed bear. He kissed me on the Ferris wheel. My first kiss."

You fell in love with him?

"Like a ton of bricks. We dated all through high school. After graduation, things changed. I went to Sarah Lawrence, and he went to UConn. He studied engineering, and I studied poetry. I began to feel hemmed in by him, and he sensed it. It hurt him badly when I told him I thought we should break up."

I nearly did that with Newton, I thought. *When I thought I'd be fast-tracking it to Yale.*

"He was so sad. He'd go home to Black Hall on weekends, just hoping I'd be there, too. But I was in New York City every weekend. I couldn't get enough of it—jazz at the Village Vanguard and Blue Note, art exhibits at the Whitney and MoMA, poetry readings at coffeehouses and drinks at the

Cedar Tavern. I started meditating and met a Buddhist monk who told me to visit Tibet, and I went there for a year and studied with a healer."

Meanwhile, Charles . . .

"Yes, Charles kept hoping I would return. He would go to my house to see my parents, and often Althea would be there. She went to Connecticut College to study art, and she'd often return home to sketch the river, or sculpt in the barn or her little studio by the river. Her greatest inspiration was always Black Hall. Like yours," she said, glancing around the room at my photos.

There's no place more beautiful, I said.

"Althea missed me, too," Martha said. "I think it started with them consoling each other."

Did you still love him? I asked, my pulse racing.

"I'm not sure," Martha said. "It got all mixed up in my mind, for a while, with jealousy and resentment. They married right after Althea's graduation."

Did you ever forgive them?

"It took a while. A few years, honestly. Wasted years, I think now, when I could have been spending time with my sister. Now that that's impossible, I think back on all the missed moments. They stayed together until Charles died—by then, we were all friends again. I would go to their house in New London, where Althea taught sculpture at the college, for holidays. After he died, she moved back into our family house, where I'd been living for a while."

You came home to each other.

"We did. And we had wonderful years."

Luna and Willoughby Moon.

She nodded, smiling. "Do you and Tilly have nicknames?"

Well, Tilly and Roo. She's Mathilda Mae and I'm Ruth Ann, officially. But things aren't good with us. The texts, and the accident. And . . . I hesitated, but I needed to talk, to tell this woman who knew us both, who knew how it felt to be betrayed by her sister. *She kissed Newton,* I said.

"I know, Roo. She came to my house that night. She was devastated. I am glad she told you, though. And I'll tell you what I said to her. Things between you can't be broken."

But they are.

"No. Damaged maybe. You're very hurt by the two people you love most. Even now, when I think of Althea and Charles, it feels like being stabbed. But things worked out. We both had to want that, and we tried and kept trying. That's the only way. She feels terrible about what she's done to you. If she could undo it, she would. She needs you."

I'm not sure of that.

"I'm positive of it. You have particular strength, an inner guidance system. I saw it that day in the marsh, and I feel it even more now. Tilly looks up to you, just like the moon rising in the east, every single night, even behind the clouds. She counts on you being there."

Not anymore.

"More than ever. You two speak the same language. Remember that."

I thought back to a night when Tilly and I were in middle school, when we'd greeted the moon by doing cartwheels the whole length of the beach. We didn't say a word out loud; we were dizzy with happiness. That night, cartwheels and the moon had served as our language.

"Roo, here's the secret of life," Martha said. "You get to be a sister only because you have Tilly. Without each other, that goes away. You're still beautiful and talented, but you're not a sister. It's the alchemy of sisters, Roo."

She inched to the edge of her seat, as if about to stand.

"I think Lucan needs to stretch his legs," she said. "And we had better let you rest. We're happy we visited. May we come again?"

Please, I said.

"As Tilly knows—in fact, she's working on it—I am planning an exhibit of Althea's sculptures. It will be held on the summer solstice. I would be so thrilled if you would let me show some of your photographs, too."

My heart jumped—she was inviting me to be in an exhibit! *I would be honored.*

"That's wonderful. You choose the ones you want to send, and I will arrange to have them picked up."

I already know.

"You do? I love that. You're just like Althea. She had such an artist's vision, and she would have known in an instant which works were her best, which ones she would want the world to see. Of course, I think they're all great. But you artists see things differently, more clearly."

I don't feel that way. I can't see my life at all anymore.

"Oh, I think you can," Martha said. "Just ask yourself what you want. That's the hard part. There are so many choices, every minute."

It seemed strange, her saying that to me—I couldn't choose much of anything, at least when compared to my old life. But she was right. And in a way, she was reminding me of what Christina had said about the plateau. Did I want to stay where I was, sink into despair, or use my gifts? Grab on to everything I could?

I watched her reach into a crocheted bag and pull out some tiny sachets. They had been stitched of bright silk—turquoise, orchid, peach, and vermilion.

"Roo, I brought you some herbs. They're varieties that grow wild in Black Hall, and these are from my garden. I thought you might enjoy, even be inspired, by the aromatherapy. Shall I leave them with you?"

Yes, please.

"Okay," she said, and tucked the sachets around my pillow. The smell of my hometown surrounded me and filled me with a combination of peace and excitement. If I closed my eyes, I could imagine I was on the path to Little Beach with Newton.

Thank you, I said. I didn't want her to go. I could have talked to her forever. I had a million questions, but I could see her gathering her things, clipping the red leash onto Lucan's collar. So I thought of just one more.

Martha, you studied poetry at college? I asked.

"Yes," she said. "People think they need to take economics or business, practical subjects that teach skills. But there's nothing more practical than poetry. No matter which career you choose, how can you do your best in it, understand life the way it really is, without poems?"

I agree. Who's your favorite poet?

"Rilke," she said.

Mine too.

She beamed. Then she and Lucan approached closer. He touched my cheek with his cold nose; it felt like a blessing, a kiss. She bent down, touched her forehead to mine just as Tilly sometimes did.

"'Perhaps all the dragons in our lives are princesses who are only waiting to see us act, just once, with beauty and courage,'" she whispered the quote.

And she left, leaving me thinking of those lines from Rainer Maria Rilke's *Letters to a Young Poet*, trembling with love for all the princesses, all the sisters, for Martha and Althea, Luna and Willoughby Moon. For Tilly and Roo, for the dragons on Tilly's shelf, and our secret language of cartwheels, the moon, and sculptures in a seaside herb garden.

Tilly

*T*he morning sun felt hot on my back, working outside at Martha's. Slater had stashed bottles of water under the tree, and I drank half of one and poured the rest over my head.

Getting ready for the summer solstice exhibit was heavy-duty. For one thing, the grounds were really overgrown, and we had to clear six truckloads' worth of weeds and vines— and we had to be careful, because what looked to us like weeds might, to Martha, be some precious wildflower or herb that had lived there since her and Althea's childhood.

Slater and I polished Althea's outdoor bronzes, weathered by salt air and dust, until they gleamed. The expressions of the girls' faces came alive, and their grace of movement made them seem ready to dance across the lawn.

"These statues remind me of Central Park," Slater said one afternoon. "My aunt got married in Harlem. I was a kid, the ring bearer, but they took wedding pictures in Conservatory Garden, in the north part of the park. We stood by this sculpture of three girls holding hands and dancing in a circle. It looked something like this one, maybe not as abstract."

"This one reminds me of sisters," I said, rubbing the figures' flowing hair with a soft cloth. I tried not to think of the fact that Martha had visited Roo two days earlier and, other than telling me she'd gone, had said almost nothing about it. Had Roo talked about me? Did she despise me worse than ever?

"So you like Central Park?" I asked Slater, to keep my mind off those things.

"It's really cool. Not far from the park's zoo, there's a statue of Balto, that sled dog that saved Alaskan kids by bringing them medicine. He's made of bronze, too. He has all these shiny patches on him, where kids climb on him, and touch him, and their hands rub the bronze clean."

"Do you miss New York?" I asked.

"Every minute," he said. "But I like Black Hall more."

"Why?" I asked, thinking of the times my parents had taken us to the city, to the Hayden Planetarium and to see *Audubon's Aviary*, a fabulous exhibit of rare bird prints by John James Audubon at the New-York Historical Society. Afterward we always walked through the Upper West Side to have ice cream at Café Lalo. I loved New York. My energy was totally at home there. "It's not half as exciting as the city."

"That's for sure. But my mom's doing better here. She's finally relaxing, and her symptoms are improving. She and my aunt are getting along better, too. Settling in, I guess. Plus, you're here."

"As if that's any reason."

"It is," he said.

I let that go, but inside I glowed. I kept working, but when I glanced up, I saw him watching me, and that just made the glow burn brighter. He was sixteen and had his license, so he drove the truck to and from the dump on Four Mile River Road. My muscles burned, hauling all that brush. The day was hot, so we stopped at Hubbard's Point to dive into the Sound. It was only June, schools were still in session, so summer families hadn't arrived for the season yet. We pretty much had the beach to ourselves.

"This is where you grew up?" he asked as we stood in shallow water, cooling off.

"Yep. That's our house," I said, pointing up at the rock ledge towering over the beach. We both wore shorts and T-shirts, and waded in a little deeper because the day was hot and the water felt so good.

"Really nice," he said. "You're lucky."

"We *were*," I said.

"*Are*, Tilly. Still are."

At that, I couldn't help myself. I dove straight under, not caring that I was dressed. I was a fish, and I needed to swim. When I came up, I shook my head, and the water splashed Slater. He pulled his shirt off, tossed it onto the beach, and ducked underwater. I slid under, too. We came up for breath right in front of each other and started swimming, then raced to the big rock about fifty yards from shore. He beat me there by two seconds, but I climbed out faster.

"It's weird," I said, out of breath as I hauled myself onto the ledge, giving him a hand and helping him up.

"What's that?" he asked.

I didn't answer right away. We lay back on the rock, looking up at the blue sky. After a minute I caught my breath. "I just realized this is my first swim of the year, the first swim since Roo's accident. I can't believe she won't ever get to go into the water again."

"You don't know that," he said.

"I pretty much do. She's paralyzed."

"We were out of hope when my mom first got diagnosed. The researchers are making strides every day. She can do a lot more than we thought she'd be able to."

"Well, MS is different from locked-in syndrome."

"No doubt. But still. Disabled people can have good lives, too. Keep an open mind."

"Yeah, I'll try." I dove in so I wouldn't have to talk any more. I heard him splash behind me. We swam back to the beach, not racing this time. I slid through the water, thinking of the mermaids Roo and I used to be, how swimming was as natural to us as walking. And I thought, what if Slater was right, what if we could somehow get her to the beach, hold her afloat?

When I came up for air, in the shallow water back at the beach, I saw Slater standing there in the gentle waves, waiting for me. He smiled, beaming at the sight.

"What is it?" I asked.

"You," he said. He reached out, touching my hand, but I backed away. Swimming with boys, it got me in trouble.

"Let's go back to Martha's," I said, blushing and feeling embarrassed, somehow confused and undeserving of whatever Slater was thinking.

"Okay, Tilly Mae," he said.

We'd worked so hard on clearing the back property, Martha told us to take it easier for the rest of the day. She had opened the wide doors to the barn, where part of the exhibition would be held, to air it out. The space was filled with old farm equipment; she said her father had raised Christmas trees for twenty years. Later they had added a flower farm, rows of zinnias and snapdragons that they would sell at a stand out on Ferry Road, on an honor system where passersby would buy bouquets in mason jars, leave money in a tin box.

Martha's idea was that we should keep the farm equipment in the barn, just the way it was, so people could see the tractor and carts and plow and rusty old rakes and shovels, and remember how things used to be. We would hang Roo's work on the silvered board wall.

Until we had the actual photos, we wouldn't know the position of each one, but since I knew the size of her prints, I could estimate. Slater measured the height from the floor and the width between frames, and I hammered in nails, so the barn gallery would be ready and waiting for Roo's pictures.

"Hey, Newton," Slater said, and I glanced over to see him walking in. Was it my imagination, or was there a tone in Slater's voice?

"Hi, Slater," Newton said.

They stared at each other with definite attitude.

"Can we help you?" Slater asked. I caught the *we*.

"Tilly, your mom told me you were here," Newton said.

"Yeah, I'm working here now," I said. Duh, wow, I could be brilliant sometimes. But I felt awkward. There was a tense vibe between Newton and Slater, and it felt like it had to do with me. Was Slater jealous of the kiss? And Newton seemed to be giving him a serious once-over. It made me nervous, but also gave me a secret thrill, honestly. Slater let it go and kept measuring.

"I don't want to interrupt," Newton said. "But can I try something out on you?"

"Like what?" I asked.

"Well, you and Roo have the same-shaped face, right?"

"Basically. Only hers is gorgeous, with perfect cheekbones, and mine is plain."

"Hey!" Slater said warningly. I blushed hard.

Newton gave him a look, but basically ignored him.

"I'm talking more about your eyes," Newton said. "Their shape, and the distance between them. I remember you used to steal each other's sunglasses. And if Roo was using binoculars, and passed them to you, you wouldn't have to adjust them, right?"

I thought about it, trying to remember. "Right," I said. "That's true."

"Okay, come here a second," he said. He had definitely lost weight in the last few months, making him skinnier than ever. He hadn't gotten new glasses since that disaster at the bight — his old ones, black-framed and ungainly at best, were now held together with electrical tape.

I stood in front of him, with Slater right there watching. Newton frowned as he removed a six-inch ruler from the pocket of his blue-checked shirt. He balanced it on the bridge of my nose.

"Close your right eye," he commanded, squinting. "Now your left. Now open both."

"Like that?" I said.

"Yeah, thanks."

Then he measured the length of my nose, the width of my forehead, the distance from the top of each ear to my cheekbones. He seemed to be doing calculations in his head, then jotting numbers down in a small notebook. I started off feeling self-conscious, then realized the tension between us was gone. I was more focused on the fact that Slater was watching.

"I think I have what I need," Newton said.

"You doing something for Roo?" Slater asked.

"Yeah," Newton said. "Trying to."

"That is so cool."

"Thanks," Newton said, seeming to relax with him a little. He gave the closest thing I'd seen to a smile in weeks.

"Whatever it is you're making for Roo, I'm glad," I said.

Newton just nodded. When he left the barn, I turned to Slater. Afternoon light slanted in through the open doors, and specks of dust glinted and danced in the sun. Slater was watching me, his eyes serious. I thought of him touching my wet hand as we'd stood in the water at Hubbard's Point an hour ago, and I slowly reached out, linked my finger with his now.

"Thanks for letting me be here with you," I said.

"It works for me," he said.

We stood there holding each other by one finger for a long time. I didn't want to let go, and I knew he didn't want to either. Sometimes the smallest connections are the biggest ones of all.

Chapter Fourteen

Roo

The front of the postcard was a hazy, soft-focus shot of a beach, with rippling white waves rolling in, and a girl standing at the water's edge.

Dear Roo,
Your photos are so much better than this one, and I hope you are
ready to make this big leap and return to the camera. I hated to
leave without saying good-bye, but there was an emergency, and
sometimes my job doesn't allow for real good-byes.
You are a wonderful, talented girl. I am proud of you and
honored to have worked with you. Keep going, Roo! Nothing can
hold you back.
With admiration,
Dr. Tim

Dr. Gold stood by my bed, backlit by bright June light flowing through the window, holding the card so I could read it.

Thank you for delivering it to me, I said.

"You're welcome," she said. "I know he feels strongly about you, and he felt terrible about the way he left."

So many patients, so little time, I said to disguise the emotion I felt.

"Not too many like you, Roo," she said.

I stared at the card. I had felt embarrassed by having a crush on my doctor, especially thinking maybe he'd been flirting with me. What kind of idiot was I? No one would ever want me, not in a romantic way.

I want to write him back, I said.

"I'm sure he'll appreciate it," she said.

What did he mean by "this big leap"? How can I return to the camera? He was going to help me with that.

"I'm going to have to let someone else answer that question," she said, smiling.

Newton came through the door, carrying two large boxes and a sheaf of paper. He hadn't been here for two weeks, and I tensed up at the sight of him. He looked uncomfortable, too, and ungainly, all elbows and angles, and he moved as if he was afraid he might drop everything all over the floor.

"I know you'd rather not see me," he said. "I understand, Roo. I respect your wishes, and after this, I won't come back if that's what you want."

"Roo, Dr. Howarth and I spoke a few minutes ago, and he asked me to stay until Newton came into the room. I'm supposed to ask you if it's okay for him to stay," Dr. Gold said.

It is, I said.

"Okay, then," Dr. Gold said. "I'm going back to my office, but I'm just a phone call away. Ring for Christina and have her page me if you need me."

I didn't respond. I was too busy looking at Newton. When something cataclysmic happens between two people who love each other, it's like the planet going through an ice age. The world isn't destroyed, exactly, but it's not the same, either.

Newton looked older, and skinny. His skin was pale, as if he'd spent all his time indoors lately. That was like him; I'd been the one to get him outside, into a kayak, or onto a trail. He would never sit on a beach if it weren't for me telling him how good the hot sand would feel on his back, how refreshing the salt water would be. If it were up to Newton, he'd spend all his time with his books, in a lab.

You look terrible, I said.

"You look beautiful," he said.

You never used to lie to me.

"That's not a lie," he said, still laden down, his arms full as he stared at me. "You're Roo. You're the most beautiful girl in the world."

How did Dr. Howarth know you would be coming into my room at this very moment? I asked, letting that one pass.

"I called him."

But he's not here anymore.

"I tracked him down in Toronto. We've had some long conversations and emails."

I thought you hated him.

"I had my reasons. Okay, I was jealous," he said, which gave me a little jab in the heart. I felt like smiling.

So why did you track him down?

"Because he's the one who started developing a system for you to take photographs again. He developed the software, and he had the interface all figured out. All he needed was someone to invent the right headgear."

Headgear?

"Yes," Newton said. He placed the boxes on the shelf beside my bed. He seemed so nervous; his broad forehead was beaded with sweat, and he bobbled the papers he was holding. They flew onto the floor, and he bumped his head on my tray table, gathering them up.

What are the papers? I asked.

"They're the blueprints," he said. "The master plan that Dr. Howarth came up with. He sent me everything I need to know about connecting the camera to the computer. You can control the settings exactly the same way you do the cursor on this laptop."

Camera settings?

"Yes. Once we open the page, you'll have every choice you need—exactly the same ones you'd find if you were holding your Canon."

But I can't hold my Canon.

"Ah!" he said, holding up his left index finger. "But you can."

I watched him rummaging around in one of the boxes. He removed a slinglike collection of nylon straps, a bicycle helmet, an aluminum frame, and a six-inch-square wooden box painted glossy black, and placed them on the window ledge. Now that he was into his project, his nervousness was gone. He moved with the focus and economy of movement I had always found so attractive.

He pulled a delicate screwdriver from his shirt pocket, the kind I used to use to fix his glasses, and unscrewed a one-inch plastic frame from the back of my camera.

"I'm enlarging the viewfinder," he said.

That little window you looked through, to set up the shot. Then he placed the camera in the box, threaded the straps through small holes in the box's sides, and attached the other end of the straps to the helmet.

I watched, remembering the ease that had always been between us. We'd do homework together at my family's dining room table for hours, barely speaking, our feet touching under the table. I felt that way now. One time, Newton built a water filtration system out of junk he found in the basement. Tilly had called him a mad scientist, a geeked-out genius. Maybe he was both. But watching him work calmed me down.

"Okay," he said when he had finished assembling. "The challenge is that you're so good. If you just wanted to point and shoot, I could hold the camera for you, and you could direct the computer to click the shot. But you shoot stars, sky objects. It's dark out, and there's movement. So I needed to figure out how to hold the camera steady and stable long enough for you to get the settings right."

I probably won't be going to Little Beach to photograph stars any time soon.

"Yes, you will."

How?

"I'm working on it. Let's just get you familiar with the apparatus first. We'll do some test shots in here before we go out to do fieldwork. Can we get you into the wheelchair?"

Call Christina. She's on today; she'll do it.

"We don't need Christina, Roo."

He lowered the side of my bed, made sure all my IV lines were out of the way. My catheter was there, too, and I felt mortified. But he just unclipped the bag of urine and hooked it to the side of the chair, as if it was no big deal.

He slid his arms around me. He held me for a minute that way, wedged beside me on the bed. I couldn't move my arms, but if I could, they would have slid around him. My hands would have touched his face. He smelled so good, that quintessential Newton combination of salt air, soap, and pencils. He brushed his face against mine, and it made me laugh to be jostled by his glasses. A tiny little grunt actually escaped my mouth, but from Newton's chuckle, I could tell he knew it was a laugh.

Then he lifted me up. He held me against his chest; I felt his heart beating through his shirt. His body felt warm, and I wanted to stay right there all day. From up here, I had a better view out the window—of the Charles River, a bridge filled with traffic, and the sky. But I barely saw. I just wanted Newton to hold me.

Finally he put me into the wheelchair. He strapped me in, then made sure my wire harness was connected to the computer. He placed the helmet on my head; it was my own, the one I'd worn on hundreds of bike rides. There was a scuff mark from where I'd wiped out in the beach parking lot.

He secured the small, almost delicate, wooden box holding my camera to the aluminum frame—I recognized it as the modified frame from a backpack; he had cut it down a third of its size, and instead of putting it on my back, he strapped it to my front—to support the camera and balance the weight.

The box had cutouts on two sides—one that pressed against my right eye, the other to accommodate the camera's lens. The straps looped from the box sides to the temples of my helmet, to hold the box in place. Once he had the whole thing put together and strapped it to my body, I was gazing straight through the camera's viewfinder.

I looked through the camera, but because the muscles of my left eye were paralyzed and I couldn't close my eyelid, too much light came in. Newton had anticipated that. He slid a pirate-style eye patch over my right eye, and that made a huge difference.

He had positioned me to face the window. I saw seagulls wheeling around in the blue sky.

"Dr. Howarth told me how to program this in, hang on a sec," he said, looking through the pages of notes. He ran the camera cable from the back of the box to the USB port on the laptop. Then with a few keystrokes he got the computer to recognize the camera.

"This part's complicated," he said. "The computer is used to responding to the cursor and expressing your words. Now it needs to hear your thoughts about taking a photo. The basics are up for zoom, left for distance, and right for click the shot."

He came around front, made a few adjustments to the frame and the way the camera rested in the box.

"Ready?" he asked.

Because I couldn't see the keyboard, I wasn't able to answer. But we were in synch, so he took my silence as a yes.

"Go for it," he said.

I watched gulls wheel and turn in the blue sky, saw the patterns they were making in relation to the dark horizon. When one gull soared past the window in a perfect glide, I moved the cursor right and heard the camera click.

"You did it!" Newton said, standing by the monitor.

He was right, I'd taken a photo. I felt like throwing my arms around him, I felt like flying.

I wanted to zoom in on a building across the river, a brick factory-looking edifice with five tall chimneys spiking the sky. I directed the cursor to move up, and I heard the lens motor whir as zoom engaged and the building enlarged within the viewfinder. Shadows fell from the chimneys, creating an effect that filled me with longing, made me think of trees. I took the shot.

I spent some time on that building—the color of afternoon light on the bricks, the juxtaposition of chimneys against the blue sky, arched windows broken and empty, pigeons roosting on the window ledges. I took many shots. It felt limiting because the camera was in a fixed position—I could only shoot what appeared exactly in the viewfinder, and I had no lateral or vertical motion.

And it felt weird to not be able to just check the monitor, keep the photos I wanted, and discard the rejects along the way, but I kept taking pictures anyway. The building, the sky, more seagulls, different patterns, a plane on its final approach to Logan Airport.

The more I did it, the more I felt lost in the pleasure of taking pictures, and I forgot the limitations and actually began to enjoy the challenge of finding the best photo possible with a completely stationary camera. I knew this was brand-new technology, and that Newton had worked so hard to invent it for me, but I quickly went from marveling about the newness to feeling like myself again, connected to the camera and the thrill of taking photos.

After a while I felt tired, so I stopped. Newton was in tune, and he unhooked me from the camera-holding apparatus and lifted me back into bed. He switched the computer program back to the keyboard, but left the monitor open with all the photos I had just taken.

"Look, Roo. Look what you just did."

I gazed at my shots and wondered, is it true, I really took those?

They were all right. A few were blurry, out of focus, but a few were pretty decent. They weren't so different from photographs I would have taken if I were mobile, not paralyzed. My eye was the same, drawn to dark and light, shadows and sun, sky and birds and nature, the warm red of the bricks, the luminous blue of the sky, the desolation of broken windows, the freedom of seagulls.

Thank you for doing this for me, I said to Newton. *Making it possible.*

"You made it possible," he said.

That whole setup, with the camera and harness, it really works. How did you come up with it?

"I let myself be you for a few hours," he said, sitting on the edge of the bed. "I imagined I was you, and then I tried to figure out what I—you—would need to take beautiful pictures. Then everything just fell into place."

You did a good job of being me.

"There are so many things I want to say to that."

Say them.

"I would be you if I could. Take this away from you. But I know I can't. I feel bad saying anything's hard for me, considering what you go through, but that is hard for me. Seeing you suffer in any way. So instead of being you, I just want to be *with* you."

I thought about that. My stomach flipped, wanting his words to be true, so true they would last forever.

Tilly, I said.

"I know. I can't even explain or excuse it, Roo. Some kind of insanity took me over—her, too. We are both lost without you, and she is such a part of you. The fact that you can stand to look at me says a lot—I can't stand to look at myself."

Get over that, I said.

"What do you mean?"

I thought of Martha. Of what she and Althea went through, how they battled their demons and stuck together till the end. They chose each other, and they forgave each other for being human.

We belong to each other, I said to Newton. *We claimed each other when we were young. I don't expect you to stay with me; you can't. But I want us to be friends. That means all three of us.*

"That sounds nice," he said. Why did those words feel like a dagger in my heart? Then he took my hand. "But it's total bull."

No, it's not.

"Yeah, Roo. It is. You and I can't be friends. Not like that. You think I can undo everything we are to each other just because you're in this bed? Because I can't."

Not undo. Just recalculate.

"Nice try, but I don't think so. 'Recalculate'? As if we're on GPS, a navigation system? A machine? You *are* my navigation, Roo." He touched my head. "You're my north star. Will you try to keep going with me?"

I'm so afraid we're going to hurt each other.

"Because of what I did?"

I hesitated, wanting to tell him the truth. *I don't believe you can handle this. No one could.*

"After all this time, you don't know me if you can say that. Inside, you're the same as ever, so beautiful and smart, making me keep up with you."

We won't be able to do anything. Go outside, use our telescopes, run to Little Beach. Kiss, I said, but inside I felt my resolve weakening. What if Newton and I COULD be together in spite of everything?

"Hey, Roo? We can still do that," he said.

But, I began. He interrupted me, hand on my wrist.

"Remember that night, the Leonids, what I said?"

Yes. My heart began to pound.

"I still feel it," he said.

So did I. What is love? It's only everything.

And he kissed me. He put his arms around me and held me against his body, and I felt his lips on mine. The thing about a kiss, it either fills you with stars or it doesn't. And this one filled me with stars.

Tilly

ate Thursday afternoon, the third week of June, I went to Martha's after school.

I hadn't seen much of Nona and Emily lately; TEN wasn't together that often anymore. Sometimes I wasn't sure whether it was just normal growing up, or whether all the drama had driven a wedge between us. I hoped it hadn't. But the thing was, I didn't seek them out the way I had before Roo's accident. They were fourteen and innocent, and I was fourteen and had lived a few lifetimes. I wanted to spend time with people who got it.

I had also distanced myself from Isabel. I couldn't get over what she'd done. Telling on me had started a gigantic avalanche in my life, and I was still digging out. Sometimes I wondered: Would I have come to it myself, told my mom about the text? Would Mom still have given that interview if she and I could have really talked first? I didn't know; I probably never would. But the TV trucks were gone, on to the next tragedy, and we were left here with ours, trying to put our lives back together.

The two people I most wanted to spend time with, it turned out, were Slater and Martha. They didn't judge me. I needed people like them.

That afternoon, I stood on a stepladder, washing the windows in Althea's old studio. I'd mixed up a bowl of cool water and white vinegar—Martha's recipe—and polished every pane of glass with old newspaper. Years of dust and grime came off, making them sparkle.

Martha's property had several small outbuildings on it, abandoned and overgrown. Slater concentrated on the barn, preparing it for the exhibit, but I had gravitated to the studio, a tiny one-room house. When the sisters were young, Martha told me, it had been their playhouse. Later, after Althea moved back, she turned it into a place to make sculpture.

It was magical. The walls were hung with photographs of sculptures by Elisabeth Gordon Chandler, Camille Claudel, Louise Bourgeois, and other women sculptors; postcards of places Althea had visited—both when she was married to Charles and at other times with Martha; some handwritten quotes from favorite books; and shelves holding plaster casts, shells, beach stones, and a collection of birds' nests. A beehive kiln stood in the corner.

I left the door open to air out the musty space. There was a small refrigerator in the corner, humming away. I wondered why it was still plugged in, when no one was ever in here.

"You're doing a great job," Martha said, walking in.

"Thank you," I said.

"You have no idea how many hours Althea spent here," she said. "It was her favorite place."

"It's really cool," I said. "I like the kiln."

Martha nodded, smiling at me. "Althea did, too. What's your art, Tilly?"

"My art?" I laughed uncomfortably. "I don't have one."

"Everyone needs art, a way to express themselves. For me, it's poetry and working with herbs. Althea had sculpture. Your sister's a photographer. What about you?"

I shrugged and just kept working. Memories smashed into me like a tidal wave, of how I used to wish I had a gift, just like Martha was suggesting. But I kept those thoughts to myself.

Martha crouched by the small refrigerator, her amber velveteen skirt trailing on the floor. She pulled out a plastic bag filled with clay. Lucan looked over her shoulder, very interested.

"This is the last of Althea's clay," she said. "I've kept it in the fridge to keep it moist, but I think it's time to do something with it."

"You want me to throw it out?" I asked.

"I want you to sculpt something."

"Me?" I asked doubtfully.

"Roo's photographs are remarkable, and I can't wait to hang them for the show. But they made me wonder, what do you do, with all you have inside?"

"It's funny," I said slowly, remembering that time last July when Roo had sat on my bed, braiding my hair. "I was just wondering the same thing. Roo and I talked about it once."

"What did she say?"

I laughed, embarrassed. "It won't make sense. You had to be there."

She stood still, waiting to see if I would say more. Maybe I would have, if I could have. The thoughts were too powerful and confusing to put into words, though.

"Well, I'll leave you with the clay," she said, smiling after a minute. "Don't think too much about it. Just get your hands into it. That's what Althea used to say she did. 'I let the clay tell me what it wants to be.' "

"As if it has a life of its own," I said, trying to laugh.

"Just see what happens," she said.

It seemed weird to be playing with clay; that's what it felt like—playing, when I was supposed to be working. But Martha had told me to do it, and she was my boss. I glanced around the room, hoping for inspiration. Martha stood by the door with Lucan.

"Can I ask you one thing?" I said.

"Of course. If it's about technique, I don't know. You just have to feel your way, have fun with it."

"It's about Roo. When you visited her, did she say anything about me?"

"Yes, she did."

My stomach fell; I wasn't sure I wanted to know, but I had to ask. "Can you tell me?"

"We spoke about love between sisters, and we spoke of princesses and dragons," Martha said, a smile twinkling in her eyes as she and Lucan walked out the door and headed toward the barn.

Too mysterious for me, I thought. Pulling the stool close to Althea's worktable, I stared at the lump of clay. I remembered middle school, making Christmas ornaments, and how we'd needed water to keep the clay moist. So I pulled a sage-green bowl from the shelf and filled it.

When I returned, the clay stared at me. It seemed to be daring me. Martha had it all confused. Roo was the artistic one. She had the talent. But I kept thinking about what both Martha and Roo had asked me, at separate times: What do I do with all I have inside? And I had plenty. I had anger, fear, dreams, hope, sorrow, and love for my sister. I thought about the anger, how mad I was at myself for texting her, and, surprisingly, how mad I was at her for texting back, going off the road.

And now we were so distant. We were so far apart. I felt grief for how we used to be, how badly I wanted that again. My fingers found their way into the clay. I wasn't really thinking or trying; I was just feeling. Martha's words echoed in my ears: *love between sisters, princesses and dragons.*

And words of Roo, from last summer: *poetry of . . .*

Not of owls, not of life, but something else.

The clay felt slippery and smooth. It was pale gray, and turned my hands white, as if I'd dipped them in flour. My mind filled with a story about sisters who were princesses, who lived in a castle in the clouds, and who were attacked by dragons. I pushed and pulled the clay, fighting Roo's dragon, wanting to slay it for her. Althea had said the clay tells you what it wants to be, and as hard as I tried to make a wicked, evil beast, it didn't work out that way.

When I was finished, I had a cute little dragon on the worktable. She was about the size of an orange, round and compact, with a scaly tail and off-kilter wings. Her face looked a bit like

Lucan, including a tongue that lolled out. I was so proud of her, I wanted to show Martha and Slater.

As I ran, holding her in my cupped hands, she began to wilt from the heat. I entered the barn and saw that Newton had dropped off Roo's framed photos. He must have left right away. Martha and Slater were standing back from the wall, trying to figure out where each one should go.

"I did it," I said. "I made this."

"Cool, a stegosaurus!" Slater said.

"With wings?" I asked, scoffing.

"It's a dragon," Martha said. "And a very good one, Tilly."

"This is what I had inside me," I said. "A dragon." *Roo would get it*, I thought. All my funny little creatures: Who knew they had been there for such an actual, real, productive reason? To save me. And to save Roo.

"Maybe you'll find she has sisters," Martha said. "Friends and relatives. You might have a whole family of dragons in there. Well, we can get you more clay so you can sculpt them all. Meanwhile, you have to glaze and paint her. We'll fire up the kiln."

I knew I should tell her not to bother, it was too much trouble; but the truth was, I felt excited, good about what I had done. And she was right: I had more dragons inside. I felt them smashing around inside my chest, a thousand wings.

I propped up Sage—her name, after the color of the water bowl and one of my favorite herb beds in Martha's garden—the best I could on a table in a corner of the barn, while Martha went down to start the kiln. Slater and I began hanging Roo's photographs.

Each one was so familiar. I had seen every place, every face that appeared in her pictures. In some cases, I had been standing with her while she'd taken the shot. Would that ever happen again? My mother had told me Newton had rigged up some kind of mad-scientist apparatus that allowed Roo to take photos. Apparently, Roo was happy she could take any at all, but so far, they weren't the same caliber as these.

Another dragon, I thought: the my-sister-can't-take-photos-the-way-she-used-to dragon. There were so many: the my-sister-and-I-were-texting dragon; the will-my-sister-ever-forgive-me-for-kissing-her-boyfriend dragon; the my-sister-is-in-the-hospital-in-Boston-and-I-want-her-home dragon.

"Should we hang this one right here?" Slater asked, standing by an empty spot, holding up Roo's time-lapse photograph of last year's Leonid meteor shower.

"No, that should be the central piece," I said. "It's her favorite. Let's put it right in the middle."

I took the picture from Slater's hands and walked it to the place of honor—the center of the back wall—so it would be the first thing people saw when they came through the door. I hung it on the nail, then stood back with Slater to admire it.

"Looks great," he said.

"I wish she could be here to see," I said. "We'll all be celebrating, and she'll be up there in Boston."

Slater didn't reply. We continued hanging the rest of Roo's photos, and it surprised me to realize how excited I was about firing this dragon and making many more. It surprised me to realize I felt excited about anything at all.

"I'm going back to the studio," I said, and couldn't wait to get there.

"Sounds good," Slater said. We smiled at each other.

Then I took my droopy little dragon and ran down the hill to Althea's studio, to see Martha and find out when the kiln would be ready.

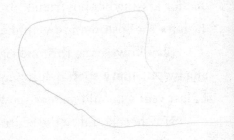

Chapter Fifteen

Roo

*T*hese are fantastic," Dr. Gold said, early Wednesday evening, viewing my photographs on the computer screen. "I knew you'd made progress, but you have blown me away with how much."

Thank you, I said, beaming inside at the praise.

"You have really mastered this computer interface, Roo."

The camera hardware helped.

"Yes, Newton did an amazing job," she said.

She and Dr. Hill stood beside my bed, conducting my exam together. They examined my head, the incision where the sensor had been implanted. They shined lights into both my eyes. They stuck tiny pins in my fingertips and looked pleased when I flinched ever so slightly. Inside, I was yelping with pain, which I knew was a good sign.

"She moved!" Isabel said, standing at the end of my bed. She had come up to show me her finished portfolio and look at the pictures I'd taken with Newton.

"She reacted," Dr. Hill said, correcting her.

"That's a new development, right?" Isabel asked. "Does it mean she's getting feelings back, she's got a chance of much greater recovery?"

"Everyone," Dr. Gold said, "Roo is right here. Could we stop referring to her as 'she'?"

Thank you, I said again, inwardly smiling because she sounded like Dr. Howarth. It didn't bother me so much anymore, being spoken about in the third person, now that I could communicate. At the same time, I realized I didn't really miss Dr. Howarth anymore; I only had room in my heart for one crush.

"You're welcome," Dr. Gold said.

"Yes, Isabel, you did observe a reaction," Dr. Hill said. "It is too soon to know exactly what to expect, but we are certainly heartened. I think it's time to discuss next steps."

What next steps? I asked.

"We can begin to think about a rehab facility. Closer to home, so your family can make the trip to visit you more easily."

"*Gracias*, that is great news," Isabel said.

Can I go home? I felt breathless at the thought—both excited at the prospect, and really scared. But if there was any way to actually go, I knew I'd get through the fear.

"There is no reason why you can't *visit* home, but Dr. Hill and I would both feel better if you were living in a place where people could respond to all your needs, and where they are prepared for all contingencies," Dr. Gold said.

A nursing home? I pictured Marshview, across the river from Black Hall. Our school visited each year, sang Christmas carols to the residents. Old people, some with Alzheimer's, sitting in wheelchairs while someone played the banjo and sang old-time tunes. The smell of diapers was strong. My heart twisted. Did I belong there?

"That might be a possibility," Dr. Gold said. "I would want to make sure they had first-rate physical therapy, and a medical staff that's tops, and would be willing to work closely with me, Dr. Hill, and Dr. Danforth."

Dr. Danforth? I asked, and my heart literally skipped. In spite of the idea of being moved to an assisted living home, the idea of being reunited with her filled me with pure happiness.

"Yes, of course. She has continued to consult with us, and she would really like it if when you returned to Connecticut, she could take over as your doctor. She is as good as they come, in my book. How would you feel about that?"

I'd like it.

"We'll discuss it much more," she said. "I'll leave you two friends together now. Enjoy your visit."

Thank you, I said.

Isabel and my nurse, Nina, helped me into the wheelchair, and Isabel pushed me down to the solarium. During her frequent visits, Isabel had gotten to know some of the patients. My friends.

At first I had disliked coming here. The other disabled patients shocked me into realizing I was just like them—or worse. Morgan and Dani, the two patients I had seen on my first foray out of my room, had been discharged to rehab units, but other patients had arrived. And we had become friendly.

Laura, a slim blond eighteen-year-old, had dove into a shallow bay when she was twelve and broken her neck; paralyzed from the neck down, at least she could talk, and she had learned how to control her motorized wheelchair. She had some health issues and was in here for what she called "a tune-up."

Patsy, twenty-three and newly married, had spina bifida. She'd had birth defects, been born with a split spine, and as a child her nerve endings and spinal cord had bulged through her vertebrae and caused her brain to swell. She was mentally acute, but her body was frail, her bones deformed, and she had to be in a wheelchair.

"Hey, Roo," Patsy called now. "How's it going?"

"Having a good day, Patsy," Isabel answered for me. "How are you?"

"Pretty good, thanks."

"How was your exam today, Roo?" Laura asked.

I felt closer to Laura than any other patient I had met so far. We were closer in age, and in spite of her diving accident, she still loved the ocean.

I might be transferred closer to home, I said.

"That would be awesome," Patsy said. "What kind of place?"

Nursing home.

"Oh, goodie," Laura said. "Where you can be the youngest one by fifty years."

"Hey, be positive," Isabel said.

"We're just kidding around," Laura said. "DH—disabled humor. You're so serious, Isabel!"

"You have to find the right facility," Patsy said. "Some know how to handle young people, others just warehouse us, keep us clean and fed, not much else. I've been disabled since birth, so

I've seen it all. The best places really get it. You need doctors who understand. Like the one I've got now, she's helping me with fertility treatments."

"You want a baby? That's so great," Isabel said.

"Yeah, I want a baby! I always have. Jerry and I went to one doctor, and he was so skeptical. Spina bifida can be genetic, and he was all, oh, you might pass it on to your child. And I was like, why shouldn't I want someone like myself? As if a baby with my condition isn't worth having." She shook her head. "So I found someone new. A woman doctor."

"Of course," Laura said. "A woman would understand."

I thought about Newton and me, wondered whether we'd ever be thinking this way, wanting to have a family. Would it even be possible? Before my accident, deep down, I'd pictured us with kids someday, playing on the same beach where we'd grown up.

"Do you live at home or somewhere else?" Isabel asked.

"I go back and forth," Laura said. "My family wants me home, and I love the idea. But it's hard, I can't lie to you. I'm here right now because I've got a urinary infection that spread to my kidneys. My family has to lift me, and clean me, drive me to classes, and they take me down to the beach, push me along the boardwalk, and they do their best. But my mother's getting older, and sometimes I can see it in my brother's eyes he's kind of over it."

Will that be Newton? I wondered. He had lifted me so easily, and he said we were forever. But this could wear anyone down.

"What classes?" Isabel asked.

"I go to Lesley University," Laura said. "I'm studying art therapy."

"She's great at it, too," Patsy said, smiling warmly.

Laura rolled her eyes, but she also smiled. "Well, I'll have to get a master's degree if I want to work anywhere good. But Lesley has a graduate program, so I'm aiming for that. When are you going back to school, Roo?"

I don't know, I said. The truth was, I had given up thinking I ever would. I felt so destroyed, so ugly and alien. But seeing these women, just a few years older than I, made me see other possibilities.

"She's coming back for senior year," Isabel said.

I looked at her, feeling surprised.

"You are, *chica*," she said, squeezing my hand as if she'd read my mind. "Don't say you're not."

"Isabel is right," Laura said. "You are the only one who can stop yourself. The school will find a way for you to be there. I was a disabled kid through half of middle and all of high school."

Wasn't it weird being there with the . . . I hesitated, searching for the word.

"Normal kids?" Laura asked, supplying the word, laughing. "Totally, although actually we say 'typical,' or 'people without disabilities.' Why should they be the 'normal' ones?"

"Yeah, we're all normal, or none of us are," Patsy said.

"So true," Laura said. "Anyway, after growing up with them, being on the soccer team, acting in school plays—we did *The Wizard of Oz* the year before my accident—and suddenly I was paralyzed. No one knew how to act, including me. But it got easier."

"I thought I was—here's the word again—'normal,'" Patsy said. "Because I always had spina bifida. I had no idea I was different until I went to first grade and the kids started calling me Big Head."

"They called me Gimp and Wheelchair Girl. Then they got tired of it and figured out I wasn't all that different than I was before, and it all seemed kind of normal after a while," Laura said.

"You just want to have an ordinary life," Patsy said.

I never did before, I thought. And I thought how much my family used to make of the fact that I was extraordinary—how I was going to go to Yale, and win academic awards. And you know, I still wanted to be different, wanted to do the best I could.

"You don't have to scale back," Isabel said, as if she could read my mind. "You're still my amazing Roo. That has not changed."

"She's right," Laura said. "I didn't know you before, but I think you're pretty amazing."

"True," Patsy said. "Dr. Hill wants you fast-tracked into communicating, getting back to your life as soon as possible."

"Wherever you go, just make sure you find other disabled kids," Laura said. "As wonderful as Isabel is, she doesn't know what it's like to wear a diaper and not be able to scratch that itch on your nose. No offense, Izz."

"No offense taken," Isabel said.

"You need us," Patsy said. "And there are lots of us. I'm in this online club, the nicest people you ever want to meet."

"And wicked and irreverent. Lots of kids with brain injuries, actually," Laura said. "You'll find good ways to keep your people on their toes. Like, using person-first language. We're not our disabilities. I'm not 'the quadriplegic.' I'm a person with a spinal cord injury."

"I used to go to school on what everyone called 'the handicapped bus,'" Patsy said. "Made it sound like the bus was on crutches."

"You don't say 'handicapped'?" Isabel asked.

"No, we say 'disabled,'" Patsy said.

I was really starting to like my new friends. I'd have to get used to the language, though. Disabled started with "dis," a negative. And these were some of the most positive and *most-abled* people I'd ever met.

What's the club called? People with Disabilities? I asked.

"Nope. The Society of Remarkable Alpinists," Laura said.

Alpinists? Mountain climbers?

"Yeah," Laura said, smiling. "Because we've all climbed mountains higher than most people even imagine. And we do it with style, and we do it every day!"

We do, I said. Inside I was grinning because I liked the name; they'd gotten it so right.

I felt tired, and after we said good-bye, Isabel wheeled me back to my room. She sat with me while I dozed. It was strange, but I was looking forward to those chat rooms. I was an alpinist, and I had a lot of questions. And I was even looking forward to seeing kids from my old life, even though it seemed a million miles away. I thought of Tilly. I had always been her champion, stood up for her and protected her. It was weird to think I might have to lean on her quite a bit if I was ever going to return to school. I wondered what it would be like to have our roles reversed.

On Saturday morning, very early, I woke up to see my mother sitting by the bed. That wasn't unusual; although she'd gone back to work, she often came on her days off.

But Sunday was our regular time, the day she settled down beside me with the Sunday papers, homework, and whatever novel she was in the midst of reading. Besides, today was the solstice: the exhibition at Martha's.

I was surprised, and even a little disappointed, that she was here. I hadn't seen Tilly, but I knew from my mother and Newton how hard she had been working on the exhibition. Newton had delivered my photos to hang in Martha's barn. I'd thought my mother would want to see. I gazed at her; she was wearing her favorite summer dress and the necklace of Hubbard's Point moonstones I'd made for her.

Why are you here, Mom? I asked.

"Is that a way to talk to your mother?" Dr. Gold asked. "She's come all the way to Boston, looking lovely I might add, to see you."

"Thank you," my mother said.

But I thought you'd be with Tilly, I said. *At Martha's.*

"Oh, that's right," Christina said, brushing my hair. "Today's the exhibition."

"I can't imagine your mother wanting to miss that," Nina said, easing my feet into a clean pair of white pressure socks.

"The exhibition," Dr. Gold said.

Today's the solstice, I said.

"Yes," Dr. Gold said.

Althea's sculpture show, I said, looking at my mother, wishing she would go to it.

"And your photographs will be shown there as well, I am told," Dr. Gold said.

Now I saw my mother, Christina, and Nina grinning, as if they knew something I didn't. My heart began to race.

What is it? I asked. *What's going on?*

"It's a long day, down to Black Hall and back," Dr. Gold said. "I wouldn't feel comfortable with you going without a doctor along."

Me? With me?

"You have to tell me, Roo," Dr. Gold said, getting down to eye level with me. "It's a major event for a talented young photographer. And I don't want you to miss it. But it's a lot of stress, a trip like this. You have to tell me if you're up to it. I just want to be sure you're ready."

Today? Right now? I get to leave the hospital?

"I want to give you the choice," she said.

"I've hired an ambulance, but you can pretend it's a limousine, honey," my mother said.

My vision blurred with tears. I could only imagine how much that cost. I wanted nothing more than to do this, but everything felt so new, so precarious. I hadn't left the hospital

since arriving in March. What if I had a seizure? Or even
another stroke?

Can I really do this? I asked Dr. Gold.

"You have to tell me how you feel. I'll be with you, Roo, the
whole time."

"And I'll be in the car right behind you," my mother said.

Dr. Gold looked up, toward the door, beckoned someone to
come in. "And so will this young man."

Newton.

He walked into the room wearing the suit he'd worn to last
spring's prom. It was black, with a white dress shirt, and a
skinny black tie. He looked like the handsomest geek in the
world. He held a box. He opened it and took out a bouquet of
beach roses.

They're beautiful, I said.

"I picked them for you at Little Beach," he said. He removed
one from the bunch; hands shaking, he pinned it to my hospital gown.

Are we really going back to Black Hall? I asked.

"Only if you're ready," he said. "Otherwise we'll stay right
here. We'll celebrate either way."

It was up to me. I stared into Newton's face and thought
of how recently I'd thought of giving up. Just weeks ago I
had wanted to slip away. But now I was getting my life back,
and that meant I wanted to make the choice that would keep
me here.

So I made my decision.

Tilly

*T*hat morning, the day of the Solstice Art Celebration, I couldn't keep my eyes off the driveway. I was staring right at it when Nona, Emily, and Isabel showed up early to Casa Magica to volunteer. Isabel had given them a ride. It was a kind of old-time pulling together, and it made me feel emotional and grateful—even to Isabel. When she walked over, it was the first time we'd hugged since she'd found the cell phone.

Slater and I showed them the barn and the studio, and the gardens that people might want to wander through. We set up a table near the herb garden for tea and cookies. Martha had bundled up tiny bouquets of dried herbs; whatever was sold would benefit Roo's care.

I wore a blue halter and long flowered skirt, dressed up for the occasion, and I blushed when Slater smiled and nodded, letting me know he liked it.

"Where's Newton?" Emily asked me. "I thought he'd be here helping out."

"So did I," I said. "He dropped off Roo's photos a few days ago and hasn't been back. He's on a mission."

"Is your mother coming?" Nona asked. "Considering Roo's photos are part of the exhibit."

I didn't answer. My mother and Newton were on the same mission. They had driven up to Boston that morning. Mom had told me that Dr. Gold was going to arrange for Roo to show up today. It was so much to hope for. Everything had to line up: Her vital signs had to be completely stable, which they hardly ever were, her brain scan had to be perfect, and a doctor, preferably Dr. Gold, had to be available to accompany her. That meant no emergency admissions or surgeries.

More than anything, Roo had to feel well enough to make the trip.

"Tilly's in the art show, too," Slater said. "Did she show you?"

He led my friends into the barn, where Martha had set up a table for my dragon family. During the last few days, I had spent every spare moment with my hands in clay. After Sage, my first droopy dragon, I'd made ten more. All small, all with Lucan's face, painted bright colors and fired to a high glaze. Some were flying, some were sleeping, two were fighting, two were kissing. They all had tails and wings.

"These are adorable!" Emily said. "I want the orange one!"

"How sweet," Nona said. "The way you painted tiny daisies down the spine of the purple girl."

"And hearts on the spikes of the pink one," Isabel said.

"Do they have names?" Emily asked.

"This one should be Squishy-Face," Nona said, holding up my first dragon, the poor girl who'd melted in the heat before I'd figured things out.

"That one's Sage, but the rest have secret names," Slater said. "She won't tell anyone."

It was true. I'd named them after the emotions that had been swirling around while I made them. All were girls, and I thought of them as being my team, my club. Dragon Power, I thought.

It seemed perfect that the dragons stood on a table by Roo's photographs, as if they could protect her, and guard everything she held dear. It killed me that she was being honored this way, and she might be stuck in a hospital bed a hundred miles away. The dragons made that just a little better, as if they could spread their scaly wings and fly to her, carry to her my love and belief in her strength.

And I felt happy, even a little proud, that the dragons had helped me realize maybe I can be an artist, too. In my own way.

People began to arrive. I felt strange and a bit intruded upon—Slater and I had had Martha and her magical property to ourselves for weeks. If I were honest, I'd say the only person I wanted to be there was Roo. But I'd gotten no word from Mom. She probably didn't want to give me the bad news. The idea of Roo actually showing up was so impossible, so heartbreaking to consider, I named the feeling Angst and decided she would be my next dragon.

"You okay?" Slater asked as we watched Marlene and Debbie walk into the barn. It was strange how Marlene seemed changed by Roo's accident. I had thought her collecting donations had been an act for the reporters, for the national Don't Text campaign. But here she was today, and there were no TV cameras in sight.

"I guess so," I said. "Not completely."

"I can tell," he said. "You get a very Tilly look on your face sometimes."

"What does it look like?" I asked.

"Well, you look very determined, but there's this little hint as if you're afraid it won't work out."

"That sounds kind of pathetic."

"Actually, it's cute."

"Huh," I said, blushing. "But in this case, it won't. Work out, I mean."

"Your sister?"

It was perfect June weather in Black Hall. The sun shined, the river and tributaries and Sound sparkled bright blue, and Martha's roses and gardens were in bloom. People had come to celebrate Roo's photos and Althea's sculpture, but Roo wasn't here.

"Yeah," I said. "It doesn't look as if she's going to get here."

"I'm sorry," Slater said. He put his arm around me and kind of shored me up, a good-friend thing to do. Was it crazy of me, under the circumstances, to notice that his touch felt electric? I leaned into his chest to keep the charge going.

"Slater, aren't you going to introduce us?"

We turned, and there was his mother. I recognized her from that day I saw them at the Big Y. Dressed in black pants, a white silk shirt, and broad straw hat, she was in a wheelchair being pushed by a young woman with intricate beaded braids.

"Mom, this is Tilly McCabe. Tilly, this is my mother, Yvonne Jones, and my cousin, Arlene Franklin."

"It's really good to meet you, Mrs. Jones. Hi, Arlene."

"You too, Tilly. I've heard a lot about you. You and my son have done a great job pulling this day together."

"Thank you," I said, feeling a big smile on my face when she said that. "He's pretty great to work with."

"If my mother says it's good, that's something," Slater said. "She worked at the Metropolitan Museum of Art. So I'll take it!"

"Me too," I said.

Arlene and Mrs. Jones went through the herb garden, stopping at each of Althea's sculptures, regarding them from every angle. Other people from town came, kids from school, my friends' parents, and total strangers. I watched them looking at Althea's bronze dancers, then move into the barn to stop in front of each of Roo's photos, and my feelings began to change.

I felt proud. My sister's photos were on display, and now I was glad crowds had arrived. I watched people stand in front of each of her pictures, taking in the beauty she'd seen and captured. It hit me once again how she had photographed local scenes but made them look so radiant, so important, they seemed to transcend the map. They were the whole world.

Slater held my hand. We looked at Roo's "Star Trails" photo. He put his arm around my waist.

"This makes me want to go to the Hayden Planetarium together," he said. "We can take a train from Old Saybrook, as soon as school gets out."

"I can't wait."

"To go to New York?"

"Yeah. And for this school year to be over. It's been the worst ever." But I caught myself and gave him a smile. "Well, most of it."

He kissed me so lightly on the lips, I felt weak in the knees. I grabbed his elbows. I was filled with emotions, a whole new bunch of dragons: excited, euphoric, tempestuous, enthralled, feisty, pumped.

Just then a weird noise sounded—rhythmic beeps that I'd heard before, when Roo was being taken from New London up to Boston, when the ambulance had gone into reverse.

"What's that?" I asked, breaking away.

"Here she is," he said, staring over my shoulder, and I turned to see an ambulance backing into the property.

We tore out of the barn, past the herb garden to the gravel drive. Behind the ambulance, driving slowly, was my mother's car. She was behind the wheel, and Newton was beside her.

A crowd began to gather. Martha came toward me, Lucan bounding beside her. He went straight to the back of the ambulance, as if standing vigil. Newton walked around back just as the attendant swung the door open. It was dark inside the ambulance, but Martha pushed me closer so I could see. Dr. Gold was there. She waved to me.

Hello, Tilly came the voice, but it wasn't Dr. Gold's.

I scrambled up the bumper, crashing past Newton to get into the back, pushing past Dr. Gold to throw my arms around my sister.

"Roo, you're really here," I said, my voice breaking.

She lay flat on a gurney, held in place by red straps. My mother had brought real clothes to the hospital, so Roo was wearing jeans and a white T-shirt, her favorite beige cashmere sweater draped around her shoulders. Her hair was less than an inch long, just growing in after the chip implant, and her blue eyes were as wide and staring as ever. But I thought she looked beautiful.

I am, Tilly. I wouldn't have missed it, Roo said, her voice coming through the computer as Newton finished adjusting the cables.

And Dr. Gold had to pry my arms from around my sister so she and Newton could lift her down into her wheelchair, her first time back in Black Hall since the accident.

Chapter Sixteen

Roo

I t smelled like home. The fresh air of the exact spot where the Connecticut River poured into Long Island Sound, and I felt surrounded by the fragrance of tidal marshes, and new leaves, and beach roses, and mountain laurel. Getting air into my lungs took all my energy at first, because the sight of my family, and so many friends, literally took my breath away.

Newton held tight to one hand, Tilly to the other. My mother kept watching me, as if she was afraid this wasn't real, she'd open her eyes and realize she'd been dreaming. I felt the same way. Isabel ran over to hug me, sticking right by my side.

Martha bent down, kissed my forehead. Lucan nuzzled my hand. I held it together, but that was one moment that overwhelmed me: to be at the house of the woman I could have killed, whose dog I had injured, filled me with the knowledge of how close I had come.

"You're here," Martha said. "And we're so glad."

So am I.

"Would you like to see the exhibit? Your photos?" she asked.

Althea's sculptures, I said.

Martha pushed my chair. Tilly and Newton stayed right with me. We went down a narrow path lined with boxwood. Herbs grew everywhere, in tidy beds. I smelled sage, thyme, lavender, and mint. It reminded me of the little sachets Martha had brought me, and I savored the moment, knowing that from now on, their scent would remind me of this day.

The sky was bright blue, the sun warm on my arms. Friends from school circled around, wary or shy. If I could have, I would have called them over. I felt them assessing me, saw them whispering as if I weren't there. My stomach twisted; I thought of Laura, Patsy, and Ellen, of what they had said about how hard it was to enter into an ordinary life again, how it was all they wanted.

I wanted it, too, I realized, more than anything. I wanted the ease of jumping up, running around the yard and seeing everyone, gazing at Althea's beautiful statues as long as I could.

"This is one of my favorites," Martha said, stopping in front of two girls holding hands and dancing.

"I've always thought it was you and Althea," Tilly said.

"It is," Martha said.

Willoughby Moon and Luna, I said.

"Your nicknames?" Tilly asked, sounding delighted, getting it immediately.

"Yes," Martha said.

"It captures what sisters are like," Newton said.

"How would you describe that?" Martha asked. "From the sculpture, I mean."

He was quiet for a moment. Although I couldn't turn to look at him, I could imagine the pensive expression in his eyes as he regarded the statue, formulating his thoughts.

"The girls are together. They're individuals, obviously—one is taller, the other wears glasses; the tall sister has shorter hair and is wearing pants; the shorter one is laughing, wearing a skirt. Different personalities, but so obviously together. They're almost one."

"Yes, they are," Martha said.

"*We* are," Tilly said, squeezing my hand.

"Do you know, this is the first time I've ever seen you two together?" Martha asked, looking at us. "You're two years apart, and you have very different talents, but oh, you are so close. You are so alike."

"Thank you," Tilly said. "I always wanted to be like Roo."

Not now, I said. *You wouldn't want to be.*

"I would," Tilly said, bending down, putting her head on my shoulder. "I always want to be like you."

Martha pushed me around the garden to see Althea's other work: a young girl reading, another kneeling, with her face tilted up toward the sky.

Is she looking at the stars? I asked.

"She might be," Martha said. "She might be making a wish."

I stared at that little girl for a long time. She was kneeling just as a real girl would, the backs of her thighs resting on her heels, feet splayed out. Her arms were straight down, palms on the ground supporting her. She wore glasses. I glanced at Martha.

It's you, I said.

"Yep. She always said I inspired her," Martha said.

My sister inspires me, I said. *Besides Newton, she's the person I most like to photograph.*

"Seriously?" Tilly asked.

Your face, I said. *You're just like the weather, changing every second. I love to watch your eyes, see the emotions there. I was horrible; I sometimes teased you just to see your face change. I would say something scary, then happy, because I loved to make you smile.*

And Tilly smiled then, which made me happy.

"You're Tilly's inspiration, you know," someone said. He was standing out of sight but came around front so I could see him: Slater Jones, the kid who had started Black Hall High right around the holidays last year.

"Roo, this is Slater," Tilly said.

I remember. Hi, Slater.

"I'm glad you came," he said. "Especially because Tilly's over the moon right now. She saw you pull up and, wow."

"Yeah," Tilly said. "It's true. I essentially had the best nervous breakdown anyone has ever had, when I saw you pull up."

"You're still kind of having it, aren't you?" Slater asked.

"Yes, about one hundred percent."

She likes him, I thought. A lot. Tilly has a boyfriend. I looked at them, saw them smiling at each other. Tilly's face looked as if it might crack with joy and love, and I have never regretted not having a camera more than in that very instant.

Martha began pushing me toward the barn, and when we went inside, I felt choked up. My photos were hanging on the wall opposite the door. They had all been matted and framed, and they looked professional. It felt like an art gallery. My mother, Dr. Gold, and Isabel were walking slowly in front of them, studying each one. Many other people milled about, too. I heard them whispering, saw them turn when I entered.

"It's Roo!" Marlene said in a loud whisper.

"She better keep away," Tilly said under her breath.

But Marlene came right over, dressed in a tight pink tank and cutoff shorts.

"Oh, Roo," she said, crouching down so our faces were close. "Thank God you're alive."

Her eyes were filled with tears, and amazingly, now mine were, too. Marlene and I had never been friends, never had anything in common. I was shocked to see her act this way.

Thank you, I said.

"We've all been hoping you'd get better, that you'll come back to school."

I'm trying, I said.

"Marlene collected a lot of donations in the cafeteria," Isabel said.

"She did," Tilly said, and that shocked me, too. She had never been a fan of Marlene, and she had never been one to fake her feelings—but she sounded genuine, and grateful.

I appreciate it.

"We'll keep the fund going," Marlene said. "Me and Deb."

She hugged me hard, seeming to not want to let go. I smelled perfume, gum, and powder, and I felt her shoulders heaving with little sobs.

She had broken the ice, and now other kids and teachers came to say hi. Nona and Emily hugged me, Teddy Messina and Isabel's cousin Melanie said they liked my photos, and Mr. Gordon told me he was very proud of me and looked forward to helping me return as a senior as soon as I was ready. My heart raced at his words, and I felt excited by the possibility of going back to my school.

"You okay?" Dr. Gold asked, leaning down to whisper in my ear. "It can be very tiring to feel so much emotion. Just say the word, and we'll leave."

No way, I said.

She laughed.

Martha and Lucan went to give new arrivals tours of the sculpture garden. Dr. Gold backed off, and went to view the exhibition.

Newton and I admired Tilly's dragons. They were arrayed on a table next to an old plow, small round creatures painted primary colors, their spines and tails decorated with stars, hearts. Their expressions were a combination of ferocious, tender, frightened, and brave.

After a few minutes, Newton balanced the laptop on the table and walked away with Slater, leaving Tilly and me alone.

She crouched down next to me, looking into my face.

"I'm glad you're here," she said.

Me too.

"I wasn't sure we'd ever be together again."

We're sisters, I said, and that really did say it all.

She put her arm around my shoulders, touched her forehead to mine. Her eyelashes fluttered against mine. I tried to breathe steady, because I could tell she was really agitated.

"I'm sorry," she said.

You've said that enough. Let's have it be over, I said.

"I want to."

Good. Then it is. And sometimes it was that simple. *I love your dragons.*

"I made them because of you," she said.

Because I'm a dragon?

"No," Tilly said. "And not because you slay them, either. Because of that poem by Rilke. 'Perhaps all the dragons in our lives are princesses who are only waiting to see us act, just once, with beauty and courage.' Martha told me, and it's you, Roo. You do everything with beauty and courage. So I wanted to try."

I thought back to last summer, when Mom and Dad had praised me so hard, and Tilly had felt left out. And I'd followed her up to her room, my sensitive little sister, and I'd tried to make her feel better.

I could see the sun setting over the beach, the light coming through the window, and I felt the same as I did then, wanting her to believe in herself and find a way to express herself.

You've more than tried—you've done it. You have . . .

"I have . . . what?" she asked, beaming. And I could feel her waiting for it.

The poetry of dragons, I said.

"We have the same memory," she said, tearing up.

My eyes welled, too, spilling over, and she wiped the tears from my cheeks.

It washed over us, all we had been through, our lives together, our lives apart. Memories of our happy childhood, and of this last ferocious year. This was how we knew we were sisters—we had a language for it, deeper than words, that no one else, even our parents, could know. We spoke it both awake and in our dreams, and it told the story of us.

I wished Tilly could see my smile. It might not have been on my face; I couldn't control those muscles. But it was inside, filling my heart.

"I want you to have the dragons," Tilly said. "In the hospital, till you come home. To keep you brave and remind you I love you."

She hugged me hard, just as Newton came back. Tilly stayed by my side another minute, and I felt something shimmer between us. She hesitated, looking into my eyes, not wanting to leave me. But it was okay now, and I wanted her to feel it, too. We had found our ways back to each other, to the place we'd started from the day she was born, the day she became my little sister.

"I'm going to find Slater," she said. "Meet us down by the river, okay?"

Okay, I said.

Tilly gave me one more hug, then ran off.

Newton pushed my chair out of the barn, down the narrow, wooded path to the Connecticut River. Saturday boat traffic was in full swing, one of the first really warm spring days. The train bridge was down, and boats circled, waiting for it to open so they could pass again. The river sparkled all the way down to Long Island Sound; it was late afternoon, and I saw the glint of the lens at the Outer Light.

"Hey, it's the first day of summer," Newton said.

Summer. I can't lie. The idea of it filled me with such longing, such wistfulness for all the summers he and I had spent together, all the beach walks, and swims to the big rock, and lazy afternoons at Foley's, and the sailing and kayak expeditions along the coastline. I thought of times we'd taken the ferry across the Sound to Orient Point, ridden bikes along North Fork roads through potato fields, apple orchards, and vineyards, then back to the ferry dock, where we'd look toward Hubbard's Point, try to make out my family's cottage.

The sun was going down now, and I thought of sunsets we had seen, times the sky had turned bright red, letting us know the next day would be blazing hot. And we wouldn't care, because we could swim, and read in the shade, and let the sea breeze cool us.

I didn't know what we had, I said.

"You and me?" he said.

Yes. And me and Tilly. All of us. I didn't know how lucky I was. I took a lot for granted. Just look at this.

The river sparkled as the sky turned from bright blue to dark blue to violet. The crescent moon swung low in the west, cradling Venus, just above the deep-red sun. The view looked so beautiful, I wanted to drink it in so I could carry it with me when I returned to the hospital.

"This is just the first sunset of summer," Newton said. "There will be so many more, and the best skies come in winter anyway. That's when they're so clear, and the stars are so close."

Truer than true.

"Here it is," I heard Tilly call. She came tearing down the path with Slater, holding the box I'd first seen when Newton had brought it to the hospital: my camera and the rig he had built.

I stared out at the water while Tilly held my camera, and Newton assembled the box, frame, straps, and helmet, and Slater stood by the water's edge, watching the current. A boat sailed past, leaning into the wind. The breeze caught the sail, and the setting sun painted it gold.

Newton set me up and, without asking, pointed my chair exactly toward the moon and Venus. He had emailed Dr. Howarth again, and they had worked out the bug where previously the software could perform only one function at a time, so I had had to choose between shooting photos or speaking.

Now, by switching with a sharp glance upward, I could toggle between camera and communication. I looked through the viewfinder, spotted the silvery sky objects in the rose-colored twilight. The sailboat bisected the window, and I clicked one photo, then another.

Tilly checked the monitor and gasped.

"Roo, these are so good. You can definitely include them in your portfolio, and good old Serena Kader Barrois won't know what hit her!"

We have to hurry, I said. *The light is perfect.*

I zoomed in on the sky, took a shot of the moon and planet that caught the moon's thin edge of light and shadowed disc, along with Venus's bright glare.

Could you turn my chair? I asked.

"To face away from the sunset?" Newton asked.

Yes, because I don't want you to be backlit.

"Me?"

Yes, I'd like to take your picture.

"I can't," he said. "I have to hold the computer."

"I can do that, man," Slater said, bounding over. Newton showed him how the cables worked, told him not to get them tangled, told him to keep the computer steady.

Newton pivoted my wheelchair so I had my right side to the sun, moon, and Venus. I was facing downriver, toward Long Island Sound; there were the two lighthouses at Fenwick, one blinking white and the other green. Newton could imagine what I was seeing through the lens, and he stood directly in view.

Tilly, now you, I said.

"Where?" she asked.

Next to Newton, I said.

She seemed shy, and he looked nervous. But they did as I asked, stood side by side, arms barely touching as they faced the camera. I saw sadness and regret in both their faces, but I thought of Tilly's dragons, and sent them chasing those old emotions away, sent them riding down the deep blue river on a fast current.

I wish you could see me smiling, I said.

"Smiling?" Newton asked.

Yes. Because I'm taking a picture of two people who love me. And who I love back.

That made them both grin. And this happened: I swear, even though the sky was deep blue and not fully dark yet, a single meteor plunged from heaven toward earth, blazing through the blue just behind their heads, and I took the shot and caught the moment.

"Should we go back now?" Tilly asked. "Are you getting tired?"

A little, but I want to stay longer.

So the four of us sat by the river, looking out at the moon and the sunset, and waiting for something else, something beautiful, maybe another shooting star, just for us.

Acknowledgments

Deep thanks to Susan Robertson for her understanding of the effects of trauma on the mind and heart, and for helping me translate the language of dreams.

I am grateful to Saffron Burrows for sharing her experience and compassion as someone who has long campaigned for the rights and equality of disabled persons. Thank you also to Alison Balian for the wonderful conversations we had during the time I was writing this novel.

My gratitude to Richard Rieser and Susie Burrows for working toward inclusion and against the bullying of disabled children and people of all ages. Richard's generosity in talking to me about his own experiences helped me imagine a child's long hospital stay and understand more about the challenges of moving forward.

My mother had a brain tumor, and during her long illness I learned a lot about loving someone with a brain injury. The grace and humor she showed through her suffering has always inspired me. She was an artist, and she never gave up looking for beauty and meaning.

The brilliance and kindness of her neurosurgeon, Dr. Isaac Goodrich of Yale-New Haven Hospital, helped me see how critical a truly caring and never-giving-up doctor is to a patient's well-being, both physical and emotional.

Sharon Salzberg's teachings on mindfulness and loving-kindness have been invaluable to me, and now, to Roo.

I am grateful to my editor, Aimee Friedman, for her insight and sensitivity. Thanks to everyone at Scholastic, including David Levithan, Ellie Berger, Lori Benton, Alan Smagler, Betsy Politi, Nikki Mutch, Sue Flynn, Tracy van Straaten, Jennifer Abbots, Caitlin Friedman, Bess Braswell, Lauren Festa, Lizette Serrano, Anna Swenson, Elizabeth Parisi, Emily Cullings, Joy Simpkins, and Jennifer Ung.

My agent, Andrea Cirillo, and I have been together forever and a day, and I never forget how lucky I am to be part of the Jane Rotrosen family: Jane Berkey, Meg Ruley, Annelise Robey, Christina Hogrebe, Amy Tannenbaum, Rebecca Scherer, Peggy Boulos Smith, Danielle Sickles, Donald W. Cleary, Christina Prestia, Julianne Tinari, Michael Conroy, Liz Van Buren, Jessica Errera, Ellen Tischler, and Don Cleary.

Much appreciation to the incomparable Ron Bernstein.

So many thanks to Joe Monninger, my great friend and New Hampshire guide, for his constant encouragement in and out of the woods.

I am very grateful to all librarians, with special thanks to Amy Rhilinger, assistant director of the Attleboro Public Library, for her incredible support to readers and writers everywhere.

About the Author

Luanne Rice is the *New York Times* bestselling author of several novels for adults. Altogether, her novels have sold upward of twenty-two million copies and have been adapted into TV movies and miniseries. *The Secret Language of Sisters* is her YA debut. Visit Luanne online at www.luannerice.net.

J-16